DOUBLE PLAY

Zulu crossed up onto a little mound, then he dropped as though into a chute or cleft, vanishing before Pharaoh's eyes. A *thud*, a rustle of boots and falling rocks, then nothing.

What the . . . ? Had he fallen into a hole? Had the ground collapsed? Had these bastards been tunneling? No way—the ground was way too hard for digging.

He came up onto the mound, looked down. Zulu lay right there, rolling over, about to sit up. Oh, he'd tripped. The ditch below had just shielded him from Pharaoh's view. But as the sergeant looked up, his gaze tracked to Pharaoh's left shoulder.

"Captain!"

He whirled, trying to get his hands back on his rifle, but what he saw made him extend his arms and reach outward. An Arab had come around from behind him.

Whether he had been lying in wait in the ditch and had tripped Zulu was not clear, but the knife jutting from the bottom of his fist presented no questions, only facts.

DIRECT ACTION

SPECIAL FORCES AFGHANISTAN

Peter Telep

BERKLEY BOOKS, NEW YORK

THE BERKLEY PUBLISHING GROUP
Published by the Penguin Group
Penguin Group (USA) Inc.
375 Hudson Street, New York, New York 10014, USA
Penguin Group (Canada), 90 Eglinton Avenue East, Suite 700, Toronto, Ontario M4P 2Y3, Canada
(a division of Pearson Penguin Canada Inc.)
Penguin Books Ltd., 80 Strand, London WC2R 0RL, England
Penguin Group Ireland, 25 St. Stephen's Green, Dublin 2, Ireland (a division of Penguin Books Ltd.)
Penguin Group (Australia), 250 Camberwell Road, Camberwell, Victoria 3124, Australia
(a division of Pearson Australia Group Pty. Ltd.)
Penguin Books India Pvt. Ltd., 11 Community Centre, Panchsheel Park, New Delhi—110 017, India
Penguin Group (NZ), 67 Apollo Drive, Rosedale, North Shore 0632, New Zealand
(a division of Pearson New Zealand Ltd.)
Penguin Books (South Africa) (Pty.) Ltd., 24 Sturdee Avenue, Rosebank, Johannesburg 2196,
South Africa

Penguin Books Ltd., Registered Offices: 80 Strand, London WC2R 0RL, England

This is a work of fiction. Names, characters, places, and incidents either are the product of the author's
imagination or are used fictitiously, and any resemblance to actual persons, living or dead, business
establishments, events, or locales is entirely coincidental. The publisher does not have any control over
and does not assume any responsibility for author or third-party websites or their content.

SPECIAL FORCES AFGHANISTAN: DIRECT ACTION

A Berkley Book / published by arrangement with the author

PRINTING HISTORY
Berkley edition / January 2008

Copyright © 2008 by The Berkley Publishing Group.
Interior text design by Kristin del Rosario.

ISBN: 978-0-425-21895-2

BERKLEY®
Berkley Books are published by The Berkley Publishing Group,
a division of Penguin Group (USA) Inc.,
375 Hudson Street, New York, New York 10014.
BERKLEY® is a registered trademark of Penguin Group (USA) Inc.
The "B" design is a trademark belonging to Penguin Group (USA) Inc.

PRINTED IN THE UNITED STATES OF AMERICA

10 9 8 7 6 5 4 3 2 1

For my father,
William David Telep,
who taught me how to be a man.

ACKNOWLEDGMENTS

I owe a special thank-you to my editor, Tom Colgan, for his trust, insights, and encouragement during the years we've worked together on various projects.

Randy McElwee is a retired master sergeant, U.S. Army, and decorated Special Forces combat veteran with eighteen years' Special Operations experience, including service in Afghanistan. Randy provided me with invaluable advice on my storyline and characters, helping me to walk the tightrope between drama and accuracy. I am incredibly fortunate to work with him.

Vietnam veteran and Chief Warrant Officer James Ide, a fellow Floridian with twenty-one years of active naval service, brought his considerable experience to this book, helping me create the story from the ground up and reading every page of the manuscript. He is a great collaborator and a true friend who never stops inspiring me.

Troy L. Wagner, TMC(SS), EOD, USN, is a retired chief torpedoman, a submariner, and a specialist in explosive ordnance disposal who helped me design a very particular scene, and I couldn't have blown stuff up without him.

Major William R. Reeves, U.S. Army, has served as a technical advisor on many of my novels, and once again he's brought so much to this book that I could never repay the debt.

Mike Noell is the president and CEO of Blackhawk Products

Group, recognized as the world's leading supplier of military and law enforcement equipment. Mike gave me complete access to any and all equipment I was writing about.

Tom O'Sullivan, director, Government and Military Programs at Blackhawk, has been a great technical advisor and friend over the years. Tom helped clarify many of my equipment questions, drawing upon his long and distinguished career as a lieutenant colonel in the U.S. Army.

Michael Janich, a brand manager at Blackhawk, is one of the world's leading edged-weapon experts, the creator of the Jani-Song, and author of numerous books and instructional videos on self-defense. He has more than fifteen years of distinguished military service and has studied and taught martial arts and defensive tactics for more than twenty-five years. Mike answered my many questions and helped me choreograph many of my combat scenes to keep them technically accurate. I deeply appreciate his assistance and am truly honored to know him.

Steve "Mato" Matulewicz, command master chief, Navy SEAL (Ret.), is director of Special Operations at Blackhawk and was kind enough to answer questions on both equipment and the "character" of Special Forces operators. Mato is a true operator in every sense of the word.

Brent Beshara of Besh Knives has been a member of the Canadian military for more than twenty-four years and is a former member of their most elite Special Forces unit—the successor of the First Special Service Force or "Devil's Brigade." He is the designer of the XSF-1 combat dagger, a unique tactical knife from Masters of Defense and Blackhawk Blades that you'll read about within these pages.

Laura Burgess, public relations agent for Blackhawk, and Robin Hart, also of Blackhawk, were exceedingly helpful in regard to much of the equipment described here.

Michael Rigg, manager of sales and marketing at Paladin

Press (paladin-press.com), provided me with many nonfiction resources as part of the extensive research process involved in writing this book. His enthusiasm for the project and great sense of humor really helped through some long writing days.

Lieutenant Colonel Jack Sherman, U.S. Army, has been a great friend and offered keen insight on my outline. He introduced me to Matt McGucken, a former staff sergeant in the U.S. Air Force Special Operations Command, who answered many of my logistical questions regarding Forward Operating Bases and other issues. Their help is deeply appreciated.

Larry M. Chase, former U.S. Navy missile technician and military enthusiast, sent pictures and inspirational material that influenced the early stages of this book.

Darrel Ralph, custom knife maker extraordinaire (darrelralph .com), advised me regarding the kinds of custom weapons a Special Forces operator might carry and answered quite a few of my nagging questions.

Scott Whitney, director of business development at Kwikpoint (kwikpoint.com), provided me with the company's incredibly useful Visual Language Translators, which are carried around by many soldiers in Afghanistan.

Carole McDaniel took James Ide's concept for our Afghanistan map and created a very nice graphic for the book to better orient you to all the locations. I thank her and her husband— my teaching partner—Dr. Rudy McDaniel, for their help and support.

The listing of these individuals is a humble way to express my gratitude. None of them were paid for their services. The fact that their names appear here does not constitute an "official" endorsement of this book by them or by any branch of the U.S. military.

Special Forces Creed

I am an American Special Forces soldier. A professional!

I will do all that my nation requires of me. I am a volunteer, knowing well the hazards of my profession.

I serve with the memory of those who have gone before me: Roger's Rangers, Francis Marino, Mosby's Rangers, the First Special Service Forces, the Jedbrughs, Detachment 101, and the Special Forces soldiers of the Vietnam War, who earned seventeen Medals of Honor, and ninety Distinguished Service Crosses. I pledge to uphold the honor and integrity of all I am—in all I do.

I am a professional soldier. I will teach and fight wherever my nation requires, to liberate the oppressed. I will strive always, to excel in every art and artifice of war.

I know that I will be called upon to perform tasks in isolation, far from familiar faces and voices, with the help and guidance of my God, I will conquer my fears and succeed.

I will keep my mind and body clean, alert and strong, for this is my debt to those who depend on me.

I will not fail those with whom I serve. I will not bring shame upon myself or the forces.

I will maintain myself, my arms, and my equipment in an immaculate state as befits a Special Forces soldier. My goal is to succeed in any mission—and to live to succeed again.

I am a member of my nation's chosen soldiery. God grant that I may not be found wanting, that I will not fail this sacred trust.

Special Forces Motto

DE OPPRESSO LIBER

To Liberate the Oppressed
or
From Oppression We Will Liberate Them

Special Forces' guys are young, capable, smart, dedicated. I'll use the term remarkable, absolutely remarkable; very, very, brave men. They were introduced in the country of Afghanistan in a great many locations in very small numbers. It sounds a bit dramatic, but they were inserted in the dead of night, alone but unafraid. They took a great deal of capacity with them—a capacity to communicate, a capacity to be able to identify and engage targets at a considerable distance from themselves, using air-to-ground forces, close air support. It was remarkable; a remarkable effort. I predict that people will be writing about the exploits of these young people well into the future.

—General Tommy Franks, U.S. Army (Ret.),
on the efforts of U.S. Special Forces
in the months following 9/11

CAST OF CHARACTERS

ODA-555 (TRIPLE NICKEL)

Captain James Pharaoh—detachment commander, call sign *Titan 06*

Chief Warrant Officer 3 Dennis Bull—asst. detachment commander, call sign *Tempest*

Master Sergeant Robert "Zulu" Burrows—operations sergeant, call sign *Zulu*

Sergeant First Class Michael "Hojo" Johnson—asst. operations sergeant, call sign *Thunder*

Sergeant First Class Jason "Mr. O" Ondejko—weapons sergeant, call sign *T-Rex*

Staff Sergeant Gregory "Gator" Gatterson—asst. weapons sergeant, call sign *Tombstone*

Sergeant First Class Jonathan Figueroa—engineer sergeant, call sign *Tarzan*

Staff Sergeant Larry Sullivan—asst. engineer sergeant, call sign *Tomahawk*

Sergeant First Class Steven Borokovsky—medical sergeant, call sign *Triage*

Staff Sergeant Anthony Grimm—asst. medical sergeant, call sign *Trauma*

Sergeant First Class Jerry Weathers—communications sergeant, call sign *Talk Radio*

Staff Sergeant Rudy McDaniel—asst. communications sergeant, call sign *Typhoon*

OTHERS

Major Barry NurenFeld—Operational Detachment Bravo (ODB) commander

Abdul Abdali—president of Afghanistan

Rafiullah Mojadeddi—a young Pashun and Abdali's aide

Eric Newberry—former Force Recon Marine and Abdali's bodyguard

Victor Auss—former Navy SEAL and Abdali's bodyguard

General Malim Kahn—warlord working with al-Qaeda

Fahim Kahn—brother of Malim and second in command

Sheikh Abu Hassan—new al-Qaeda leader in Afghanistan

"Rock"—CIA operative in Badakhshan Province

"Scorpion"—former CIA operative

Khodai Noor—G-chief and Tajik militiaman from Shah-e Pari

Haji Khyal Najid—Noor's right hand

Zemeri—former mujahideen fighter and village elder

Sandra Hildebrand—hardened combat reporter for NPR

Tracy O'Donnell—founder of nonprofit organization War Crimes in Afghanistan

Rich Oswaller—NPR producer

Bill Neggy—NPR engineer

Walsh—chopper pilot for NPR crew

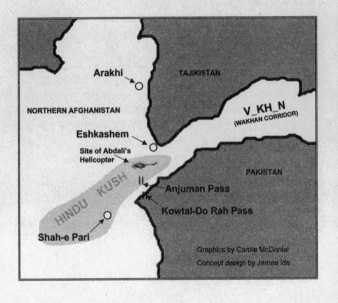

1. AUDACITY

Captain James Pharaoh bolted across the ridgeline, drawing volleys of rifle fire from the steeper hills overlooking the pass, muzzles flashing like cameras across a stadium of cold, dark rock. His pulse thundered in his ears, and he fought to clear his thoughts: no fear, just instincts, *move!*

The ground erupted around him as he neared the deeper shadows ahead, hit a patch of ice, lost his footing, then cursed and dove forward, crashing onto his gut, the woolen *pakol* sliding down into his eyes. He shoved up the hat and tugged down the heavy Afghan scarf covering his nose and mouth, the wool dragging across an inch of newly grown beard.

Team Sergeant Robert "Zulu" Burrows dropped in just behind, all six feet, three inches of him hitting the earth with an appreciable *thud*, gravel and dust flying. "Captain," he managed between labored breaths. "We're not doing too good. Khodai and Haji's men can't hold these guys. And you heard Bull. He's got three more moving toward the SUVs."

"Let McDaniel and the other guy take them."

"The guy who was supposed to guard the trucks with him ran off, and now McDaniel's left his post and says close air support is a no-go. Weathers is working to see if he can get help from another FOB."

"Damn it!"

Zulu tugged down his own *shemagh* to reveal crooked teeth and a bushy, reddish-brown beard wired with gray. "Sir, we're running out of options here." His tone turned sarcastic. "Any thoughts?"

Pharaoh shuddered. "Yeah. How many in all?"

"Bull still isn't sure. Maybe twenty."

Pharaoh pushed himself up on his elbows. It was time to make a decision, and he knew full well that Zulu was ready to make that decision for him if he panicked. The team sergeant was giving him just enough rope to hang himself.

In the span of seconds, everything that had just happened replayed in Pharaoh's head:

The trek up to the Kowtal-e-Do Rah Pass, his twelve-man Special Forces Operational Detachment Alpha (ODA) team dressed like the Tajik militiamen they were training . . .

Khodai and Haji revealing that they had spotted an enemy force of Arabs stealing their way across the border from Pakistan several days earlier but admitting they had failed to keep them under surveillance . . .

And Pharaoh nearly choking Khodai, the young guerilla leader—or "G-chief"—swearing he had not led them into a trap, even as the first few rounds of the ambush split the air, striking and killing three of Khodai's men . . .

"Captain?"

Zulu needed an answer. The entire team did.

They were ODA-555, nicknamed "Triple Nickel," a storied band of operators who had made a name for themselves in Afghanistan just after 9/11, laser-designating targets and helping to dismantle the enemy in record time. They were a scuba team now fighting on land because they went where they were needed most. And while none of those original men were in country, the Triple Nickel legend lived on. They were experts in unconventional warfare, now tasked to help NATO forces shut down the ratlines used by Taliban and al-Qaeda fighters. They were the quiet professionals, trained to liberate the oppressed.

With boots like that to fill, Pharaoh had been humbled and awed to accept command, and he sensed the spirit of every man who had ever served on 555 with him.

But that was a blessing . . . and a curse. He didn't want to let them down, not a one of them, even if this was his first time in combat.

Game on. Test of fire, baptism of fire, welcome to Afghanistan, welcome to the gun club—if you survive.

He took a deep breath and put some steel back into his voice. "All right, Sergeant, you tell Khodai to get his men to split up, two teams to flank these guys up in the hills; Haji takes that other team. They each leave one guy behind to run and gun, making them think they haven't changed their position."

"Nice. They can handle that."

"I'll tell Bull to keep our guys to the south and get some grenades and more two-forty fire on them, this way he'll also draw their fire down into the pass while Khodai and Haji put their boys to work. But Gator and Ondejko should maintain their position and keep that sniper fire coming. Keep 'em tied up until we're all ready to fall back. You and I go for the SUVs."

Zulu's lip twitched. "Can I make a suggestion?"

Pharaoh was about to roll his eyes when the team sergeant added: "Just call me Zu. And stay close."

Pharaoh almost grinned. "Roger that."

The team sergeant had never been so informal during the three weeks they had been together, and Pharaoh had assumed that Zulu deemed him just another token officer assigned to the ODA for twelve to eighteen months to be trained by the NCOs, only to move on to command companies and battalions. Smart captains were supposed to let their team sergeants run the entire show, while they sat back and took care of administrative duties.

But Pharaoh was a sponge, wanting to soak up as much as he could while still acknowledging that Zulu was the master and he the apprentice. Pharaoh figured that if he just rolled over and let Zulu do everything, he would only learn half as much. But he didn't want to endanger or alienate the men, either, which was why he double-checked everything with the team sergeant.

Zulu grabbed Pharaoh's arm and softened his tone. "Hey, first time out, you're doing okay. And trust me, you'll learn that experience is a beautiful thing. It lets you recognize a fuckup when you do it again." Zulu flashed a crooked grin.

Pharaoh nodded. "Let's get 'em moving."

They keyed their multiband inter/intra team radios and issued the orders. Then, after stowing the MBITRs, Pharaoh asked, "Ready?"

Zulu's face lit in an evil smile. "Always."

Pharaoh pried himself up and bounded for a string of boulders to his right, jagged teeth rising as high as his shoulders in some places, their surfaces alive with sparking rounds.

Thus far the enemy hadn't thrown anything more than small-arms fire at them—no mortars, RPGs, grenades, nothing. They were either holding back or poorly equipped, and the thought gnawed at Pharaoh.

He led Zulu behind the rocks, where they crouched

down and exploited the cover, working their way farther south and west, a white noise of constant popping and hissing rounds overhead punctuating their footfalls.

Now they shifted and sidestepped down the pass, toward where they had parked the SUVs at the bottom of the hill.

He stole a look back. Son of a bitch, Zulu was right there, humping his thirty-nine-year-old ass over the mountain like he was fifteen years younger, Pharaoh's age.

"What?" asked the sergeant.

"Uh, nothing, let's do it!"

Suddenly, a hand slammed on the back of his woolen coat and dragged him back toward the outcropping on his right.

"Sorry, Captain, wait a minute." Zulu dropped to his knees, brought his night vision goggles (NVGs) to his eyes, then peered down toward where their pair of black Nissan Pathfinders were already coated in a thick layer of frost. The vehicles were packed with all the goodies that Special Forces operators liked to take with them in the field and enemy forces liked to steal and/or destroy.

The most important piece of equipment mounted inside each vehicle was the Blue Force Tracker (BFT) computer, a satellite-based tracking and communication system, basically the electronic umbilical cord attaching them to Forward Operations Base (FOB) Asadabad, 250 miles to the south.

"All right, I got them," said Zulu, shifting slightly and leaning forward with the NVGs, scarf now around his chin. "Three guys, maybe we can cut them off in time, but—oh, shit. There's one I really don't like."

"Why?"

"Ah, maybe not. Captain, what we're about right now is audacity."

Pharaoh grinned behind his scarf. " 'Audacity, more audacity, and always audacity.' "

That was a quote from Georges Jacques Danton, a leader

of the French Revolution, and it became one of the mottoes of General George Patton.

Zulu shoved the NVGs into Pharaoh's gloved hands, and he spied the hillside for himself.

"See the guy on the right? He's mine. You take the guy on the far left. The middle guy is up for grabs. We're still out of range. Move."

Pharaoh returned the NVGs to Zulu, then adjusted the V-Tac sling on his rifle. The Special Forces Combat Assault Rifle-Light (SCAR-L) was a 5.56mm replacement for the old M16 and M14, had a thirty-round magazine, and put out six hundred rounds per minute. Pharaoh's weapon also had an enhanced grenade launcher module (EGLM) able to fire fuse programmable ammunition.

Zulu carried the bigger SCAR-H, a 7.62mm version that accepted "battlefield pickup" AK-47/AKM magazines with 7.62 M43 ammunition.

But their rifles didn't mean a damned thing if they couldn't put themselves in position.

This time Zulu led the way, taking them toward a little gully on their left that fed into a long stretch of smaller rocks and withered vegetation that, in the starlight, shimmered and flowed like the rains in spring.

"Just a little closer," said Zulu, pausing as they slid into the gully and crouched down.

"Are you serious? They're coming into range now."

"You don't want to miss, do you?"

"Sergeant, I think we should hang here. I mean, how close you want to get?"

Zulu raised a gloved hand, rubbed his eyes. "Captain, I told you I'd work with you, train you, let you fight this team—to a point—but we can't be taking a piss back here for much longer. If something happens up in the hills, you don't need to be explaining what we were doing down here."

"I understand, but—"

"Come on." Zulu gave him no time for further protest. His Blackhawk assault boots were already kicking up snow, ice, and gravel.

Pharaoh bit his lip and fell in behind the man as they barreled down the hill toward the Pathfinders, dropping to their guts as they reached the rear wheels of the nearest one on the right. The trucks were parked side-by-side about three meters apart and facing north. The trio of al-Qaeda fighters were coming down the hillside from the north, working their way closer to the truck on the left.

"They didn't see us," said Zulu.

"You're sure?"

"Yeah. Sort of."

"Comforting."

"Remember, I got the guy on the right."

"You really want him, huh?"

"We can't take any chances. I think our little buddy has turned himself into the guerilla's version of a precision guided munition."

"You mean a suicide bomber?"

"I like my description better."

"Shit." Pharaoh crawled around the truck, slid beneath, then peered up at the scrub and rocks ahead—

Just as three pairs of legs emerged.

The fighters ran toward them, black turbans barely visible, AKs bouncing. They were demons, all right, shouting excitedly to one another.

"Captain?" Zulu stage-whispered. "Here we go! Wait for my shot."

Pharaoh swallowed, sighted his first target, and thought, *Audacity. AUDACITY!*

2. THE HIGHEST MOUNTAIN

As the gates of the presidential palace closed behind his
dust-covered and dented Range Rover, President Abdul Abdali felt compelled to look back at the stoic-faced guards
and brick walls he was leaving behind. A chill worked its
way up from the base of his spine and branched off like
lightning into his shoulders.

"Are you all right?"

Beside him in the backseat sat his aide for the past year,
Rafiullah Mojadeddi. The young Pashtun, barely thirty, had
been educated in the UK and had, years earlier, worked
with Abdali at Usocal, the American oil company that had
bid on the contract to build a pipeline from Uzbekistan
through Afghanistan and on to seaports in Pakistan.

Abdali was nearly twenty years Mojadeddi's senior, but
they had become close friends during their tenure at Usocal, fostering connections not only with each other but with
the American executives who had taught them a great deal

about Western business practices in the boardroom and on the golf course.

Abdali cleared his throat. "Yes, Rafiullah, I am fine—despite your prophecy of doom."

With a shrug, Rafiullah pointed out, "You've never discouraged me from my voicing my opinion."

"I've never discouraged you from agreeing with me, either."

"On this we will never agree."

"Oh, come on. If there were another path, I would take it. But this is the one we must follow. And as the old proverb says, there is a path to even the highest mountain."

"This one is too high."

Abdali drew in a long breath, then sighed in frustration. He understood his aide's trepidation, but if their new government was going to work, he would need to reach out to all Afghans despite their ethnicity, reach out with kind yet bold gestures, give and impress, so that trust and truth would come together to form the foundation of their great land.

He and the rest of his staff had already been accused of being out of touch with the provincial governors and their staffs, as well as with the local citizenry, especially those in the northern provinces. The media reported that Abdali kept himself cloistered behind his fortress walls, and when he did come out, it was with hordes of security.

There were too many walls, both figuratively and literally, between himself and his people.

Before they had left the palace, Abdali had spent a few moments staring at himself in the mirror, asking, *Are you ready? Are you truly ready?*

Gone were his trademark tan tunic and trousers (*shalwar kameez*) and his green-and-white coat. Gone was his famous—or infamous—gray *karakul* made of lamb fetuses that sat upon his head like a sophisticated and contemporary crown. The hat had been discussed in countless news articles; in fact, Abdali had complained in an interview with Sandra Hildebrand on National Public Radio that his clothes received more press coverage than his ideas did.

He now wore a simple tunic and coat and a brown *pakol* on his head, making him appear more farmer than statesman. Rafiullah could not persuade him to abandon the trip, but he had resigned himself to the clothing.

Abdali glanced up at Eric Newberry, an American from the private military company DynCorp and former Force Recon Marine, one of two bodyguards along for the ride. Newberry rolled the wheel, heading northeast up Kabul's airport road, Bibi Mahro, newly widened and with light traffic this late on a Sunday night. Seated in the passenger seat was Newberry's partner, Victor Auss, a former command master chief (SEAL) who had retired to take on private security work.

Abdali felt generally secure in taking a little helicopter ride north to the farthest reaches of his country with two highly trained, highly decorated American military men at his side.

Of course, Rafiullah had argued that they wouldn't be enough, that he needed a large team, that the risk they were taking was not worth it. He had even accused Abdali of acting impetuously, of listening more to his ego than to reason.

Within a few minutes they reached a small, private hangar on the outskirts of the airport, where they exited the SUV and hurried toward an old Soviet-made MI-8 helicopter, its five-bladed main rotor already beginning to spin. The helicopter was a troop and transport carrier, frequently seen in the skies above Afghanistan.

Abdali clutched his hat, climbed the wooden steps, and

shifted into the dimly lit cabin, where three more Americans from DynCorp—the pilot, copilot, and crew chief—greeted his bodyguards while he and Rafiullah took seats and reached for the restraints.

"It's not too late to change your mind," said Rafiullah.

"Omar is a man of his word. And so am I."

"He's manipulating you."

"I know."

"Then why are you letting this happen?"

"Because I'm manipulating him, too."

Opium production in Badakhshan Province had tripled in the last two years, and the province's governor, Hajji Mohammad Omar, was dealing directly with warlords and al-Qaeda leaders now. He had once been under control, his drug money replaced by American dollars in order to ensure his loyalty to the new government. But that funding had dried up with America's attention focused squarely on Iraq.

So Omar had been forced to go back to his old ways. He was a cherubic family man with four children, and Abdali firmly believed that he wanted to do the right thing. Consequently, Abdali had negotiated with the Americans, struck a new deal, and was ready to present a request that Omar gradually reduce poppy cultivation, sever his ties with the warlords who were being bribed by Taliban and al-Qaeda leaders, and return law and order to his province—in return, of course, for lots of money. But he would not let Omar believe he was being "bought" once again by the Americans, which would damage his pride; no, he would tell the man that he was manipulating the Americans into giving him what he needed, that they, the leaders of Afghanistan, were always in control.

For his part, Omar was ready to negotiate, but he had insisted that Abdali come to him as a sign of good faith, and that he come with only a small party. Omar himself was being closely watched by the drug traffickers, who reported back to the warlords. If they discovered Omar was striking a new deal with the president, the warlords would execute him immediately. Omar knew exactly what he was doing.

And Abdali believed that if he demonstrated his faith and trust in Omar, he would have the same in return. Omar had already expressed that he would much rather be supported by Abdali's government than by the warlords and Arabs sneaking across the border. The only things you could rely on with them were their greed and hatred for America.

In point of fact, Abdali was also under tremendous pressure from Washington to demonstrate "democracy in action," to show the world how a Muslim nation, once liberated, would reach out for freedom and strive for entry into the global market and the family of peace-loving nations.

Afghanistan was the coalition's first great experiment at true "nation building," and Abdali fully supported that effort. In fact, a CNN report once referred to him as the Abraham Lincoln of his country, a battle-scarred survivor of the Soviet debacle, a veteran in-fighter accustomed to putting his life on the line.

So yes, he had to admit there were healthy doses of ego involved.

The helicopter slowly rose from the tarmac, then its nose pitched slightly, and the engine revved even higher.

"Mr. President, is there anything I can get for you?" Auss asked from his seat just in front of Abdali.

"No, thank you. About how long?"

"Figure three hours, with one stop to refuel. Security has already been arranged for that, sir."

"All right, thank you."

"You might try to get some sleep."

Abdali took a deep breath. "Impossible. There's too much on my mind."

"I understand, sir. No fears, though. We'll make sure the landing zone is secure before we get near it."

He nodded.

Rafiullah glanced over at him, pursing his lips, then he widened his eyes. "This mountain is too high."

Abdali leaned back, closed his eyes, and imagined himself scaling sheer rock walls. Nothing could stop him.

3. BULL'S-EYE

Zulu's rifle brought thunder to the valley, signaling Pharaoh to take his shot.

With his arm wrapped in his sling, stabilizing his weapon, the cam-lock buckle holding fast, Pharaoh gritted his teeth, squeezed his trigger.

And while his 5.56mm rounds tore into the chest of the fighter on the left, Zulu's guy dropped back to the dirt, pieces of his head still airborne.

Before Pharaoh could shift fire, Zulu's guy suddenly exploded in a raging fireball that rose a half dozen meters into the night. Along with the echoing boom came a wave of heat that rushed forward, carrying clouds of dust and debris.

Pharaoh shut his eyes and glanced away for a moment, then as the fire began to dissipate, Zulu cried, "He really went up! Goddamn!"

Only then did Pharaoh realize that the explosion had taken out the middle guy: his remains were strewn across a patchwork of rocks and snow, the blood like black ink, the stench of C4 hanging heavy—death's perfume, some called it.

"Hey, Sergeant?" Pharaoh craned his head, spotted Zulu crawling out from beneath the truck.

"Short memory? It's just Zu!"

"Yeah, still getting used to that. Let's go!"

Pharaoh wrestled himself out from beneath the Pathfinder, then got on his radio and called his assistant detachment commander as he fell in behind Zulu. "Tempest, this is Titan 06, over."

As he waited for the reply, Zulu shouted, "Captain, we should head back up to those boulders, near our original point."

"Do it." Then Pharaoh repeated his radio call to no avail.

Chief Warrant Officer 3 Dennis Bull was a little busy at the moment his young captain decided to call. He had just set a six-second fuse on a grenade and had sent it flying with his assault rifle's launcher.

The grenade dropped squarely into a little depression where two rifle-toting Arabs had been pestering the shit out of him. Three seconds later, a solid boom and puff of smoke silenced their AKs.

Bull dropped down to his elbows, tore the scarf away from his face, and shoved the MBITR up to his hairy cheek, no fancy helmet or boom mike for him. "Titan 06, this is Tempest, sorry for the delay, go ahead, over."

"SITREP!"

"We're continuing to draw enemy fire while Tribe 1 and Tribe 2 get their men into flanking positions, over."

Gunfire ripped across the rocks no more than a meter

from Bull's face. He cursed and rolled, digging himself backward, eyes scanning for the source of that fire, somewhere above.

"Tempest, you copy, over?"

"Say again, Titan 06, over."

"What's the delay, over?"

"No delay, they're still moving. Goddamn hill is steep on those sides. It's taking them a while to get up. Then they'll attempt to come in from behind, over."

"Roger that. Talk Radio? Typhoon? I want you guys to fall back to the trucks and set up there, over."

"Titan 06, this is Talk Radio, roger, falling back, out," replied Sergeant First Class Jerry Weathers, the team's communications sergeant.

"Titan 06, this is Typhoon, roger, falling back, out." That was Staff Sergeant Rudy McDaniel, the assistant communications sergeant.

Both of the commo guys carried light weapons and heavy radio packs and would be better off guarding the trucks, which was where McDaniel had been posted in the first place. Good call on Pharaoh's part, but then again, old Zu might be calling the shots through the kid.

Bull grinned to himself. It felt like yesterday that he was a kid in the woods behind his house in upstate New York, ducking behind trees and throwing dirt bombs and digging little traps that he covered with twigs and leaves.

Shit, he'd been in Special Forces since he was ten. Or maybe earlier—maybe he'd been running a black op inside his mother's womb. Probably.

The kid would be all right. Bull's first impression of him was that he had an interesting name: Pharaoh, the ancient Egyptian title for a ruler. The Arabs in these mountains would not be impressed. And yes, Zulu would school the kid in the deadly arts, the stuff you learned in country, not in training; they all would, but Zu, who was a little too much in love with himself for Bull's taste, ran the show and ran it well. You couldn't take that away from the narcissistic bastard.

Bull glanced across the hillside, where the team's two engineers, Figueroa and Sullivan, were laying down fire with their M240B machine guns, one on a bipod, the other a tripod, both pumping out six- to nine-round bursts so as to buy more firing time before they had to change each weapon's barrel. Ammo belt links flew from the sides of the rattling guns like metallic confetti, while shell casings thumbed to the ground beneath. Those guys couldn't remain in position for much longer, lest one of the Arabs up top lob a grenade on their heads.

After a deep breath, Bull checked his watch, pricked up his ears, and listened for the sounds of Haji and Khodai's men engaging from the flanks. That'd be the team's cue to boogie, giving the bad guys room to flood down the hillside and into the trap. But shit, nothing so far, and that wasn't good.

After another handful of seconds, Bull keyed his mike: "Tribe 1, this is Tempest, over."

"Tempest, this is Tribe 1, yes?" came Khodai's thickly accented voice. The young Tajik still wasn't used to talking on the radio, but he was getting better.

"Are you there yet, over?"

"We're almost there."

"Move your asses!"

"What?"

"Hurry! Tempest, out!"

Bull fished out his NVGs, brought them slowly to his eyes, then panned the ridgeline above him, its pockmarked surfaces holding any number of al-Qaeda knuckleheads trying to ruin his perfectly good evening.

And if those bad guys kept up this shit, he had a good mind to retire. Again. Been there, done that.

He'd started out as an SF commo guy, but he'd gotten sick and tired of his radios not working half the time and decided he wanted to become an officer. He'd gone to warrant officer school and had graduated as a WO-1. After working as a staff member at several SF headquarters, he eventually got to work on teams, earning promotions along the way. He had retired just months prior to 9/11, but once the global war on terror (GWOT) got into full swing, he'd been paid a huge bonus of more than $20K to come back to active duty—pushing his paycheck into six figures, which some folks outside the Special Forces community couldn't believe. But the Department of Defense (DoD) apparently wanted his ass to remain where it was, so he'd taken the money, the headaches, the bullets flying over his head, and, worst of all, the divorce.

He still carried Melissa's picture in his wallet, still told his fellow operators that he was happily married. They needed to believe that someone could juggle a career in Special Forces and a marriage. But in truth, even his two daughters barely spoke to him. They were women now, in college, had their own lives. And so it was that the women in his life might be his greatest regret.

He shrugged, squinted harder through the NVGs, then heard the beautiful cacophony of Tajik militiamen firing their U.S.–supplied M-16s.

Music to his ears.

"Titan 06, this is Tempest, over."

"Go ahead, Tempest."

"Tribe teams are engaging. I recommend we leave T-Rex and Tombstone in position, but have the rest of our team fall back to the southeast side of the pass, over."

"Roger that. Everyone rally to the southeast side, then spread out. Wait for them to come down the hill."

"Hey, Hojo!" Bull cried to the man about five meters to his left. "Let's break now!"

Assistant Operations Sergeant First Class Michael "Hojo" Johnson, his brown beard and long hair hidden behind a *shemagh*, rolled onto his side, pulling his SCAR-H into his chest. Then he sprang up, Bull doing likewise; together they ran across the hillside.

Despite being built like a brick shithouse and fit as a man half his age, Bull was 45.6 years old according to his Swiss-engineered watch, as he liked to point out, and running around when the footing was not good just pissed him off. A week prior he'd sprained his right ankle, and it was already beginning to throb. But he'd never complain about it. One of the wonderful challenges of being the oldest dude on the team: you had to keep your mouth shut about the aches and pains so the rest wouldn't start calling you "old man." He'd never abide that crap!

Yes, it was just fine to be traipsing around the Hindu Kush Mountains, a no-man's-land of towering peaks, ridgelines, and snow-filled defiles. If the landscape or weather didn't kill you, the tourists flooding in from Pakistan would.

Hojo beat a nice path, booting the larger rubble out of Bull's way as they descended about twenty meters, then cut sideways across the hill, racing toward an opposing wall.

The engineers were already on their way, moving much slower, lugging their big machine guns.

The two medics, Borokovsky and Grimm, were out ahead of them, their packs a little larger and heavier than the rest. Borokovsky was the senior medic, Grimm the new guy who'd come from the same Q-course class as Pharaoh. That the team actually had two medics was a stroke of luck, since on deployments one was typically forced to stay behind to keep up with the intense training schedule and qualifications.

Much farther to the northeast, hidden somewhere along the ridge, were Ondejko and Gatterson, the snipers.

With so many call signs and nicknames floating around, Bull sometimes resorted to calling his teammates "You, with the gun" or "You, with the radio," just to raise a grin or two.

After nearly eighteen months in country, the team had come up with their "Hollywood" call signs, all starting with the letter "T" since their ODA was designated "Texas 10" to identify it to commanders or higher and aircraft support.

Bull didn't care what any of their names were at the moment, though, so long as they were ready to pounce on those Arabs once the Tajik militiamen forced them into a final descent.

"Are we there yet, Mom?" he called to Hojo.

"I think so!" With that the operations sergeant slowed, then worked his way straight up the hill toward a rocky outcropping along which lay several good-size boulders.

Bull followed, digging his boots into the hard earth until he reached the rocks.

"Tempest, this is Titan 06, over."

"Captain likes to hear himself talk on the radio," said Hojo with a smile as he fished out his NVGs.

"Like I've said, we could've done a lot worse. This one actually wants to learn something. And I trust he doesn't want to screw up." Bull then answered Pharaoh's call: "Titan 06, this is Tempest, go ahead."

"Everyone in position?"

Bull looked at Hojo, grinned. No shit we are. "Uh, yes, sir, we are in position."

"Hey, Bull, better have a look," said Hojo, handing him the goggles.

Heralded by a chorus of gunfire, fifteen to twenty figures came rising over the opposite hill, silhouetted at first
in the grainy green imagery of the night vision goggles: al-
Qaeda fighters running directly toward them.

"Titan 06, you see them?"

"Roger that. Let's take 'em out!"

Bull's heart leapt. God, he was born for this. He took up
his SCAR and sighted the lead guy.

4. THE VALLEY OF THE SHADOW

Pharaoh wasn't sure who had taken out the lead fighter, but he vowed to question the men later. That Arab had succumbed to a perfectly executed head shot and was dead before his body hit the hill. Amazing.

While the radio was silent, the team's guns weren't. Between the big M240s, the assault rifles, and the grenades being lobbed down at the oncoming Arabs, Pharaoh couldn't hear himself think let alone anything else. Didn't matter. He put his own rifle to work, targeting a fighter who was scrambling toward his left.

Pharaoh's first volley fell wide, so he adjusted his aim and finally put steel on target, the guy no more than a fluctuating shadow against a sheet of snow-dappled rock.

That silhouette staggered a moment, then fell as the hot gases emitted by Pharaoh's weapon blew in Pharaoh's face.

Tugging his sling adjustment and lowering the rifle, he took up his NVGs, studying the effects of the rest of the team's fire: a half dozen more Arabs lying dead across the hill. The Tajik militiamen began to appear along the summit, shifting parallel to the kill zone, muzzle flashes occasionally marking their positions.

After a second inspection that yielded no more enemy movement, Pharaoh thumbed his mike: "This is Titan 06. Hold fire! Hold fire!"

Once the last shot had echoed off into the distance, Pharaoh shifted over to Zulu's position. "Think we got 'em."

"Have the tribe guys move down into the valley. Then we'll come down and see what we got."

Pharaoh nodded. "Tribe 1? Tribe 2? This is Titan 06. Advance into the valley, over."

"Roger, Titan 06," replied Khodai, failing to identify himself, but Pharaoh recognized the man's voice. Haji responded after him.

"All right," said Zulu, staring through his NVGs. "Now we see if they remember what we taught them."

He was referring to the many drills the Tajiks had run for the past two weeks; Zulu had worked those men hard, incredibly hard, following which he had issued them little pins according to their ranks. Some were stars, others bars, none truly official, but they wore those pins with great pride, shifting them onto whatever they happened to be wearing so that they would always be displayed.

Now twenty-six Tajiks wound their way down through the ditches and rocks, across the smaller ridges and hogbacks, branching off and holding points around the men they had helped to kill.

The ambush, it seemed, was finally over, and the ambushers had become the victims. Pharaoh could hardly beat back the rush. His team had turned the situation around and, with the help of their indigenous militia, had pounced on the invaders. This was a career-building moment.

"T-Rex, this is Titan 06," he began, calling up Ondejko, who sat in his sniper's perch. "You got any more movement, over?"

The weapons sergeant responded curtly, "Titan 06, this is T-Rex. I got nada. If any of those guys got away, I didn't see, over."

"Roger that, you and Tombstone maintain your observation, out."

"All right, they're waving us down," said Zulu, with a sigh of frustration. "They should be calling us on the radio."

Pharaoh shrugged. "Cut 'em some slack."

"For now. They pay later."

As he dropped in behind Zulu, he called Bull, told him and Hojo to cover them as they descended to link up with Khodai and Haji. Then he added: "You take out that first guy?"

"Affirmative," Bull replied.

"Nice!"

"Thank you, sir, Tempest, out."

Zulu crossed up onto a little mound, then he dropped as though into a chute or cleft, vanishing before Pharaoh's eyes. A thud, a rustle of boots and falling rocks, then nothing.

What the . . . ? Pharaoh thought.

Had he fallen into a hole? Had the ground collapsed? Had these bastards been tunneling? No way—the ground was way too hard for digging.

He came up onto the mound, looked down—

Zulu lay right there, rolling over, about to sit up. Oh, he tripped. The ditch below had just shielded him from Pharaoh's view.

But as the sergeant looked up, his gaze tracked to Pharaoh's left shoulder. "Captain!"

He whirled, trying to get his hands back on his rifle, but what he saw made him extend his arms and reach outward.

An Arab had come around from behind him. Whether he had been lying in wait in the ditch and had tripped Zulu was not clear, but the knife jutting from the bottom of his fist presented no questions, only facts.

This bearded man with the turban on his head was a True Believer, trained in the most harsh conditions to kill men like Pharaoh, and his eyes bulged as he reared back with the blade, his breath coming heavy, a cry erupting from the back of his throat.

Pharaoh thought of the .45 in the Blackhawk SERPA holster on his thigh, but there wasn't time.

He locked both hands on the guy's wrist, forced him back while trying to get his leg around the fighter's to trip him down and away.

You could train forever, take every combatives course known to fighting man, but every situation was different, and all you could do was react and instinctively apply your training, not think about it but do it, second nature.

Yet this son of a bitch was powerful, wouldn't budge, and suddenly the blade was coming down fast toward Pharaoh's shoulder, near the collar of the armor vest he wore beneath his woolen coat.

Pharaoh directed all of his energy into his arms, every ounce of strength he had, consciously realizing that if he didn't stop that blade, he was dead.

And realizing now that this guy had much more momentum, a little more strength, and Pharaoh's grip began to falter.

He screamed, as did the Arab.

It was clear: within the next few seconds one man would live; the other would die.

Pharaoh's entire being was focused on the man, on the blade. Then, out of the corner of his eye, he saw Zulu rushing up from behind. The team sergeant held an XSF-1 combat dagger in his right hand in a reverse grip, its triple-edged point hovering menacingly above the Arab's shoulder.

The sergeant's left hand reached over the Arab's head and his fingers dug deeply into the Arab's eye sockets as he wrenched the guy's head back.

At the same time, he drove his knee into the back of the Arab's knees, instantly dropping him and stretching his neck backward to expose the throat.

Pharaoh dropped his gaze to the now kneeling Arab just in time to watch all 6.4 inches of Zulu's dagger plunge into the hollow between his collarbone and the top of his sternum. With the knife still deep in the Arab's upper chest, Zulu worked the handle in a rapid circle, using the collarbone as a lever, the blade shredding everything it touched inside the Arab's body.

An inhuman noise burst from the Arab's throat as he crumpled to the ground. Zulu made sure the job was done with a final thrust into the base of the Arab's skull, severing the spinal cord and ensuring that he was out of the fight—permanently.

Wearing a grimace, steam rising from his mouth, Zulu cleaned the chisel-tipped dagger on the Arab's tunic before sliding it back into its Kydex sheath.

Pharaoh stood there on wobbly knees, speechless.

"I was going to shoot him," Zulu said with a slight shrug. "But your head got in the way."

Pharaoh would've laughed if he weren't trembling as he came down from the adrenaline rush. He wanted to thank the sergeant without coming across as some weakling who hadn't been able to hold his own at the crucial moment. But what to say, exactly?

God, he'd been wanting so badly to fit in, to prove himself, and all this had done was reinforce the bitter truth that he was just a tourist, a visitor stopping by to watch the real men, the NCOs, fight the good fight.

"Damn it!" he cried between gritted teeth. "Goddamn it!"

"Hey," called Zulu. "Forget him."

Pharaoh crouched down before the dead man, picked up his rifle, tugged free the magazine: empty. "He was out."

"Which is why he resorted to his blade. We call it CCC: cheap Chinese crap. Terrible knife. Guess they couldn't afford to buy him a pistol. And you know, Captain, these guys are either drug traffickers packing light and trying to move through quickly, or someone sent them up here to keep us busy, knowing they were expendable, which would explain why they're so poorly armed—don't want to waste the assets. But we ain't got time to bullshit about it now." He started off, limping slightly.

"Hey, uh, Zu?" Pharaoh took a deep breath.

The team sergeant lifted his chin.

"Thanks, man."

"Yeah." He lifted his index finger. "And if I ever need you to return the favor, you'd better be there."

"I will."

"Good."

Two minutes later, they linked up with Khodai and Haji, the young G-chief thrilled over his first victory. He held up a fist and cried in heavily accented in English, "We are the champions, my friends!"

"Have you been listening to Queen CDs or what?" Pharaoh asked.

Khodai scratched his short beard. "Queen, oh, yes! Yes! We are the champions!"

Haji, Khodai's second in command, held up his own fist. He was taller and leaner, his features more birdlike than human, his beard patchy. He would follow Khodai into a hail of machine-gun fire—of that Pharaoh was certain.

"Titan 06, this is Triage, over," came Borokovsky's voice over the radio.

"Triage, this is Titan 06, I see you right over there, go ahead, over."

"We got about three or four guys with minor gunshot wounds, but two are in bad shape. I got one whose femoral artery got nicked, he won't last thirty minutes. The other's not bleeding out as bad, but he needs surgery A-SAP, over."

Zulu looked at Pharaoh and shook his head.

"My men are dying, I know," said Khodai, the celebration evaporating from his face. "Helicopter!"

"Not available."

Khodai got so flustered that he burst out in Dari: *"Ber'eye cheh-moo-daht?"*

"I don't know how long," said Pharaoh after a moment to translate. Despite studying Pashto and Dari back at Fort Bragg during his twenty-six weeks of Special Forces detachment commander training, Pharaoh sometimes only caught every fifth word because the Tajiks spoke so damned fast.

The G-chief seized Pharaoh's wrist and began to drag him away, hollering, "Please!"

Pharaoh tugged out of the man's grip but followed him anyway, across the valley toward where the team's two medics were treating the injured men, both lying across beds of rubble. One man's leg was drenched in blood. Grimm rushed to establish IVs, while Borokovsky was trying to clamp the dying militiaman's artery.

Khodai raised his palms emphatically. "Please, Captain! My men!"

Pharaoh swallowed, glanced back at the hill, at the dead Arabs strewn across the ice and clumps of weeds, at the men bleeding before him. He called Weathers, who was still waiting to hear back on their chopper request.

Without warning, a shadow passed over the entire scene, made Pharaoh's legs grow weak. Was he about to pass out? *No! I'm okay.*

"I'm sorry, Khodai. We'll do what we can. But I don't think these guys will make it."

The G-chief didn't understand all the words, but the look on Pharaoh's face assuredly told him enough.

Khodai began muttering in Dari, a prayer perhaps.

Pharaoh squatted down between the two medics. "Can you prep these guys to move out?" he asked Borokovsky.

The sharp-jawed blond man glanced back, pursed his lips, and seemed to grow impatient. "Captain, I can't even stop this guy's bleeding, let alone move him. We'll just kill their pain. That's all we can do without a medevac."

The medic's tone hinted that Pharaoh should've already known that. "Uh, right. Do what you can."

Pharaoh rose, stroking his chin, cursed under his breath.

Zulu came up behind him, leaned into his shoulder. "You having fun yet?"

He shot the sergeant a dirty look.

"Shit, Captain. Couple guys? This ain't nothing."

But it *was* something—an assault on Pharaoh's senses, his emotions, his intellect, his everything.

And he stood there, in the shadow of it all.

5. EASY HANDSHAKE

President Abdul Abdali nodded as his American bodyguard Auss informed him that they were just thirty minutes
out from the small village of Arakhi, located approximately 240 kilometers NNE of Kabul and only a few kilometers west of Tajikistan.

They had landed to refuel without incident and were
now thumping loudly over the Badakhshan Province, an
L-shaped territory of approximately 44,000 kilometers
deep within the northern hinterlands.

With valleys almost entirely isolated from one another by
great shoulders of frozen rock, the province's people relied
upon the many mountain passes for their very existence.
However, these passes also allowed the drug traffickers and
al-Qaeda and Taliban forces to bring heartache and despair
to the region. Abdali needed to purge these men from his
great country—

But he could only do that with the help of Governor Hajji
Mohammad Omar, whose broad grin and easy handshake

awaited. Abdali had met the governor once before, at a party he had thrown at the presidential palace just after his election. Omar had never stopped talking about his children and their accomplishments, and about his dreams for a peaceful and stable nation. Though Abdali had only spent a short time with the man, he had learned that Omar had the same dream but that there were many forces working against him in Badakhshan.

Abdali brimmed with excitement over the meeting, but one look over at Rafiullah tempered his emotions.

"The trucks were there, weren't they? Filled with guns and shells and antiaircraft missiles."

"That doesn't mean anything."

"It was a sign of trust. A sign of good faith."

Omar had said that he would turn over two large weapons caches that Taliban forces had been storing in the mountains just outside of the province capital of Feyzabad. Six trucks in all had been driven into the city and delivered to NATO forces. Omar had taken a tremendous risk in doing that; his risk must be answered by Abdali's, and so it would be. Abdali would not turn his back on Omar, especially after the governor had kept his promise.

"Rafiullah, what will it take for you to believe that this man will help us, that this man believes like we do that the future of this country depends upon peace and stability?"

"He thinks like we do, but we've failed him once before. He believes we will fail him again."

"Then why would he agree to meet? Why would he risk his life by turning over those weapons?"

"I don't know," the younger man admitted.

Abdali held back a snort. "There, you see? Yes, they've always been mistrustful of us Pashtuns, but the time has come for them to join us."

"You talk like a man half your age."

"But I'm not as naïve, trust me on that. We'll see what he says, but I suspect there will much tea and much talk about his children before we ever get down to business."

"Even at this hour?"

"Oh, yes. Even at this hour."

The next twenty minutes blurred by like the ground below, and suddenly Abdali felt the helicopter begin its descent. He leaned over, but there wasn't much to see from the window: tiny lights below, shadows broken by rows of mud-brick huts nestled in the small valley.

"All right, Mr. President," called Auss, who was at one of the windows and staring through a pair of night vision goggles. "Looks like a small welcoming party down there. I think I have Omar himself IDed. Got some armed men, see at least two with RPGs. It's up to you if you want to land."

"Take us down, Mr. Auss. Those men are Omar's bodyguards. I appreciate his show of force."

Auss moved forward and spoke quickly with Newberry, who muttered a few words, withdrew his pistol, chambered a round, and holstered it; then he took up his rifle from a rack built into the hull. Auss did likewise, then spoke with the pilots as they came down even closer toward a narrow strip lying fifty meters or so from the nearest building. In a minute they would be on the ground.

Abdali's satellite phone began to ring. He recognized the number and answered excitedly, "Hello, Omar, yes, it's me. Can you see our helicopter?"

"Yes, we can. Stand by. We're coming out to meet you. Thank you for coming. This will mean a lot."

"I am a man of my word, Omar."

Abdali waited for a response, but the governor had already ended the call.

"He's there, Rafiullah."

"Maybe you were right, Mr. President. He wants the same thing we—" Rafiullah's mouth fell open as he peered through the window.

"What is it?" Abdali leaned forward as an orange fireball bloomed in the glass.

There was only time to gasp.

And then it hit, the impact reverberating through the entire chopper as Newberry, who had shifted back, threw himself across Abdali, shielding him from the flames and flying metal ahead.

"Take off, goddamn it, take off!" screamed Auss, as the racket continued, louder now, the rotor wash deafening, icy cold air rushing into the cabin, more sounds like gunfire ricocheting off metal, the helicopter shuddering once again.

Abdali couldn't see much now, with Newberry's entire body pressed against him, but what he heard chilled him: screams from the cockpit, the chopper's engine wailing, the bulkheads quaking. Then came waves of black smoke and a horrible burning smell that left him gasping and gagging.

The dim green lights began to flicker, and Abdali felt something warm washing over his neck as he tried to pry Newberry off his chest. But the man was not moving, and that warm sensation had to be blood. For a moment, he couldn't breathe, felt only more smoke blowing into his face.

But then Newberry fell away, and there was Rafiullah, out of his seat, his mouth working, but Abdali could not hear him above the rotor's din.

Another smell now, sickly sweet: fuel.

Abdali's neck twisted as the helicopter banked hard right in a vicious turn, the restraints digging into his shoulders as Rafiullah fell away and slid across the cabin.

"Mr. President? Are you all right?" Auss screamed, dragging himself up to Abdali's chair.

"I think so!"

"They fired an RPG—hit the fuel lines! Copilot's dead; pilot's been hit with shrapnel, and he's bleeding out bad. We're flying south but losing fuel, heading for the nearest Forward Operating Base. Do you understand?"

"Yes!"

Abdali reached for the buckle on his seat belt.

"No, stay right where you are," cried Auss. "I have to go help the pilot!"

As Auss pushed himself away, Abdali saw the chopper's crew chief lying on the deck, facedown, next to Rafiullah, who was rubbing his head.

Why? Why had Omar betrayed him—even after delivering the weapons? Was there really no path for either of them?

The chopper dipped suddenly, sending a bolt of fear through Abdali. He clutched his seat and began to pray.

6. THE SECRET OF SHAH-E PARI

Khodai's two men died on the mountain pass, and he asked if Pharaoh would transport them and his other three casualties back to Shah-e Pari, thirty minutes away, where they might be buried. They wrapped the bodies in several coats donated by the militiamen and tied them on the roofs of the Pathfinders. The rest of Khodai's men would ride pack mules down from the pass.

They had confiscated the enemy's weapons and had left the bodies where they were, not bothering even to align the Arabs with their heads facing Mecca, as was the Islamic burial custom. Leaving them littered across the hill bothered Pharaoh, and he suggested policing them up and putting them in a mass grave, but Zulu told him not to bother—let that be someone else's headache. "And besides," the team sergeant had said. "We send a message to the next guys who come through here."

Now Pharaoh sat up front in one of the Pathfinders, with Zulu at the wheel. They followed a winding dirt trail along several ridges down into another valley, where they picked up the main road, a dirt-and-ice affair that had Zulu jerking the wheel to avoid potholes and prevent the vehicle from fishtailing. Pharaoh estimated that it was only ten or twenty degrees Fahrenheit outside, and the heater struggled to warm them and the other four guys jammed in the back.

He got on the BFT computer and contacted their Operational Detachment Bravo (ODB) commander, Major Barry NurenFeld, updating him on the situation, casualties, and their curiously under-armed opponents.

About a thousand potholes later, they arrived at their "safe house" in the village, the largest mud-brick structure around with a six-foot stone wall running along the perimeter. The house had a kitchen, a single bathroom, four bedrooms, and a small living room. It was a mansion by local standards. For the past two weeks, the team had been operating out of the house, which had been rented for them by a CIA field agent named Rock.

Just Rock. No one knew his real name.

The spook was standing outside the house, wearing his dirty *pakol* and a long coat that reached to his knees. The tip of his cigar flared as he took long pulls, grimacing and squinting at the smoke blowing in his eyes. His beard was unkempt, his hair pulled back in a ponytail, and with that dark complexion you'd swear he was a local; deep lines fanned out from his eyes as though he'd spent a lifetime in the poppy fields. He routinely wore a shell-shocked stare that made you think he wasn't listening to you, but then suddenly he'd reply.

Pharaoh hopped from the SUV, along with Zulu, who directed a few of the other guys to get the bodies down from the roofs. It was still dark out, the village mostly asleep save for an old man shambling up the dirt road.

"You didn't answer my calls," said Rock, after removing the cigar from his mouth.

Pharaoh shrugged. "I figured it could wait." He moved toward the house. "I need a drink to warm up."

Once inside, he headed for the kitchen area, popped the top off a bottle of Rock's whiskey, and poured himself a couple fingers into a dirty glass. After adding a little water, he took a sip as Zulu joined him, fetching himself a drink.

"So you lost five?" asked Rock, leaning in the doorway. "All Khodai's guys?"

Pharaoh nodded and sighed into the whiskey's burn.

"How many they lose?"

"All," snapped Zulu.

"So, young captain, you did well up there?" Rock smirked, then eyed Zulu.

The team sergeant raised his brows. "He did all right."

Rock's smirk turned to a full-on grin. "Thanks to my raw intel."

Rock had used the Agency's assets to gather information on enemy forces moving through the pass, and he had handed over that information directly to the team without sending it back to Langley first, which would've resulted in excruciatingly long delays. Raw intel like that was a luxury, and Rock repeatedly made sure they appreciated the favor. He was the kind of guy who'd send you a thank-you card, and inside remind you of how thoughtful he was being.

"Don't give yourself too much credit," said Zulu. "It might go to your head, like your cheap whiskey." The team sergeant held up his class, toasted, took another sip.

"Now boys, I got some bad news—but first a question. How long you figure till Khodai and his boys get back?"

"Shit, a couple hours or more. Mules are pretty slow," said Zulu.

"That should give us enough time."

"Time for what?" asked Pharaoh.

"Well, let me put it this way . . . Khodai and Haji haven't been exactly honest with us."

Pharaoh exchanged a troubled look with Zulu.

Outside, Bull and Borokovsky were speaking with the old man in the turban and tattered coat, who had come to the gate of the compound as Bull was preparing to lock the gates.

"What's he saying?" Bull asked the medic, who held up his hand: not now.

Borokovsky's Dari was pretty good, and he said quickly, *"Koo-jaw-yet zakh-mee show-dah?"*

The old man flinched, then leaned over and clutched his back while putting a hand to his head. He muttered something about his pain.

"Let them come in," said Borokovsky. "This guy's sick. He looks like he's running a fever."

"Hey, Hojo?" Bull called to the ops sergeant, who was busy unloading packs from one of the Pathfinders. "Can you help us out?"

Hojo trotted over. "What's up?"

Before Bull could answer, Zulu, Pharaoh, and Rock came bursting out of the house.

"Bull, I need you and Borokovsky right now! Saddle up!" cried Zulu. "Make sure you got your lights. The rest of you stay put."

"Where we going?" asked Bull. "Not back up there. No way. What happened? They get hit on their way back?"

"Negative. You know those first two huts up on the hill? That's where we're going," said Pharaoh, climbing into the Pathfinder.

Borokovsky cried out to Grimm to take care of the old

man, but Zulu waved off the junior medic. "No, the old man's coming with us."

"He's got a fever."

"He's got a lot more than that," said Pharaoh.

The man began hollering as Zulu took him by the wrist and began dragging him toward one of the SUVs.

"Ah-raam baash," urged Zulu. *"Ah-raam baash."*

But the man wouldn't calm down; in fact, his voice grew even louder.

"Who is this guy?" asked Bull, thoroughly confused now. "I haven't seen him in the village."

"He's one of the elders," said Rock. "His name is Zemeri."

"So where's he been?"

"He's been doing a little organizing, a little trading, the kind of business that interests us."

"It'll be okay," Bull told Zemeri, speaking slowly in Dari. "Just relax. We're going to help you."

"You know why he's sick, don't you?" said Rock. "Because he's doing business at all hours."

Once all six of them were crammed inside the Pathfinder, with Zulu at the wheel, Bull asked, "Sergeant Burrows, you mind filling in this chief warrant officer on what's happening here?"

Zulu groaned. "You'll see."

"Hey, Bull, all these little villages up here?" began Rock. "Every one of 'em's got a secret."

"And this old man knows the secrets?"

Rock snickered. "I think so."

"Then why'd he come walking up here at this hour? Just because he's sick? Or because he wants to tell us the secret? Ah, shit, guys, you're giving me a headache. If somebody don't give me a heads-up in five seconds, my brain's going to implode."

"I called him, Bull. Told him to meet us," explained Rock. "And hey, Zu, right up there." Rock pointed at the two huts at the top of the hill. Zulu hit the gas, and they began climbing the dirt path.

"Please help me," said the old man in Dari. "I don't know what you're talking about."

"Yeah, you do," said Zulu in English.

After a serious bump that nearly made Bull bite his tongue, they reached the top and pulled up alongside the two huts, each about twenty-by-twenty square, with machine guns mounted on their roofs: home security, Afghanistan style. No one was manning those guns; in fact, no one had even come out to meet them. And no one could've slept through the racket of their engine drawing near.

"Borokovsky, you hold back here with Rock and the old man," said Zulu. "We'll call you. Captain, you ready?"

Pharaoh drew his Heckler & Koch .45 caliber compact tactical pistol, the USP45CT, dubbed CT for counterterrorist by insiders and developed for U.S. Special Operations use. Everyone on the team carried one, along with a Blackhawk Gladius illumination tool, a high-tech light about the size of a cigar. Pharaoh withdrew his and hit the thumb-activated push-button tail cap, then worked the rotary dial with his thumb and forefinger, selecting the channel he wanted: momentary on. Bull did likewise.

They had practiced moving in and clearing buildings in low-light conditions so many times that Bull could do it in his sleep. And sometimes he actually did, reliving those particularly bad moments where he'd had close calls, like nearly shooting a young girl. Her face flashed in his dreams.

A wooden door caved in under Zulu's boot, and they swept into the first building, their lights playing over the empty Coke cans and Meals Ready to Eat wrappers on the floor. Some of the stuff had been supplied to the locals by the coalition's Provincial Reconstruction Teams (PRTs) in the area, while the rest might've come over from Pakistan.

"Clear," said Zulu.

The word echoed again.

So they hustled out to the building next door, whose door was hanging half open.

Inside they found more garbage, but then Bull, who'd gone into the forward room, spotted a trapdoor in the floor. "Hey, got something here."

Once Zulu and Pharaoh were in the room and had positioned themselves around the door, Bull reached down and lifted the hatch. His light revealed a small wooden ladder leading to a dirt floor some two meters below.

Bull's pulse quickened. He gave Pharaoh a hand signal, urging him to the back corner and away from the hole. Then he reached into a pouch on his web gear, withdrawing a flash-bang grenade.

Zulu shook his head vigorously, no go. He didn't want to use that much force yet. He dropped to his gut, slid forward, and leaned down into the hole, holding his pistol and light, while Bull instinctively held the sergeant's ankles so he wouldn't fall in. Zulu switched his light to strobe mode, which would disorient and severely affect the equilibrium of anyone hiding in the dark below.

"What do you see?" Bull whispered.

7. THE GOVERNOR OF CHANGE

Hajji Mohammad Omar, provincial governor of Badakhshan Province, stood in tense silence as General Malim Kahn took the young man by the neck.

"So you are the one who fired the rocket?" the warlord cried. "You are the one?"

The boy, no more than seventeen, could not answer. Kahn's grip on his throat had already cut off his air.

"Why?" Kahn demanded. "Why did you fire?"

The boy's empty RPG-7 grenade launcher slipped from his hands and dropped to the ground. He got up on his toes as Kahn lifted him higher by the neck.

"He's just a boy," argued Omar. "He got excited. He made a mistake."

"A mistake? A *mistake*?" Kahn's voice echoed up into the mountains surrounding Arakhi.

The warlord had instructed Omar's men not to fire upon the president's helicopter, not to do anything until it landed. Then, as the president emerged, they would shoot him and destroy the chopper. A small crew from al-Qaeda's media production company, as-Sahab, had been ready to film the assassination for future broadcast on the Al Jazeera television network.

President Abdali's murder would be a devastating political and moral blow to the combined efforts of the United States and its coalition and a recruiting boon for the Taliban and al-Qaeda. The image of his body and the burning chopper behind him would be seen all over the world.

Or would have been.

Deep down, Omar could not be happier that Abdali had escaped, hopefully unharmed. He had agonized over what he was doing, agonized over betraying a man that he truly believed wanted peace, a man who had given his word.

But Kahn and his supporters in al-Qaeda and the Taliban had placed too much pressure on him. They had told him in no uncertain terms that opium production would continue, that all would be well, that if he wanted to see his family prosper, he would do as they asked.

They had not openly threatened him or his family—but the implications were clear.

And furthermore, they had reminded him how Pashtuns like Abdali were not to be trusted, that they had a reputation for lying to leaders of the northern tribes and provinces.

But Omar no longer believed that. He knew that joining Abdali's new government was a better path for his people. The Taliban and these Arabs were only there to hide from their enemies and exploit his land.

Gritting his teeth, Omar wished he had the courage and conviction to stand up to them. If only the faces of his children were not so prominent in his thoughts. He could not allow them to lose their father—

As another father was about to lose his son.

Omar shivered as Kahn released the boy, who slumped to the ground.

In one quick movement, Kahn drew his pistol, aimed at the boy's head.

Omar flinched as the round cracked.

"*This* is the militia you've trained?" Kahn stormed on by and shouted orders to his half dozen men and the camera crew as he holstered his weapon.

Omar rushed over to the boy as one of the captains in his militia urged him to stand back. He pushed the captain aside, leaned over, and took the boy's bloody head in his hands.

You fired a little too close to the chopper, but you did well, poor boy, you did well. Just as I asked. Please forgive me for what I have done to you. Forgive me . . .

Omar gently returned the boy's head to the ground, his hands bloodstained, a knot forming deep in his stomach.

"Governor, what will happen now?" asked the captain.

Shuddering through a sigh, Omar rose and turned toward the mountains where the chopper had disappeared. "I don't know. But they were losing fuel. They may not have escaped." Omar turned to face Kahn's direction. "And if that's the case, I'm sure he'll be right behind them."

General Malim Kahn was out of breath by the time he reached the truck. To have planned something so thoroughly for so long—only to see it all fall apart because of a trigger-happy youth was almost too much to bear. He was fifty-seven years old and more than fifty-seven pounds overweight. His heart could barely handle the news. His temples felt about to explode, and he raked nervous fingers through his graying beard before reaching for his ringing satellite phone.

Sheikh Abu Hassan was the new leader of al-Qaeda forces in Afghanistan. He had broken out of a prison in Bagram and was the mastermind behind this mission to assassinate the president by using Omar as the bait. Kahn had been asked to lead the mission; he had a reputation for success fighting the Soviets and warring with other tribes.

The sheikh did not even say hello; his voice came slowly, deliberately, like a blade driven into Kahn's gut. "Is he dead?"

Kahn did not hesitate. He would not show weakness. "No."

"What happened?"

Kahn took a depth breath, swallowed, explained.

"We shall keep this simple. If you do not find and kill him, I will find and kill you. Do you understand?"

Hassan's Dari was not very good, but Kahn understood all too well. "Yes."

"And you will take the media people with you. I want all of it captured on film. I will call you later. I hope you will have good news."

Kahn thumbed off the satellite phone and whirled to face his brother Fahim, second in command of their militia. "The maps! Get the maps. Where are they headed? Who do we know south of here?"

For the next ten minutes they sat in the cab, poring over several maps, making predictions about which way Abdali's pilot would head, how far he might get, what cities and towns lay in his path.

"He will land soon," said Kahn, trying to convince himself of that fact. "He must."

"He will, brother. Look here . . ." Fahim traced his finger over one of the relief maps, leading southwestward from Arakhi, running parallel to the border with Tajikistan, and moving down to the village of Eshkashem. "His bodyguards are Americans. They will advise the pilots to head back to the nearest operational base."

"Why wouldn't they head back to Feyzabad?"

"I think he's well aware of our contacts and influence there."

"We will call them anyway."

"Of course, but I think this is their path."

Kahn clutched his chest. The shooting pain was getting worse.

"Are you all right, brother?"

"I will be. How many men can we get here?"

"Another twenty, thirty, but it'll take some time."

"Get them. And we'll follow your path south."

"Your trust is welcome."

Kahn placed a hand on Fahim's shoulder. "I hope it is well put. Let's get to work."

"All right, but one more item. Omar."

"What about him?"

"I saw him looking at the boy, just as the chopper approached. I saw him whispering something to himself. I think he put the boy up to it."

"You have a vivid imagination."

"Listen to me. Omar does not want to work with us. He doesn't say that, but he thinks it."

Kahn chuckled under his breath, causing more pain in his chest. "You read minds now?"

"No, but he has a huge ego. He has told me on more than one occasion that he does not want history to repeat itself for the people of his province. He wants to be the governor of change."

"If you'd like, before we leave, we will confront him with this. And if you can coerce the truth from him—"

"Then we will kill him."

Kahn raised his finger. "Careful, brother. Hassan would not approve. Omar is worth more alive than dead."

"No, you will be governor."

For a moment, Kahn found that utterly amusing, but then, the more he thought about it, the more attractive the idea became.

He would be remembered not for his deeds against the Soviets or the infamous cases of torturing his prisoners that had found their way into the media's hands, no.

He would be remembered as the true governor of change, the governor who by exploiting the Taliban and al-Qaeda brought untold riches to his people.

And to himself.

8. A MOUNTAIN TOO HIGH

"We've lost too much fuel! He has to put us down on the side of the next mountain," shouted Auss, the bodyguard's chiseled face twisted in a grimace. He tore off his ball cap and wiped sweat from his shaved head.

President Abdali nodded and glanced at Rafiullah, who had strapped himself back into his seat. "This was a mountain too high!" cried the young man.

Abdali pursed his lips and looked away. He could not understand—he might never understand—what had happened.

Now they were hurtling toward a mountainside with a dying pilot at the controls of a crippled helicopter.

The copilot was already dead, along with the crew chief and Newberry, who had saved Abdali's life.

"I'm sorry," shouted Rafiullah.

Abdali felt overwhelmed by the bloodshed and death, the rush of cold air into the cabin, and the tremendous whomping of the rotors. But the utter fear clutching his aide's face made him realize that he needed to remain strong.

"It's okay," he cried. "He'll get us down there. We will make it!"

"Mr. President, I want you to know what a great honor it has been. I want you to know that I'm thankful for everything. I still believe in what we're trying to do."

"We're not going to die! Not yet."

"All right, I called NATO for help," Auss said from the copilot's chair. "It's going to be a while, but at least they'll know where we are! Now get ready; we're going down. Brace for impact!"

The helicopter pitched forward, throwing them hard against their straps. Abdali's head snapped back as the air seemed to grow colder and rush more violently through the holes in the fuselage. The engine revved higher, sounding as though it might rip from its mounts.

Outside the round windows, snow swirled against a black canvas, and there was no telling up from down, west from east, no telling how close they were to touching down—

Until the engine changed pitch, deepening as the bird dropped once more, as if through a chute of air, falling; then a slight bank left, leveling off, yawing a little to the right, and suddenly they rotated a moment, the centrifugal force hard, then gone, then Abdali got thrown back in his seat.

Twin thuds reverberated up from the landing gear and into the cabin. Auss shouted something, his voice lost in the rotors, lost in a scraping sound that worked up into the floor, across the bulkheads, as the engine began to whir down.

"We made it," said Rafiullah, chuckling through his words. "We made it! We're on the ground!"

Abdali took a deep breath. He had never been so thoroughly exhausted, so drained of life.

And then a sensation, like the ground suddenly giving way beneath his feet, took hold, seemed to grab him by the stomach and drag him down.

"We're sliding," shouted Auss.

The entire fuselage shook so violently that fire extinguishers and other gear attached the bulkheads began tumbling to the deck.

Suddenly, the chopper turned, or at least it felt so, then began to tip onto its side.

Abdali clutched the arms of his seat as the rotor blades chewed into the mountain, a sound so loud, so violent, that he couldn't fully register it.

Pieces of rock and ice torn free by the blades began pinging off the fuselage like gunfire, like a catastrophic hailstorm beating on metal, some pieces shooting in through the shattered fuselage and blasting overhead.

A piercing whine erupted from somewhere outside, followed by a grinding noise—the engine beginning to seize up—and Abdali imagined that the rotor blades were being snapped off as though they were made of balsa wood.

The whine gave way to a tremendous boom; glass shattered as the cockpit lights flickered off and a long, slender silhouette appeared just out of arm's reach.

It dawned on Abdali that the silhouette was actually one of the rotor blades; it had snapped off and sliced through the fuselage, crashing down and jamming itself in the steel.

After another jolt and more echoing creaks of metal, the chopper rolled completely onto its side—even while continuing to slide down the mountain. Rafiullah hollered. Auss let out a groan, a curse, a scream.

With his feet hanging in the air, and the chopper shimmying so much that he feared it would just break apart, Abdali bowed his head and surrendered to his fate.

Perhaps it would come quickly.

Perhaps his senses would fail him at the end, spare him the terrible pain.

Yet even as he considered that, pain did come. Something had broken free from the wall and slammed into his side, knocking the wind from him, crushing his arm and ribs—

And then the weight was gone just as quickly.

Instinctively, he cried, "Rafiullah!"

"I'm here!"

"Auss?"

The bodyguard did not reply.

"Auss?"

Snow and ice blasted into the cabin as the helicopter seemed to fishtail a little, still sliding, sudden bumps sending Abdali slamming even harder against the straps that now dug deeply into his shoulders.

He tasted blood, reached up, felt his wet face, his runny nose. He gasped, the air suddenly thinner.

As the panic was about to take hold, he focused on his breathing, tried to slow it down. No more panting.

The pain in his shoulders was unbearable, and he knew it was foolish, but he just couldn't take it anymore. He dug his thumb under one buckle, released the left strap—

And suddenly he rolled out of his seat, his arm coming free of the other strap. He tumbled over the next seat, then dropped across another to finally slam onto the cold sidewall, snow showering across him from the shattered windows as they scraped across the mountainside.

He took a breath and wanted to scream. The straps had been unbearable, but now the pain in his ribs made him dizzy as he fumbled to grip something, wondering if the chopper might roll over again.

Darkness draped the cabin above, fluctuating as though it were underwater, shadows elongating, pierced by flying debris, the opposite sidewall undulating.

He tried to move back, away from the snow still blasting up at him, but another bump sent him into the air and back down with a hard thump.

Rafiullah screamed his name.

He glanced around, wondering when it would all end.

Would they plummet off a cliff? Would the helicopter finally break apart, crushing them beneath massive shards of steel?

And there was so much unfinished work. So much . . .

He slammed shut his eyes, lay on his side, heard only his breathing, his pulse, a faint hissing noise, a sudden muffled boom, followed by more hissing . . .

The engine noise was gone. He opened his eyes.

His entire body was covered in snow. He blinked, back-handed more snow from his eyes.

The walls creaked. The wind whistled through the jagged seams of steel. Was that moonlight?

He kept still, listening to the sound of his breathing, feel-ing the agony of it, the blood freezing on his lip. Another creak from the chopper. He grimaced at the stench of fuel. Would the helicopter explode like they did in the movies? Should they rush outside? Could he even reach a hatch?

Oh, it hurt to breathe. It hurt terribly. He wanted to stand, but he was afraid. He wanted to speak, but he feared the pain.

"Mr. President?" Rafiullah's voice sounded low and distant.

Abdali bit back the lightning in his chest. "Here!"

"I'm going to get out of my seat."

A slight rustling came from above, then suddenly a light pierced Abdali's eyes, and he raised a palm to block it.

His aide had found a light and was coming down. The thought that he was not alone was incredibly comforting. Not alone. With someone.

"Do you see Auss?"

The light panned away, shone upward, and for a moment, Abdali caught sight of the man, facedown and pinned beneath the rotor blade that had cut through the cabin.

"I think he's dead," said Rafiullah. "It's just us, Mr. President. Just us."

"Rafiullah, you want me to say you were right?"

"Don't say anything. I'm coming down to you."

"It hurts to breathe."

Within seconds the younger man dropped down to the snow-covered sidewall, where Abdali lay. Rafiullah shone the light in his face, noted the blood, and said he'd be back, that there must be a first aid kit somewhere inside.

"We have to get out," said Abdali. "Don't you smell the fuel?"

"I think we would've blown up already."

"You are the expert on helicopter crashes now?"

"Sir, don't argue with me."

Abdali shifted his weight up onto his elbows, and it hurt. "Find a way out first. Then come back for me. You do that now."

He threw his head back, wondering how history would regard him if he died on this mountainside. Would those historians brand him a naïve fool, a martyr for peace, or just a figurehead propped up by coalition forces?

Better to live and prove them all wrong.

9. RELIABLY UNRELIABLE INTELLIGENCE

"Hah-ree-cot nah-koe! Sel-lah-heh-ta par-taw!"

Zulu's voice echoed into the cellar, but his cry in Dari of "Do not move! Drops your weapons!" had been wasted.

In fact, it seemed the story of his goddamned life in Afghanistan was being a day late and a dollar short.

He remembered a mission in which they'd been tracking what they liked to call an HVT—high value target: a suspected al-Qaeda leader, Hassan's #2 man, into the mountains, only to miss capturing him by two hours. Two lousy hours.

And so it was that in the flashing light of his strobe, he took in the room from an upside-down vantage point to be sure. He saw enough to roll his thumb on the dial, turning the Gladius to constant on.

He took another look, then said, "All right, help me up."

Bull grabbed Zulu's CQB rigger belt and dragged him away from the hatch enough so that he could shift onto his side and sit up. "It's empty."

"Get the old man in here," said Pharaoh.

Zulu nodded, got on his radio. The young captain was learning fast.

"Oh, they're back to their tricks, huh?" asked Bull.

"Yep. They don't listen." Zulu crawled back to the hatch, climbed down the ladder, then dropped into the cellar, Pharaoh descending behind him.

The cellar was about half the size of the house, just dirt wall reinforced with rotting pieces of wood and a few crumbling bricks. He worked his light over the imprints in the dirt, long rectangles, squares, and lots of footprints.

Pharaoh crouched down, directing his Gladius toward a patch of ground from which he drew several long splinters of wood. He rose and took them over to the support beams along the wall. "No match here," he said.

"Of course not."

"Hey, Zu? Got the old man up here," said Bull.

Zulu lifted his chin to Pharaoh. "Captain, would you like to question him?"

The captain sounded tentative. "Got any tips?"

Zulu reached into his pocket and produced his favorite EDC (everyday carry) knife, a unique piece called the Jani-Song. Inspired by the Filipino balisong, or butterfly knife, the Jani-Song had an outer handle, an inner handle, and a blade that all rotated on a common pivot pin. With practice, the knife could be opened incredibly quickly and firmly locked into position, ready for action.

Zulu could do things with the Jani-Song that had the other guys shaking their heads in disbelief. As a personal friend and student of the blade's designer, Michael Janich, Zulu had an inside track on the knife's unique design and carried it with pride and deadly confidence. Every chance he got, Zulu practiced his manipulations with the knife. Right now, he wanted to instill the seriousness of the moment into young Pharaoh. With an instinctive up-down-up movement, he had the blade out and locked into position with its familiar click. He held the knife before Pharaoh's eyes. "You have to be firm."

"I'll get what we need." Pharaoh quickly ascended the ladder, and Zulu made a few more deft openings and closings with his blade before pocketing it and turning to the ladder.

Up top, Pharaoh began his questioning, while Zulu waved Rock outside to the yard behind the houses.

"You know, Rock, I'm beginning to wonder about you," Zulu began, accepting a fresh cigar from the CIA agent. "You get us all riled up . . . for what? More bullshit and bad HUMINT?"

"Well, can't win 'em all. Reliably unreliable intelligence is how some of the boys back home describe it. But come on, Zu, we both know they just moved it. What do you want from me?"

"I want the location."

Rock removed the cigar from his mouth, turned away to face the mountains. "You know, my mother was a psychic. The Army hired her to predict enemy troop movements in Vietnam. She had a ninety-three-percent success rate."

"Well, maybe you inherited the gift. Lead the way."

"Wish I could. But the old man knows. Let's see how your new stud is making out."

They drifted back into the house—

Where Pharaoh had his gun pressed up against the old man's forehead screaming, *"Coo-dja? Coo-dja?"*

"Jesus Christ, Captain, I suggested firm, not this!" cried Zulu, coming up to Pharaoh and slapping a hand on his wrist. "Let him go."

"Damn right, you're going to trash a year's worth of work here, Pharaoh!" hollered Rock.

"Well, what the hell?" said the captain, pulling away. "He's not cooperating! He's a stubborn old bastard."

"Bull, you're standing right here, watching this?" Zulu asked the assistant detachment commander.

"I thought you told the captain to get what we need out of this guy . . ."

Rock moved up to the old man and said in Dari, "Zemeri, we know you keep moving them. Just tell us, and we'll get you some help. You're sick. We want to help you."

"I'm just an old man."

"You're an old fighter. Old mujahideen. You fought the Soviets. We know all about you."

"Then you know I will never tell you."

"Rock, tell him if he cooperates, we'll make a deal with him. Tell him we just want to see what he has. Tell him we won't take anything away. We just want to see," said Pharaoh.

Rock complied, and when he finished, the old man said, "You are liars. If I show you, you will call your higher command, and they will give you orders."

Zulu nodded. The old man knew exactly the way their world worked.

"Rock, tell him we'll tear this place apart if he doesn't show us," said Pharaoh.

"Captain," Zulu said in a warning tone. "These guys shut down when you threaten them, unless you plan on flying some bombers overhead. Besides, he knows what our mission is here. He knows it's against our orders."

"I'm not threatening. I'm promising."

"Let's just bribe his ass," said Rock, pulling out a wad of cash from his pocket. "How much for the location?" he asked Zemeri, waving the bills before the old Afghani's eyes.

Zemeri swiped the entire wad from Rock's hands, then pulled a cigar from Rock's breast pocket, waved it, and said, "You know the caves on the west side?"

Zulu slapped a palm on Pharaoh's shoulder. "Let's go."

The entire group filed quickly out of the house, piled into the SUV, and made the ten-minute drive across the village and up into the western hills where a series of man-made caves, constructed during the 1980s, lay just beyond reach of the Pathfinder. They got out and hiked another ten minutes along a ridge, where they found a trail of mule tracks and dozens of footprints.

Zulu spotted the first cave himself, and the old man nodded and pointed.

With that, Zulu, Pharaoh, and Bull moved ahead, leaving Borokovsky, Rock, and the old man near some talus and scree at the base of the hill. The medic began examining Zermeri: pulse, heart rate, respiration, the works.

The cave entrance was only about a meter and a half square; Zulu hunched over and slipped in first, Gladius and .45 leading the way.

The place had been reinforced with a few smaller beams. The dust kicked up into his eyes as he squeezed farther inside; then he found himself emerging into a much wider area, perhaps four-by-four meters square, with a ceiling of nearly six feet. The earth smelled sweet and damp, and there was another odor, a very familiar one . . .

"Holy shit," gasped Pharaoh.

"Yup. Holy shit," echoed Zulu.

The team sergeant liked to think that he'd been in the Army long enough so that nothing ever surprised him.

And oh, yeah, he'd been in the Army for a long time. Shit, he'd come in twenty years earlier as a field artillery observer in the airborne brigade in Italy. Three years after that he'd gone into SF and had spent fifteen consecutive years in Germany with the 10th Group as a weapons sergeant and had worked his way up to ops sergeant.

He'd thought about retiring when he hit twenty years,

played with the idea of becoming a cop, a teacher, or an athletic coach, but those boots just didn't fit right. He couldn't explain it. So he wound up reenlisting and went to the 5th Group. His COs had described him as a "hard-core warrior who neither gave nor tolerated any nonsense." He prided himself on knowing both office admin stuff and field tactics inside and out, and the voice of his father guided him every day: you can do anything you put your mind to . . . anything.

As a former weapons sergeant, he was a qualified sniper who cross trained in medical. Along the way he also became a "knife geek," collecting, training with, and mastering as many edged weapons as he could get his hands on.

Moreover, his years in Germany made him a mountaineering professional since his ODA was a mountain/high altitude team. He spoke fluent German and could fake his way through a few other European languages. Switching to 5th Group required him to learn Arabic, which didn't come easy, but he eventually picked it up, as he had Dari and Pashto, prior to arriving in Afghanistan two years ago for his first twelve-month tour.

Now he was finishing up his second tour, and would probably opt for a third so long as they let him play unconventional solider and—like Frankie said—do it his way. He'd been lucky twice so far, getting young captains who didn't give him a hard time, who seemed intelligent enough to let him fight his team, let him keep his call sign Zulu when everyone else had to come up with a one beginning with "T." It was the little things in life that gave him pleasure.

And no shit, he got a kick out of playing Merlin with these young studs, watching them gasp and walk around bug-eyed while he instructed them in the ways of the knighthood, even though they were ultimately being groomed to create fancy PowerPoint presentations on laptops and wield coffee cups instead of combat daggers.

And yes, indeed, Pharaoh was still gasping as they brought themselves to full height and panned their lights around to study the full contents of the cave.

10. COLD HOPE

The bulkhead creaked as President Abdul Abdali shifted painfully closer to the cockpit. With his left arm tucked tightly against his ribs, he stepped over the hatch that once would've allowed them to get out; but since now the chopper was lying on its left side, the hatch was pressed firmly against the rock and snow.

Rafiullah had tried to get the rear hatch open, but he didn't know how and guessed that the lack of power for the hydraulics would've prevented him from doing so anyway. He was up in the cockpit now, wrestling with the window latch on the port side, which should open skyward but wouldn't. He groaned in frustration.

"The nose got crushed when we were rolling," said the young man. "This latch won't budge. I can try breaking the glass."

Abdali pressed his head against the canopy, cupped one hand around his eyes, and stared off into a thick bank of clouds shrouding most of the mountains. "He said he called NATO."

"What was that?"

"I said he called NATO. They'll be coming for us. We have to find his phone. And the fuel . . . it doesn't smell as bad now."

"That's because you're getting used to it."

"No, I think it's okay."

"I'm not going to sit here with five dead men, Mr. President. We're getting out."

"Okay. Break the glass. Go outside. Tell me how you like the weather."

Rafiullah shifted back to the cabin, retrieved one of the fire extinguishers, and returned to begin pounding on the glass. They had underestimated the strength of the canopy, and so the aide began working on the corner latch, trying to pry it free, each thrust of the extinguisher slamming hard onto the metal and echoing through the helicopter.

After the tenth or eleventh try, Abdali cried, "Enough!"

"Sir, please . . ."

"Take a break." He gasped against the new knives in his ribs. "Take . . . a break."

Rafiullah lowered the fire extinguisher, let his head droop to one side, his breath coming hard. "I hope that after we're rescued you will seek *badal* against Omar."

"I've been thinking about that very carefully. If his plan was to shoot us down as we landed, then he would've been successful. There is no way they could've missed."

The young man shook his head, incredulous. "You're saying they took a shot at us to warn us?"

"I don't know."

"Well, we both know the code. And we both know what we must do."

Rafiullah was referring to the Pashtunwali Code, which

Pashtuns used to express their religious devotion. It was centered on honor (*namuz*) and shame (*haya*), and those 5,000-year-old cultural practices often overruled religious ones. They placed a high value on hospitality (*malmastia*), solidarity (*nang*), territorialism (*ghayraf*), bravery (*tureh*)—and revenge (*badal*).

As a Pashtun, you had to offer shelter and sanctuary to all in order to confer honor upon yourself; you had to remain devoted to families, tribes, and designated leaders who represented your tribe; you had to be loyal to your homeland and willing to defend it at all costs; you had to be brave and fight offensively, not shame yourself in defensive or security roles; and you had to take revenge upon those who wronged you—because failure to do so was perceived as shameful.

"We don't know what happened with Omar. We don't know what pressure he was under," Abdali reiterated.

"You're defending the man who just tried to kill you?" Rafiullah said incredulously.

"We don't know everything."

"We know he betrayed you. What else is there?"

"Perhaps he was ready to deal. They got to him, knew his weakness: his family."

"I say we spray his crops. We destroy all of the poppies in his province. Then we see who he turns to for financial help: the Arabs . . . or us. My hope for his support has turned cold."

Abdali glanced back through the canopy. The night was slowly washing away, but the clouds were growing thicker, darker, and the wind began to pick up, howling once more through the cracks and holes in the fuselage.

He turned his gaze to the dead pilot, still strapped in his chair, a huge bloodstain smeared across the bulkhead below. The copilot hung limply from his chair, helmet thankfully hiding his death mask. Only then did Abdali notice how much blood had sprayed across the cockpit. The darkness had concealed much of it, but now he was closer, too close.

"Sir, may I continue on this window?"

"Go ahead."

As Rafiullah's pounding resumed, Abdali slowly picked his way out of the cockpit and began his search for Auss's iridium satellite phone. He got choked up as he remembered the bodyguard carefully explaining how they would always be in touch with coalition forces via the phone. Sixty-six low-earth-orbiting (LEO) cross-linked satellites with multiple in-orbit spares created the largest satellite network in the world.

Abdali reached the man's body and, wincing, began searching through his pockets, coming up empty. He glanced around the cabin, then spotted the small phone lying near the edge of a window and crossed to it.

He touched a key, and the light green screen glowed to life. He hit the redial key, calling back to Kabul, and the man on the other end who answered gaped when he heard Abdali say, "Hello, this is President Abdali. Are you there?"

"Uh, yes, sir."

"Our helicopter is down. The crew is dead, as are my bodyguards. My aide and I are the only survivors. I don't know our GPS coordinates, but perhaps you can home in on this phone."

"That's correct, sir. We received your last set of coordinates. Stand by . . ."

"I have them!" cried Abdali.

Rafiullah released a cry of his own: "I got it! The window's open!"

11. BETWEEN A ROCK AND A HARD PLACE

Pharaoh's utter surprise had turned into anger. He shook his head at the walls of crates stretching from the floor to the ceiling, warehouse fashion.

"Don't look so surprised, Captain. You knew there wasn't strippers and booze in here," muttered Zulu.

After rubbing his eyes and swearing under his breath, Pharaoh replied, "I could use a drink and a lap dance about now. Damn, how long you think they've been stockpiling this stuff?"

"Not sure. But they're smart. I'm guessing they must have four or five hiding places and keep moving it around, adding to it, trading the old out for the new when they can. Some of it might've been part of the Northern Alliance's cache."

Pharaoh nodded.

Zulu and Bull had already pried open a few of the crates, which contained machine gun ammunition, rocket-propelled grenade rounds, 82mm mortars, mines, 107 rockets, rocket fuses, and AK-47s and ammo. There were about forty crates, a significant weapons cache for this little village, along with a dozen or so bricks of opium paste, wrapped in plain paper and stacked inside another crate. Who knew how many other boxes contained Afghanistan's #1 export?

"Triage, this is Titan 06, over," Pharaoh called over the radio.

Borokovsky responded immediately, and Pharaoh ordered him to bring the old man into the cave. The medic protested, saying his patient shouldn't be climbing and needed to get some bed rest—but Pharaoh insisted.

"Well, I know what Rock will say about this," said Bull.

"Oh, you do?" asked Zulu. "What? He'll want to confiscate the weapons then sell them back to them?"

Bull directed his light into Zulu's eyes, and the team sergeant cursed and held up his palm. "If you'd shut that hole, I'll tell you."

"Fine. I'll have my attorney contact you about my blindness."

"All right, so the spook's pitch'll start out like this: they've been holding out on us. We found that little cache when we first got here. That was our first clue. But these guys don't trust their buddies to the south, the Pashtuns, and they don't trust the Taliban or the Arabs. They don't really trust us. All they have is this little village, and all they have to protect themselves from the Taliban or al-Qaeda is this cache. That's the sympathy card Rock will play. Trust me. But don't let them fool you, Captain. This stuff has to go. They can't have it, no way, nohow."

Zulu nodded. "We either take it out or blow it—because we can't trust these guys with a cache like this."

"You don't trust the way we've trained them?" asked Pharaoh. "I thought they did pretty good up at the pass."

"That's not it. These people got nothing. Rock's been

able to bribe 'em very easily. Once he's gone, all it'll take is a couple of Arabs to come in here and flash some money, and they'll get the location of this cache pretty quick. They'll steal all this. Khodai and Haji are playing with fire. I mean, where's their security now? We strolled right in here."

"We borrowed their security, remember?" Pharaoh pointed out. "And they lost five guys."

Zulu sighed loudly. "Captain, you have to call it in, and I know higher will tell us to confiscate everything, especially the mortars and 107s. They don't need this shit. Maybe they'll send up some jingle trucks to haul this out."

Borokovsky, Zemeri, and Rock shifted into the cave. The medic's eyes widened. The old man frowned. Rock nodded, studying the crates appreciatively, and said, "Bigger than I thought."

"Captain, if you don't mind, I say we wait until Khodai and Haji get back, then we confront them and see what we're going to do," said Bull. "They're good men. We owe 'em that much."

"We don't owe them anything," said Zulu. "They stored this crap here, they didn't tell us, and who knows what else they got going on behind our backs? Opium bricks right here, deals with al-Qaeda over there . . . we can play the who do they trust guessing game, but the fact is we got this cache, and it doesn't belong here. It poses a huge security risk."

"Slow down there, Zu," said Rock. "You take away their cache, you undermine a lot of good work. I want to use this as leverage. If we play it right, this'll turn out to be our lucky day. But we have to play. I tipped you guys off in the first place to help you gain more loyalty. You owe me for that. We show them what a favor we're doing by letting them keep the weapons. I agree you should confiscate the opium."

Pharaoh shifted over to Zemeri and spoke softly in Dari. "Why didn't you tell us about this?"

The old man's eyes widened. "It's none of your business. This is our village, and this is part of our protection. You Americans will not be here for very long, and when you leave, we will be all alone."

"See?" said Rock.

"You know we can't let you keep this stuff," said Pharaoh.

"If you take it away, we will have no way to defend ourselves."

"Are you kidding me?" Zulu interjected. "We've created an organized militia here. We've trained and armed your men. That's enough."

"It's not enough. It will never be enough. The Pakistanis cannot control their border. We cannot control our border. The Arabs will come. They will not stop. This is our land. And we will defend it," Zemeri declared.

"Captain, it's your call," said Zulu. "Make the right one."

"Whoa, it's not his call," said Rock, popping the cigar from his mouth. "It's *my* call. You boys work for me. This is my show, right here, right now. My agency discovered this cache, and my agency will decided how this goes."

"Rock, that was never made clear to me in my orders," said Pharaoh.

"Of course it wasn't. Young man, let me teach you about how this works. My three-letter agency is the brains. Your four-letter agency is the brawn."

Pharaoh might have been young, might have been inexperienced, but his superiors believed in him and he, for the most part, believed in himself—which was to say he didn't have to take this brand of bullshit from the spook. "Uh, Rock, unless I hear that from my CO, it doesn't mean anything to me. So my seven-letter response to your three-letter agency's request stands." Pharaoh wriggled his brows, pleased with his verbal foray.

Rock took a moment to figure out what Pharaoh was

saying. He threw up his palms. "I'll have your CO give you a call, and he'll make it abundantly clear to you, okay?"

Pharaoh smiled darkly. "Have fun. Everyone outside. Bull, I'm posting you and Borokovsky here, but I'll send up relief when we get back to the safe house."

The assistant detachment commander nodded.

"Zulu, you told me you neutered this young stud, just like the other guy. What the hell happened?" asked Rock.

The team sergeant was wise enough to keep his mouth shut, and Pharaoh's glare helped.

Outside, they trudged back to the truck, loaded up, and drove to the safe house in silence. Pharaoh sent Ondejko and Gator back out to the cave to relieve Bull and Borokovsky.

During the hour and a half it took for Khodai and Haji to arrive, Pharaoh listened to more arguments from Zulu, Bull, and Rock. It was interesting how different things were in the field. If such a scenario were presented to him during his training, he would not have imagined the others so vigorously offering their views.

Whatever he decided would be the lesser of evils choice, a damned if you do, damned if you don't decision. Take away the weapons and piss off the Tajiks. Let them keep the weapons and risk them being stolen by the bad guys, only to be used against coalition forces. The real irony was that the United States had supplied much of the ordnance, first to the mujahideen in the 1980s to fight the Soviets, then to the Northern Alliance in more recent years. Some of the weapons might've also been smuggled in from Tajikistan.

Because Rock, Zulu, and Bull had been so passionate about the situation, Pharaoh had been willing to delay calling higher until he spoke with Khodai and Haji. A delay didn't mean much, especially with his men posted at the cache.

When the G-chief and his assistant finally did arrive, they were ushered immediately into the safe house, where they sat at a long table and were given hot kava, which was made by actually boiling the leaves. Afghans liked to drink their tea green, and the stuff was bitter enough to trigger a grimace, so it was common for them to hold a hard candy in their mouths as they sipped.

Rock made small talk with the G-chief and his assistant, expressed his condolences over their loss at the pass, expressed his admiration for their bravery, then carefully said that Pharaoh wanted to ask them a few questions.

Khodai removed his *pakol* and scratched his oily black hair and beard. He widened his eyes and a weak smile broke the dark planes of his face. "It has been a very long night."

"And I'm afraid it might be a very long morning," said Pharaoh. "We, uh, we heard some rumors about you and your men hiding some weapons, so we followed up on it." Pharaoh lifted his gaze to Zemeri, who sat on the opposite end of the room, looking more ill. "Zemeri did the right thing and showed us where you're keeping them."

The color faded from the young G-chief's face, and he slowly sat back from the table, turning a penetrating stare on Zemeri. Then he flicked his gaze to Haji, who shifted uncomfortably in his seat.

Sergeant First Class Jason Ondejko and Staff Sergeant Gregory Gatterson sat on either side of the cave entrance, their rifles draped across their laps. Ondejko was already nodding off, and he told Gator that if the younger man did catch him drifting that he should give a shout.

"You got it," said Gator, whose nickname came from his obsession—and it was an obsession—with his favorite college football team, the University of Florida Gators. The guy was a human sports computer, rattling off stats like a prisoner forced to study one subject; his knowledge of the team was scary good.

Ondejko had been awake for nearly thirty hours straight, and he had mentally prepared himself for a long snooze back in the safe house, only to be torn away and sent back up to the hills. At least it was warming a little, but that made him feel comfortable enough to drift off.

"Talk me to, Gator. Tell me a story."

"Okay, I'll tell you what happened to me at this tailgate party."

"No. Can't be related to football in any way, shape, or form. What else do you do with your life?"

"Why do you care?"

"Because I'm worried about you."

"Yeah, right. I don't do anything else. I'm an SF guy. A Gator fan. And that's it. My life is shit."

"Yeah, it is. Tell me a story."

"I'm thinking . . ."

As Ondejko waited, the mountainside grew darker and seemed to break over him, like the shale had turned to black water and washed him into sleep.

For how long? He didn't know.

A sudden shake at his shoulder sent him bolting awake.

"Yo, wake up!" cried Gator, who was hovering above him. "Got some window-shoppers."

Ondejko blinked, noted the four Tajiks moving up toward the cave entrance. He clambered to his feet clutching his rifle, careful to keep the muzzle pointed down.

The lead Tajik was Rastin, one of Khodai's lieutenants, a man Ondejko had trained himself. Rastin waved and smiled at them, so Ondejko returned both.

"My friend, a long but victorious night," Rastin began as he walked right up to Ondejko and proffered his hand.

One of the other guys, a sergeant named Parsa, reached out to shake Gator's hand.

Ondejko took a step back, tightened his grip on his rifle. Gator did likewise.

And that was when the other two Tajiks raised their rifles, one covering Ondejko, the other Gator.

But in that spilt second, Ondejko and Gator managed to get their rifles up, aiming at Rastin and Parsa.

"Rastin, tell them to back off," said Ondejko.

"No, you back off. You go to your safe house. We will take over for you here. That is our mission."

"You know I got orders," Ondejko reminded him.

"And so do I. And that is all we are, huh? Men who follow orders?"

"You got a cave full of weapons back there. You've been holding out on us, buddy. What do you want me tell you? Back off, right now."

Rastin's tone grew sharper. "No, Sergeant. We won't."

Ondejko flicked his glance to Gator, who seemed part pissed off, part shitting a brick. Then he eyed Rastin. "I'm going to call the captain. Why don't you call Khodai?"

"Okay, yes, that's right. We are just men who follow orders. No need to die over our own reckless decisions. Better to get killed and blame it on someone else."

"Yeah, whatever. Now I'm going to reach for my radio. Okay? Okay?"

12. PYRRHIC VICTORY

Pharaoh was about to say something when Khodai's satellite phone rang.

"Uh, excuse me for a moment." The Tajik stepped away from the table, then cupped one hand over his ear. He spoke quickly and quietly.

At the same time, Zulu got a call from Ondejko, and he shifted back from the table, saying, "The captain's busy right now. What do you got?"

"Haji, we can work this out, okay?" Pharaoh said. "Don't worry."

The man's birdlike face grew even sharper, his eyes narrowing in disgust. "Yes, you will work it out. You will take away our weapons, leaving us with what little you've provided, and then you will go home when your government and the coalition decide we are no longer worth the effort."

"We're helping you to help yourselves."

"Is that this week's advertisement? You only help us because the Arabs coming across the border want to blow up more of your buildings and planes and kill more of your people."

"That's not entirely true."

"Maybe you should wage war on your own arrogance before hunting down al-Qaeda and the Taliban."

"Haji, where is this coming from? We've worked together, trained together."

"Captain, we understand the role we play, and that's why we take steps to protect ourselves. You cannot deny us that."

Khodai returned to the table, but as he sat down, he nonchalantly drew his sidearm—

And suddenly that pistol was pointed at Pharaoh's head.

Chair legs screeched along the floor as everyone slid back from the table. Zulu and Bull were cursing, and Rock hollered something to Khodai.

Pharaoh reflexively threw up his palms. "Khodai? Slow down! Slow down!"

"You're not taking our weapons!" he screamed in Dari. "We won't let you! We won't!"

In the few heartbeats it took for the G-chief to utter those words, Haji was able to draw his own pistol, as were Bull and Zulu.

"Okay, buddy. I haven't called my CO," Pharaoh began.

"You posted men at the cave! Well, they are in our custody now!"

Pharaoh glanced sidelong at Zulu.

The team sergeant raised his voice and said, "Khodai, I just spoke to Ondejko, who's up at the cave. You don't have anyone in custody."

"I can order my men to fire. You know that."

"You do that, and the captain here will call in a bomber, and we'll take out this whole village. We say there's a high value target here. You know how it works. One phone call."

"Gentlemen, if we would put away these dirty guns and raise our tea glasses, I think we'd accomplish a lot more," Rock said, lifting his glass.

"No," said Khodai. "Not until the captain promises me that you will *not* be taking our weapons."

"Khodai, I can't do that," Pharaoh replied. "And you've got opium in there. Who's getting that? How the hell do we know you're not working with us *and* the Taliban and al-Qaeda? We both made a promise to be honest with each other."

Khodai averted his gaze. "I can't keep that promise. And neither can you."

"So what are you going to do? Shoot me? Will you call that a victory?"

"Khodai, do you know the story of King Pyrrhus?" Rock interrupted. "He fought against the Romans and won, but he lost all of his friends and his best commanders. There weren't even men to recruit for his army. He said that another victory would have killed him. He won. But he lost. Do you understand?"

"You're saying that if I keep my weapons, I will win, but I will lose?"

Rock stroked his beard in thought. "Let's make a deal. Let's see how much of that cache you can keep. I don't think we need to take it all. You don't need the 107s, not here. And we can talk about the opium. But I'm betting we can really do you guys a big favor and let you keep most of it."

"You will do that?"

"We're on your side. But we have superiors we need to convince. That's going to take some work on our part, and we're going to risk our careers to do it, but it might work. Just calm down, put your pistol away, and have some more tea. We'll reach an agreement. We want you to protect yourselves. That's why we're here."

Khodai's suspicious gaze turned to Pharaoh. "Captain, do you agree with him?"

Pharaoh eyed Zulu, whose expression was as emphatic as Rock's. "Yes, I agree. Zulu, call Ondejko. Tell him and Gator to remain in position but they're not to engage anyone. Tell them they're on a joint mission to guard the cave, along with Khodai's men."

"You got it." The team sergeant holstered his pistol and got back on his radio.

Khodai considered for a moment longer, then slowly lowered his weapon and barked to Haji to do the same. He eyed Pharaoh. "We fought together. We are brothers. You shouldn't forget that."

Pharaoh steeled his voice. "I won't. Never. Call your men up at the cave. Tell them to stand down."

Khodai nodded and made the call. Bull holstered his sidearm.

"Now we're making some progress," said Rock.

Pharaoh gingerly lifted his teacup and took a sip. He then took the kettle and was about to refill Khodai's glass, but the Tajik covered it and said, *"Bus."* Enough.

Pharaoh said, "Tell me about the opium."

"We have friends across the border in Tajikistan who take payment for arms. Some of the ammunition we acquired from them. This is drug smuggling to you. It is survival for us."

"But don't you understand? You pay them in opium, and you just contribute to the problem."

"What problem? What else can we produce that is worth anything to you? To them? Our farming is barely enough for us. There's nothing here!"

"He's right, you know," said Rock. "Even Abdali has admitted that he can't control opium production. Oh, he's trying. But he can't. It's all they really have. They're not making Nikes and Sony TVs in this province."

"Khodai, what makes you think the weapons are secure?" asked Zulu. "You moved them, we know. And you keep moving them. But you had no one posted there."

"I did post two young boys with radios. They must have gone home or run off. I don't know."

"How old?" asked Pharaoh.

"Ten or eleven. I needed every man up at the pass with you."

Zulu's frown deepened. "Khodai, you really think you're ready to fight, ready to use some of the stuff you got in there? Mortars, rockets? RPGs?"

Before Khodai could answer, Zemeri, who'd been utterly silent in the back of the room, held up his fist, shuffled slowly forward, and pounded the hardwood table. "They are ready to fight!" His voice came shrill and broken. "Like their fathers did with me. Like we have always done. Soviets, Arabs, Taliban . . . they all try, and they all fail . . . we are ready. We have always been ready to die for our people and our land."

Zemeri's words were striking, but even more powerful was the expression on his face, the deep blue eyes, penetrating eyes, eyes that you knew had seen more than he was ever willing to share.

And those eyes had grown heavy with tears. He was choking up, his lip quivering, his hands beginning to shake as perhaps he relived the battles of his youth, saw the faces of the friends and the brothers he had lost.

It was truly moving. Even Zulu, recruited and promoted by Satan himself, seemed taken by the man.

Rock hustled from his chair and helped the old man back to his seat.

Pharaoh stared down into his glass. And he'd thought *his* first night in combat had been tough.

Now he was faced with a choice like this? There shouldn't be any question. They'd found a weapons cache, and the only ones issuing weapons around here were coalition forces.

Allowing these locals to procure and stockpile their own weapons was wrong. Period.

But if Zulu and Bull had taught him anything, it was to slow down and ask questions. Lots of questions. And at the moment, they did have the luxury of time.

Or at least he'd thought.

"Sir, I'm sorry to interrupt," called Hojo from the doorway. The assistant operations sergeant appeared rosy-cheeked and breathless.

"Hojo, we're in the middle of something here," said Pharaoh.

"I understand, sir. But I need you to come out to the truck right now."

"It can't wait?"

"Sir, absolutely not, sir."

Pharaoh groaned, pushed back his chair, and slowly moved around the room. "Hojo, if life and death are not involved—"

"Sir, please come with me. And you'll understand."

Outside, the eastern skies were beginning to fade from deep blue into a faint orange, and the wind had gone home for the morning. Pharaoh took a deep breath, checked his palm: damn it, he was shaking just like the old man had.

Christ, what a moment back there.

"I'm almost afraid to ask, Hojo."

"Don't be, sir."

As he and the assistant ops sergeant reached the truck,

the sergeant turned to Pharaoh, grinned, and said softly, "Sir, we just got the mission of a lifetime."

"Oh, yeah? They sending us to Hawaii to infiltrate some bikinis?"

Hojo blushed. "No, sir."

The ops sergeant opened the passenger's side door of the Pathfinder and gestured to the BFT computer mounted before the dashboard. "Go ahead. Read it."

As Pharaoh climbed into the SUV, he glanced back at Hojo, who now wore a serious shit-eating grin.

Then he eyed the computer screen—

And the words he found there left him shaking his head, as though the orders weren't real, couldn't be happening, not to a green-ass captain like him.

13. GOOD ON CAMERA

Governor Hajji Mohammad Omar's eyes were swollen shut. His lower lip had ballooned. His nose was bleeding. He had wet himself, and the odor was beginning to fill the room.

Now he lay in the corner, near the broken chair, his back pressed against the mud-brick wall. He was a pitiful sight, and General Malim Kahn almost felt guilty. Almost.

"I hope we can still be friends," said Kahn, who stood next to his brother, wiping the blood from his fists.

"Yes, me, too." Fahim chuckled, despite having ruined a brand-new tunic and cursing over that moments earlier.

"We were never friends," said Omar, his voice barely above a whisper.

"But now we will be. Now that you understand what you're going to do."

"I will never resign as governor."

"Sure you will. You'll do it for your family."

Omar slowly shook his head.

"We're going to leave you here to think about it. Your bodyguards are dead. There's no transportation. We'll come back for you in a few days, once you've had time to decide. The people here have been ordered to keep you, otherwise they know what we'll do to them. Now, before we leave, I'll ask you one more time: did you order the boy to fire upon the chopper?"

"No. He was just a boy . . . too eager, not very well trained."

"All right. We'll return shortly."

"Kahn?"

He turned back from the doorway.

"You think I am weak?"

"Yes. Because of your family. That is the crease in your armor. That is your weakness."

Suddenly, Omar leaned forward. "I will have my revenge! I swear to you, Kahn! I will have my revenge!" He shook a fist at the sidewall, unable to see.

"You'll have nothing."

Kahn and Fahim left the small house and climbed back into their truck. They had procured a half dozen old Toyota Tundras from some friends in Kabul, and now their convoy would move south, following Fahim's suggested course and the new lead they had just received:

Some militiamen in Eshkashem had heard the president's helicopter fly overhead and had gone out to watch it vanish over the horizon. The chopper had been flying low and they had said they could smell the fuel. Additionally, their contacts in Feyzabad had not reported any sign of the helicopter.

Kahn had promised a handsome reward to any man in the village who could locate that chopper, and he was told that a group of about forty had already assembled under the leadership of a mercenary soldier and had begun making their way south, some on mules, most on foot.

Kahn's trucks would move much quicker, of course. They had about twenty in all now, most of the fighters seated in the flatbeds and huddling against the chill. They would follow the only dirt road south to Eshkashem and eventually catch up with the militia moving south. They were about 150 kilometers north of the village, but they wouldn't make very good time with all of the potholes and switchbacks in the road. Also, as Fahim had pointed out, a serious front would move through the area very soon, bringing with it the possibility of heavy snow.

They were the second truck in the convoy, with Fahim at the wheel, Kahn in the passenger's seat, and the three media people from as-Sahab crammed in the backseat. There was a young reporter in his twenties, lean with a long, narrow nose; a cameraman of about forty, heavy and unkempt; and an engineer, a scrawny little man who wrote furiously in a notebook.

Kahn glanced back at the group and said, "Do you think I look good on camera?"

The young reporter flicked his glance to the cameraman, who said in broken Dari, "Uh, very good. Yes. Very good."

"You hear that, Fahim? They are professionals. They can see the camera loves me."

"Do you want to be on camera? That is the question," Fahim replied.

"Why not?"

"Oh, if we successfully kill the president, you will be one of the world's most wanted men."

"An honor."

"Brother, do try to be serious."

"Yes . . ."

Kahn threw his head back on the seat and closed his eyes. He thought of the glory days, years ago.

Among his many accomplishments was one that stood out: he had controlled a key road that connected Pakistan with Kabul, via the Khyber Pass. He had set up military checkpoints that had enabled him to steal money and goods from all kinds of travelers. He'd had an army of more than one thousand, and those who opposed him were beaten with rifle butts or rubber pipes, raped, and a host of other forms of torture, including having their ears cut off.

He had used a simple but effective plan to win the hearts and minds of those in the local villages: he had employed teams of men dressed like bandits to attack, steal, and murder in these remote towns. Then he would enter as the villagers' savior, saying that if they pledged their allegiance to him, acted as his eyes and ears, then he would protect them. At the time, the American and coalition forces were powerless to stop him, and he was able to control both areas in the north and south, a feat unrivaled by any other warlord.

Some of his men had taken his orders too far, to be sure. At one checkpoint his soldiers had captured a man and turned him into a "human dog," keeping him in a hole and forcing him to eat the testicles of those they killed for challenging them.

That was unfortunate. But yes, he was renowned and feared, and he had wielded far more power than he did now. First the Americans, then the NATO forces had slowly stripped him of his deserved strength and honor. President Abdali had made a pledge to use "the stick" in dealing with warlords and their private militias. He and the Americans had forced him into hiding, stolen his equipment, brainwashed his men.

Yet the tide was turning again. And Kahn's future looked bright. His talks with Sheikh Hassan had renewed his spirits.

He must maintain that furor. He must not surrender!

He sat up, beat a fist into his palm, then glanced at Fahim. "We're going to get him."

Fahim understood all too well what was at stake. "Yes, brother. We will."

14. THE ULTIMATE WARNO

Pharaoh called back to FOB Asadabad via satellite phone to confirm the data glowing on the Blue Force Tracker computer's screen.

Yes, the WARNO (warning order) was legit, as verified by Major NurenFeld, who went over it in detail.

SITREP: A'stan president's helo ambushed during meeting with provincial governor. Helo damaged and supposedly crashed at grid 115813. Iridium contact number to follow. Dismounted threat forces closing on crash site.

Task: Conduct personnel recovery operations for A'stan presidential group. Helo crew reported dead. Recover to nearest coalition FOB possible.

Purpose: Prevent the kill or capture of A'stan presidential group by threat forces seeking to affect A'stan governmental stability or gain propaganda value.

Method: One UH-60A inbound your location, joint fire support coordination under way, immediate CAS not available, launch ASAP, send additional support requests when ready.

Following that, Pharaoh updated the major regarding the weapons cache they had discovered, and NurenFeld said he couldn't get those big cargo trucks everyone referred to as "jingle trucks" up there before the team left.

"Sir, there's been discussion about taking out the mortars and 107 rockets but letting them keep the rest of the smaller stuff. Rock's been pushing hard for that. What do you think?"

"I think we confiscate the entire cache. Period. Unless I hear differently from higher."

"Well, sir, we can't stay now. What do you suggest we do in the meantime? If we just leave the weapons without posting a pair of guys here, there's a good chance they'll move them again. And I can't afford to leave anyone right now."

"And you guys don't have time to rig a nice explosion or follow-up to be sure you've destroyed everything. Let me get back to you on this. Meantime, you prep to go. That's your priority. Not that weapons cache."

"Yes, sir. I'll brief you as soon as I can."

"Good."

Pharaoh hung up, then he got on his radio, called Ondejko, and ordered him and Gator back to the safe house.

"But what about the cache?" asked the weapons sergeant.

"Tell Rastin and those guys to guard it carefully."

Ondejko sounded surprised. "All right, I'm sure they will. See you in a few, out."

Pharaoh burst back into the safe house. "Gentlemen, this meeting is over. We've been given new orders. Khodai, we'll need to leave soon. I called my CO, told him about the cache. No decision yet. He'll get back to us. Meanwhile, you keep your men posted there, all right?"

The Tajik shrugged, glanced to Haji.

"What's going on?" asked Rock.

"Big party. Sorry, you weren't invited."

"Come on, Pharaoh, I can get on my laptop and find out in two minutes. You share your raw intel with me, I share mine with you."

Ignoring the spook, Pharaoh turned back to the Tajiks. "Khodai? Haji? You guys can go now. Go get some sleep. We'll let you know what's going on soon."

The two men stood, clearly unhappy with the turn of events, and shuffled slowly out of the room.

Pharaoh closed the door behind them. He wondered whether or not he should speak in front of Rock, but the CIA agent was right: he could easily pick up his own intel within minutes.

The three men stared impatiently at Pharaoh. He took a deep breath. "President Abdali went out for a meeting last night with the provincial governor here."

"That would be Governor Hajji Mohammad Omar," said Rock. "Nice guy. I've met him twice. Big family man. Of course, he's been looking the other way when it comes to opium production, but hey, business is business."

"Yeah, well maybe he's a drug dealer and an assassin. The president's bird got shot down. We're not sure who's responsible. We do know he's alive."

"We got his location?" asked Zulu.

"Yeah. And that's the reason they called us. We're about a hundred and twenty klicks south of his supposed grid co-ordinates. We've been ordered to recover him. You can check the BFTs for the WARNO. We have a Black Hawk en route. But we also have some dismounted guys from Eshkashem moving southwest to intercept. We're not exactly sure who they are: Taliban, al-Qaeda, could be Tajiks from across the border. I'm sure Signals and everyone else is working on IDing them. They're about forty-eight klicks away, but that terrain is rugged, so we should be able to intercept."

"We need the maps," said Bull. "I'll go get 'em out of the truck." He sprang from his chair and jogged out of the room.

"Zu, if you can round up everyone else?" Pharaoh asked. "I already called Ondejko and Gator."

"You got it. So we're going to rescue the president of this country. Damn. You walk in here, first command, and you get a mission like this? If I were religious, I'd say God has a plan for you."

"Aw, it's dumb luck. Right time, right place. We're closest to the crash site. What we need to do now is seize the day, bring home our VIP, and then—and only then—will the beers be on me."

Zulu gave a curt nod. "I'll hold you to it."

"Yeah, otherwise, this won't be the mission of a lifetime like Hojo told me. It'll go down in infamy, with our names on it. You remember Colonel Charles Beckwith's failed attempt to rescue those hostages in Iran in 1980?"

" 'The Debacle in the Desert.' But that wasn't his fault, you know. Choppers broke down, pilots weren't trained well enough in those ops."

"No, it wasn't his fault, but people are still writing about it. And they never fail to mention him."

Zulu's tone grew emphatic. "He created Delta Force."

"I hear you. And their first mission was a spectacular failure. This one has that same potential. Not just a failed mission. A *spectacular* failure."

"What are you now? A prophet of doom? Hell, you're working with some of the best operators in this community—especially me." Zulu winked, whipped out his Jani-Song, and made a couple of impressive knife deployments; then, in one fluid motion, he clipped the blade back into his pocket.

"Damn straight," Pharaoh said. "Let's get some."

"Gentlemen, if you don't mind, I need to make a few calls," said Rock. "I have a feeling I'll be receiving an invitation to your little jaunt up north."

"Glad to have you," said Zulu. "I'll pull you in front of me when the bullets start flying, that way I can leave my body armor back home. Then again, maybe you should stick around and mind that weapons cache."

"We'll see. You know I'm not up here for my health. I've got multiple agendas. We'll see how things prioritize themselves."

"Oh, yeah? What else you got on your plate?"

Rock and Zulu left the room, still talking, and Pharaoh headed outside, where he found Khodai waiting for him.

"Still here? You look very tired, my friend," Pharaoh said.

"You're going to leave us. You're going to take our weapons," Khodai repeated.

"I didn't say that."

"You are leaving."

"We have to."

"Where are you going?"

"Khodai, I can't say."

"North?"

Pharaoh sighed deeply, then gave a resigned nod.

"If you plan to drive, you will need a guide. The road won't help much, and the trails are very bad. You told me yourself that your maps are unreliable. You will get stuck without a guide."

"Can you spare someone?"

"Haji will be here with the men. I'll come."

"You?"

"Please. Maybe we can talk more along the way."

"I'll think about it. But right now I'm very busy, all right?"

"I'll stay here until you decide."

"It's up to you." Pharaoh waved over the rest of the men, who were also waiting out near the gate, and they all filed back into the safe house.

Once they gathered around the table, some in chairs, most leaning against the walls, Pharaoh gave them a capsule summary of the warning order, then told radio guys Weathers and McDaniel to designate a pickup zone and make sure they guided in the Black Hawk, relying upon their joint tactical air controller qualifications. Weathers left to find that zone and make contact with the helo, and McDaniel would update him on the rest of the briefing.

Meanwhile, Zulu and Bull had spread two maps across the table, along with a pair of laptops.

"All right, so we got some militia moving southwest from Eshkashem. No way to tell if they know exactly where the chopper is, but the fact that they're moving in the general direction is enough to get our attention," said Bull.

"Well, looks like we got another problem right here. In order to get to that grid, we'll have to cross the Anjuman Pass here," said Zulu, tapping his finger on the map.

"So?" asked Bull.

"So, that's fourteen thousand five hundred feet. You walk three steps, you take a break. You walk another three steps, you take a break. It's twice as cold and your radio batteries last half as long. Shale gives way under your feet, and down you go."

"Not to mention trying to get a Black Hawk to fly that high while fully loaded," said Pharaoh.

"If we luck into some good pilots and decent weather, they might be able to do it. Been done before," said Bull.

"But not with all of us," said Zulu. "Too much gear, too much weight."

"So it's a split team direct action mission," said Pharaoh. "It has to be. One recovery team, one interdiction team."

Zulu and Bull nodded, almost in unison.

Pharaoh continued: "Recovery team falls back to the pickup zone, gets prepped, and flies directly up to the crash site. Interdiction team packs up the SUVs, and drives up to interdict, attrit, and otherwise kick the asses of those militiamen moving toward the site."

"Sir, how many MOs we talking about?" asked Hojo, referring to the enemy militiamen by their more politically incorrect name Mohammads or MOs.

"No details yet on the size or composition of this force, but most of these little villages are barely populated, so we can't be talking about large numbers. Maybe twenty? Thirty? We'll request updates en route. Maybe we can get a Predator up here to fly over and grab some images."

"So we'll only be outnumbered five to one instead of ten," quipped Hojo. "Sounds good."

"Also remember those guys are on foot," said Bull. "That much has been confirmed. Average speed on that rough terrain is about three to four kilometers per hour. Figure they'll near the site in ten or twelve hours, not counting on any weather issues. Interdiction team should be able to intercept them in about five hours, if we leave within the hour. I figure the trucks will only average about twenty to thirty miles an hour at best, and if the hills get too steep, we may have to leave them behind. That's the part I'm concerned about."

"Khodai wants to come along as our guide," said Pharaoh. "He's reminded about how unreliable our maps have been up here. Maybe we take him."

"That's a good idea," said Zulu.

Bull nodded.

"All right. Now all we need to do is divide and conquer," said Pharaoh, shifting over to a notebook and clicking a pen.

RECOVERY TEAM	INTERDICTION TEAM
Bull (team leader)	Pharaoh (team leader)
Hojo (asst. ops)	Zulu (team SGT)
Gator (asst. weps SGT)	Ondejko (weps SGT)
Sullivan (asst. engineer)	Figueroa (engineer)
Borokovsky (medic)	Grimm (asst. medic)
McDaniel (asst. commo)	Weathers (commo)

"Bull? You get the cush job of recovering the president," Pharaoh continued.

Zulu shifted over behind Pharaoh. "This looks good. Bull, we're going to make you famous."

The assistant detachment commander grinned. "It's not the fame or fortune I seek, gentlemen. It's the beer and women."

"Hooah!" cried the rest of the team.

"All right, so let me say this." Pharaoh swallowed, anxiously shifting his weight. "I, uh, just want to thank all of you for your advice, encouragement, and support. You are the best operators in this community. So we're going to bring it to them, and we're going to bring it hard. All right, gentlemen. Let's gear up and get the hell out of here!"

Pharaoh watched as his men nodded and hurried out of the room, leaving him, Bull, and Zulu behind to finish their planning.

Before they could begin, in walked Rock. "Well, boys, you got room for one more?" He wriggled his brows.

"Probably not," said Pharaoh.

"Maybe we can tie him to the roof?" suggested Zulu.

"Or just drag him from the tailgate," Bull said.

Rock threw up his hands. "Langley sends their love too."

15. SIGNS, SISTERS, AND PORTENTS

The remarkable turnover of truckloads of Taliban weapons in the Badakhshan province capital of Feyzabad would be the lead story of the week—

Or at least that was what National Public Radio correspondent Sandra Hildebrand had thought. She had been stationed in Feyzabad for the past month, working on another piece about the renewed drug trade and its connection to terrorist activity. The interviews she had gathered were, in her humble opinion, pretty damned insightful—not to mention that she had risked life and limb in the process.

But now, as she hurried around her squalid hotel room packing a bag, her thoughts focused on the recent and more exciting news.

Her producer, the gray-haired and regal-looking Rich Oswaller, and her engineer, the heavy-set technonerd Bill Neggy, both kept in close contact with their military connections back in Kabul. Apparently, there was some activity northeast of them, near the Anjuman Pass. Rumor had it that someone in Abdali's government might be involved.

Hildebrand was not one to pass up on an opportunity like that, and she, unlike her sister, Tracy, did not mind helicopter travel; it was simply a necessary evil of her profession.

Answering a knock at her door, Hildebrand found her sleepy-eyed sister standing there in her robe, her long, gray-streaked black hair flopping in her face. "Where the hell are you going now?"

"North. Near the Anjuman Pass."

"Where's that?"

"North."

Tracy smirked.

Hildebrand darted toward a small dresser, withdrew a bag containing her toiletries. "Why don't you come? It'll be exciting to get out of this dump for a while."

"Sandy, look at you. You're forty-two years old. You're running around like you're still back at Harvard."

"But that was more work and less fun than this. Come on, Tracy. This is who we are. This is life. And if that can't get you excited . . ."

Tracy smiled knowingly. "Well, it's not the Peace Corps in Morocco, that's for sure."

"No, it's not."

Hildebrand had been reporting from Afghanistan for the past five years, and during that time she had inspired Tracy, an activist back home in Berkeley, to come out and see what was happening all over the country. Tracy had been moved enough to found a nonprofit organization called War Crimes in Afghanistan, designed to uncover corrupt NATO and American military practices that were resulting in civilian deaths and destroying Afghan society. She had more than one hundred volunteers working for her, with nearly twenty of them stationed in Kabul. She had come up to Feyzabad to keep Hildebrand company (and watch her back) while she was working there.

While Hildebrand didn't entirely agree with her sister's politics, she respected them. The military had made some grave mistakes in Afghanistan. But it had done some remarkable work as well. She wouldn't make her final assessment until years from now, when there was time to analyze and reflect.

"Go get ready," Hildebrand told her sister.

"We're driving, right?"

"All the way up there?"

"Oh, come on, Sandy. You want me puking all over you? I will not fly in that thing again."

"You will."

"No, but you'll just use that tone to guilt-trip me. You learned that from Mom."

"You should've paid more attention to her. You could've learned that too."

"Well, have fun." Tracy started back from the door.

"Be ready in five minutes."

"I'm not coming."

"Tracy, I need you."

"You don't need anyone."

"Then why are you here?"

She shrugged. "I like shitty hotels like this. I'm a martyr, don't you know?"

Twenty minutes later they were both in a car with Oswaller and Neggy speeding toward the small airport, when they found the road blocked by a pair of trucks parked in an arrowhead formation: a checkpoint of sorts.

Suddenly, their car was surrounded by five or six gunmen, all wearing black turbans.

"All right," began Oswaller, who was at the wheel and tugging nervously at his beard. "I'll talk to them. Just another toll."

"Can I pee in my pants first?" asked Tracy.

The lead gunman, a dusky-skinned, heavily bearded man with small eyes, moved up to the car and muttered something to Oswaller.

"How much do they want?" asked Hildebrand quietly.

"I don't know yet," he snapped.

Hildebrand tugged nervously at the burka covering most of her face. She itched to talk, knew that if she did she would further incite the men.

The lead gunman suddenly shifted to the back of the car and rapped a knuckle on Hildebrand's window.

Oh, shit. She slowly rolled down the window.

He reached inside and yanked down her burka. "You are the American reporter from NPR, right?"

She took a deep breath. "*Bah-lay.*"

"Out of the car," said the gunman.

"It's okay, please," said Hildebrand, then made a face and motioned as though she were bringing a glass to her lips. "My sister is depressed and has been drinking."

"Out of the car!" he screamed.

"Oh, no, no, no," said Hildebrand. "This is not how we want this to go. How much?"

"Wait a minute," said Neggy, the engineer. "Ask them if they want to be on TV."

"But we're radio," said Hildebrand. "He knows that."

"He doesn't really know," Neggy said. "I have a camera. Tell him we'll put him on TV."

Hildebrand translated exactly that into Dari, then added, "I'll interview you right now, come on!"

But the gunman had already thrust the muzzle of his

AK-47 into the car. He wasn't listening, just screaming, "Get out!"

"Sandy, what do we do?"

"Listen to him," she cried. "Just get out. Rich, show them some money."

As Hildebrand slowly opened her door, two more of the gunmen came closer and covered her. She raised her palms, glancing over her shoulder at Tracy, whose eyes burned.

Something was wrong. This wasn't a routine checkpoint set up by local thugs. These men had newer-looking weapons and seemed trained.

One of them reached in and hit the trunk release, then another two rushed to the back of the car.

"Here, we'll pay you," said Oswaller, thrusting a wad of cash toward the leader.

But the gunman ignored Oswaller to wave over his comrades. They began chatting quietly, just out of earshot.

"It's just too early in the morning to die," said Tracy.

"Why did you have say that?" asked Hildebrand.

"Because if they don't kill us, the helicopter pilot will. I have no luck today."

Suddenly, the lead gunman broke off from the group. "You are okay. For now."

"What's going on?" asked Oswaller. "We've never seen this checkpoint before."

"We're not supposed to talk about it."

"Please, tell us. Maybe we can help," Hildebrand blurted out.

The militiaman scowled at her, then said, "Governor Omar is missing. He may have been kidnapped. We've set up roadblocks all around the airport. But this morning, we know that at least one American news crew is not responsible."

"Thank you," said Hildebrand.

"Can we go?" asked Oswaller.

"Yes. The toll is five hundred dollars."

Oswaller rolled his eyes at Hildebrand, who widened hers. "Pay them. And let's get going."

16. THE CALM BEFORE

Bull felt proud to lead the recovery team. He and his merry band might get credit for rescuing the president of Afghanistan.

How could he beat that in his long and illustrious career as an operator?

It wasn't every day you were tasked with a mission of such great importance.

So why was he also feeling let down?

Because the odds were against his team seeing much action. They'd reach the chopper before enemy forces could get close enough to pose a problem, pick up Abdali, and be out of there, while Pharaoh and Zulu played hit-and-run.

And that was too bad. The firefight up at the pass had rejuvenated him, reminded him that the hunting of men cannot be duplicated, that there was no taste like it anywhere in the world. Ernest Hemingway had thought so. Bull knew so.

But it was not his day to hunt.

Take the good with the bad. Move on.

No great revelations there. Just the way it was.

For their part, Weathers and McDaniel had found a broad stretch of ground about a quarter klick south of the village, and Zulu had dropped off Bull's team to await pickup there. The temperature was dropping, and it smelled as though it would snow any minute.

They had received updated intel via spy satellite on the position and composition of the enemy force moving toward the crash site: approximately forty men with an ETA of about twelve hours, as Bull had predicted. New weather information indicated a front would begin to move through within the hour and most likely stall over their position. Wonderful.

A second bit of intel regarding the president's party indicated there were only two known survivors, the president being one of them, and that he had sustained some injuries, possibly broken ribs and a fractured arm.

Their young Captain Pharaoh had already back-briefed the CO on their plan for a split-team mission, and he had learned that a squad of Rangers was coming with the helo and would be dropped off to secure the weapons cache until such time as they could transport the weapons back to the FOB.

Bull and his men had topped off their canteens and Camelbacks and loaded up on ammo, rations, medical supplies, and any other crash/rescue equipment they could scrounge up, including portable litters and lots of spare IVs.

They would also take along the Special Operations Forces Mountaineering Equipment Set (SOFME), comprised of rock hammers, ice axes, ascenders, three types of snap links, descenders, five types of pitons, eight sizes of stoppers, cliff hangers, two sizes of piton ice screws, full body climbing harnesses, mountain rescue pulleys, crampons for their boots, two sizes of snow anchors, two sizes of tubular webbing, and five sizes of rope/accessory cords. Bull hoped they didn't have to use the gear, but getting to the crash site could prove the greatest challenge. As of yet no images had been sent.

And once they were there, they had no idea how difficult it would be to gain access to the bird, so they'd take along their tactical entry kit purchased with the team's slush fund money. The kit, manufactured by their good friends at Blackhawk, included nonsparking, electrically nonconductive hammers, rams, and other tools specially designed for such breaching activities, all stored within a quick-dump backpack.

Of course they would continue to wear their Army combat uniform (ACU) trousers per Army regulations—the JAG lawyers said they had to wear at least one article of U.S. milspec issue gear, so they always opted for the trousers, what the hell. And of course Bull would take along his goodluck charm, a challenge coin given to him by his father, an old Army tanker who had spent many years in the 1-72 AR in South Korea.

Being superstitious was not uncommon among operators, and ODA-555 was no exception. Before splitting up, everyone on the team had rubbed Ondejko's bald head for luck, a ritual started by Zulu. He said that any and all bald guys must yield their lucky noggins to their greasy palms. Captain Pharaoh had agreed with a hearty: "So let it be written, so let it be done."

As Bull sat on his pack, watching the oncoming front smother the orange streaks of dawn, his gaze swept down from the horizon to the five operators seated around him.

Hojo gave him a slight nod then returned to cleaning his rifle. He was arguably the most anal-retentive member of the team, which made him a great assistant ops sergeant and would someday make him an even greater team sergeant.

Attention to details, experience, and unwavering commitment did a world of good when you found yourself in a world of shit. For the most part he was a quiet guy, all business, and everyone liked him because he rarely did anything to get on your nerves. People said he had a forgettable face, but you wouldn't forget his expertise or bravery.

Gator, whose call sign "Tombstone" fit him well, was an accomplished sniper, humble, yet sometimes a bit too pessimistic. The dour look on his face said it all: I don't want to be here; I want to be on the interdiction team, spitting steel. He was a good guy because he didn't bitch and moan, but he didn't roll with the punches, either. He just gave you the look: I hate this. When he spoke, it was with a deep Georgia drawl of which he was very self-conscious. Bull had even caught him with a pronunciation book designed to neutralize one's accent. They'd poked fun at him for weeks over that.

Sullivan, the team's assistant engineer, liked to have fun with girls and C-4 for what he called "precision destruction and sexual operations." Additionally, he was also a dedicated Sudoku player, quipping that sharpening his logic skills not only made him a better operator but also a better lover—because "as we all know" sex and math are the same thing. Okay . . . At the moment, the fair-haired, fair-complexioned man with the ruddy red beard had his pencil working across yet another of his Sudoku puzzles in a book as thick as a rifle mag.

Medical Sergeant Steven Borokovsky had been a handsome fellow before coming up to the mountains. He could've been a TV host or a soap opera actor, but the last eight months had worn him down like the spring rains eroding the mountains. His face was now hidden beneath a dust-laden beard, his blue eyes shaded by a seemingly permanent squint. Like any good medic, he kept his own emotions in check, balancing the tears and bloodshed with a healthy dose of humor. He noticed Bull eyeing him and said in a mock Russian accent, "It is big mountain we go. And I like. We rescue important man. It will be difficult. But don't worry. I am Borokovsky. I am here."

Bull cracked a grin. "Have another glass of vodka, comrade."

"Yes, more vodka."

Last but not least was the affable Rudy McDaniel, assistant communications sergeant aka rookie radio guy, who'd gone to school with Pharaoh and could have been dismissed as a kiss-ass captain's pet. In truth he wasn't especially friendly with the detachment commander, or at least not in front of anyone, and he spoke deftly about his gear and the steps he was taking to ensure its continued operation. He carried the AN/PSC-5C "Shadowfire" tactical satellite radio, and the AN/PRC-150 high frequency and FM radio, as did Weathers. The fact that he was also Joint Terminal Attack Controller (JTAC) qualified made him an even greater asset. Though his eyes still bore the look of a teen, his even tone and technical prowess had already won over Bull. McDaniel spoke expertly with the helo pilot as the sound of whomping rotors grew more distinct.

17. THE OPTIMIST

Zulu loaded the last bag into the back of the Pathfinder, slammed shut the rear door, then jumped into the SUV. Pharaoh sat in the passenger seat, studying the BFT computer, while Khodai and Rock warmed up in the back.

The other Pathfinder was driven by Ondejko; Figueroa sat up front with him, while Weathers took a rear seat with his bulky radio pack.

"And we're off like a herd of turtles," said Zulu.

"A herd armed for bear," added Pharaoh.

Along with their personal weapons, they'd taken the team's pair of M240B medium machine guns, the M24 SWS (Sniper Weapons System), some AT-4 rockets and extra cans of machine gun ammo, some antipersonnel mines, and some demolition explosives.

Most important, they carried with them the blood, sweat, tears, and proud traditions of every Special Forces operator who had come before them.

Firepower was one thing, but if it wasn't backed up by a

hard heart ready and willing to kill, it meant nothing. Zulu was already trembling with the desire to engage the enemy. He imagined the hills, the ridges, the targets. He already heard the crack of gunfire, was already leaping into a machine-gun nest, his primary and secondary weapons already empty as he slashed the throats of his adversaries.

He shuddered even harder.

"So what's the latest and greatest?" asked Rock, leaning forward to glimpse the BFT's glowing screen.

"Well," began Pharaoh, placing his finger on the map. "Our bad guys are still moving, and they're about here."

Rock sat back, typed quickly on his own heavy-duty laptop with wireless satellite connection.

"You know something we don't?" asked Pharaoh.

"Hang on. The crystal ball's still cloudy."

"Captain, are you going to take the main road here?" asked Khodai, pointing at the map showing the gravel path leading north from Shah-e Pari all the way up to Feyzabad.

"Yes."

"We must make a turn here," said the Tajik. "Because this part of the road is impassable."

"Well, shit, that'll slow us down."

"You remember the earthquake last month? The boulders are still there."

"You know the detour?" asked Zulu.

"I do, but we've crossed it on mules, not in trucks."

"First time for everything." Zulu switched on the wipers. "Here comes the snow."

The road ahead wandered toward towering peaks more than a hundred kilometers away. The smaller hills lay barren, quickly collecting snow across their bare sides. Parts of Afghanistan were incredibly beautiful, Zulu knew, but this place was hard on the eye, broken rock surfaces amid piles of talus and scree lying everywhere.

Then the road got a lot bumpier, taxing the Pathfinder's suspension, and he checked his mirror to make sure that Ondejko was keeping up. They ran without headlights, though it was light enough now so that he didn't need his night vision goggles. He wished they were traveling at night—much better cover. Now everyone and his grandmother could take potshots at the passing vehicles.

Pharaoh got on the radio and was talking to Bull, who reported that the Rangers had arrived and were pissed that they had to walk back to the village.

"That's okay," Pharaoh said. "Tell those fat bastards I said they can use the exercise."

"Roger that. And hey, you want the good news? The helo they sent is an old 'A' model, one from the California National Guard, only one they had in time."

"What are you saying?"

"I'm saying we're in for one hell of a ride. We'll be lucky to cross the pass."

"Well, you tell that pilot he's got to push it!"

"I've already talked to him. Guy's a CW5 with like eight thousand hours of flight time. He even flew in 'Nam, for God's sake. He claims the engines will have enough ass to get us up there. But you know how those guys are. And the weather's getting shitty over here. Just an FYI, in case it goes FUBAR on us, over."

"Roger that. Talk to you soon, out." The captain shook his head. "You believe that?"

"That's not like Bull. He doesn't bitch like that, unless . . ."

"Unless what?"

Zulu caught himself. "Hey, we were lucky to get a helo in the first place. I know some people who wouldn't mind seeing Abdali rot on that mountain. They don't think he's doing a goddamned thing."

"What do you think, Zulu?" asked Rock.

"I don't."

"Bullshit, you're one of the most opinionated and ego-tistical assholes I know."

"And you mean that in the best possible way," Zulu said through a slight chuckle.

"That's right. So tell me where you stand. Tell us, on all of this . . ."

Zulu glanced over at Pharaoh. No, he wasn't about to bare his political soul. "I'm an optimist."

"And a comedian," said Rock with a snort. "What's the best way to stop the Taliban, stop al-Qaeda, and put an end to the drug trade here?"

"I'll answer that," said Pharaoh. "We have to secure the border with Pakistan, and we can do that by slipping into Pakistan and winning over all those tribes. They'll help us. And we have to provide economic support to the locals re-lying on drug money to survive, and we have to continue with direct action missions to hunt down and eliminate terrorists and those who aid and abet them."

"Hallelujah!" cried Rock.

"You got it all figured out," Zulu said, lifting a brow at Pharaoh. "Except the part where we cross the border into Pakistan."

"That can happen through joint negotiations between us, Abdali, and the president of Pakistan."

"Son," cried Rock, "you're on your way to becoming a glorious politician. Statesman and solider. But no, those aren't the answers. Zulu knows. You going to tell us?"

Zulu chuckled under his breath. "Nope."

"Come on, brother. Educate this young leader of men."

Pharaoh eyed Zulu, waiting.

He sighed loudly for effect. "All right. You'll never secure the border. Ever. You'll never stop the drug trade. You'll never eliminate all the terrorists. The answer is that there is no answer. But that's okay. Doesn't matter. We do our best. And we take it one day at a time. Like I said . . . I'm an optimist."

"Whoa, whoa, whoa, slow down," said Pharaoh, who had raised a pair of binoculars. "Got some movement up along those hills to the east."

Zulu glanced up through the window, couldn't see jack, couldn't take his eyes from the dirt path for fear of smashing into some of the larger rocks.

"Aw, hell, they got two big machine guns up there, look like DShKs. Who the hell are these guys?"

"Yeah, I see 'em, too," said Rock, clutching his own binoculars. "At least four guys running for the guns."

The DShK was a Russian 12.7mm heavy machine gun developed in the 1930s and widely used in Afghanistan and around the world. It was nearly as popular as the AK-47, capable of firing 350–650 rounds per minutes and taking fifty-round belts.

It was one piece of metal that could put a serious dent in your interdiction plans.

"And now they've manned the guns!" hollered Rock.

Before Zulu could drive another six meters, the ground ahead exploded, rocks, snow, and sand spraying across their path as the muffled *rat-tat-tat* of the DShKs came from outside.

"Ondejko, stop your truck, we're under fire!" Pharaoh called into the radio.

Zulu was already throwing it in park and halfway out the door, one-handing his rifle. He crouched down and helped Pharaoh crawl out his side, putting the truck between them and the incoming.

Rock met them a second later, breathless and cursing. "I hope you're feeling optimistic about this!"

Another salvo of fire drew closer.

Then a chill spiked through Zulu as he looked around. "Where's Khodai?"

18. THE SECOND PILLAR

Rafiullah had spent the last thirty minutes hauling the bodies of the three crew members and their two bodyguards into the cockpit.

It was his plan to carry each of them outside through the narrow copilot's window now located directly above him. He felt strongly about occupying the same cabin with them. Outside, he would align the dead men with their heads facing Mecca, and the cold would preserve them until help arrived.

At the moment he stood near the cockpit, breathless, obsessed with his mission, ready to make his first attempt to lift the heavy pilot's lifeless form into the air.

"Rafiullah, I know what you're doing."

"Yes, me, too."

"You can take out your frustration on me. You don't need to do this."

He answered through clenched teeth: "Yes, I do."

"It's time for *Fajr*."

"Time for prayer? I don't care anymore."

"You should. Allah is the one true God, and he will make sure that we are safe and protected."

Rafiullah's gaze lowered to the bodies. "Did he protect them? Now they're gone . . . and their families will suffer—all because we had a dream."

"Don't you mean because *I* had a dream? I led us up here, I trusted Omar, and I am to blame for their deaths?"

The young aide pursed his lips.

"I trusted Omar, and I still do. I think he wanted to help us, but they pushed him too hard. It wasn't his fault."

"Maybe that's true. But does that relieve both of you of responsibility?"

"No. But sometimes you must take a leap of faith. You must trust God. You must obey God."

"God told you to come up here?"

"He did not speak to me. But I believe we are here for a purpose."

"To die? Like them?"

Abdali clenched his own teeth. "Now . . . I have my *musalla*. Get yours. Time to pray."

"I will not."

Abdali moved toward the cockpit, flinching as he breathed too hard and needles woke in his ribs. The makeshift sling that Rafiullah had fashioned for him out of Auss's jacket tugged heavily on his neck.

He stared deeply into his aide's eyes and said, "We wanted to do the right thing. We failed. And that is okay. We must still thank Allah for this day, for this life, and ask him to show us the next path."

"The next path? I'm tired of walking." Rafiullah's head hung even lower, and he began to choke up.

Abdali placed a hand on his aide's shoulder. "You have walked with me a long time, and if you choose another path, I will not stop you. But I think it would be a mistake. We've done far too much work, and there is so much more waiting for us. This is what we do, Rafiullah. We were not born for anything else."

Suddenly, Rafiullah burst past him, crossed to the back of the chopper, and withdrew his *musalla* and two *kufi* caps from their bag. He set down his *musalla* next to Abdali's and handed him one of the caps.

Then he reached over and grabbed one of the canteens they had found. Before praying they needed to perform a ritual ablution, so they took some of the water and slowly washed, Rafiullah keeping his head low, Abdali stealing glances at him.

The five daily prayers, the *Salat*, were performed in units of prayer, *raka'ah*, consisting of a series of positions and movements, while specific supplications and verses from the *Qur'an* were read aloud in each position. The *raka'ah* would begin in the standing position called *giyaam* and end in the prostrate position called *sujood*. Abdali served as the imam and read the prayers aloud.

The *Salat* needed to be performed with sincere devotion (*khushoo*); otherwise it would be invalid, and Abdali feared that Rafiullah's devotion was in question. Still, the very act might remind him of how fortunate they were and that Islam must take priority over all things, even one's guilt and grief.

And so they prayed inside the helicopter, sitting on a mountain slope as the wind returned, humming through the cracks and holes, the snow beginning to flutter inside.

When they were finished, they remained there, meditating. After a few more moments, Abdali said, "Can you take me to the window? I want to see outside."

"Thank you."

"Excuse me?"

"Thank you. I . . . I am a fool."

Abdali smiled thinly at the man. "You are my best friend. You have been there through the good, and through the bad, through this. I would not abide a fool. So, will you help me to the window?"

"Why?"

"I want to see my country."

Rafiullah nodded and proffered his hand.

They moved gingerly across the cabin and into the cockpit, where Rafiullah helped him up onto the copilot's chair, now lying sideways. He stood on one armrest and brought his full height up past the window to feel the icy wind slash at his cheeks.

It was a devastatingly beautiful view:

Great hunched backs of snow-covered rock shaved off by long rafts of dark clouds . . .

And mottled hills dappled with more snow rolling out like great carpets for as far as he could see . . .

But then, when he turned his head back and glanced up the mountainside, the path they had taken, the inevitable path of their lives, lay before him, freshly hewn in the dirt, snow, and stone.

Farther back were the shattered rotors, two of which had impaled the ground at sharp angles and now jutted up like strange scarecrows marking the site.

Pieces of the fuselage, the landing gear, and the tail rotor lay farther still like signposts shuddering in the wind. He caught a whiff of fuel, but the scent wasn't as strong as it had been.

He searched for paths up to the chopper; although the slope was fairly level, the ground dropped off sharply at its end, leaving only the somewhat jagged hills behind them, to their left and right, as the only true access. Where would another helicopter land? No, he shouldn't worry himself over such matters. Leave that to the experts. He took long, deep breaths, then lowered himself back into the cabin. Rafiullah helped him down from the chair, then climbed up and shut the window.

"It's getting colder," the aide said, rubbing his palms together.

"Stay inside." Abdali raised his chin at the bodies. "We'll cover them up and leave them here."

Rafiullah sighed. "Mr. President. I know they're coming for us. But I wonder, are they the only ones?"

Abdali glanced away as the thought he'd been denying finally reared its ugly head.

Omar's associates had tried to kill him.

They had seen him flee in the damaged chopper.

They, too, had to be coming.

"Rafiullah, have you ever fired a weapon?"

"With my father, when I was a boy, but not in a long time."

Abdali nodded. "Get all of the weapons. Bring them here. Let's be sure that if the wrong people arrive first, we'll be ready for them."

19. THE GOOD SHEPHERDS

Pharaoh, rifle in hand, stole his way to the rear of the Pathfinder, dropped onto his belly, then crawled forward just behind the rear tires and steaming exhaust pipe.

Another salvo of machine-gun fire boomed from the hilltop. The second gun joined in.

Someone shouted in Dari.

The *rat-tat-tat*ing of the guns cut off.

Another shout. Was that Khodai?

With a grunt of exertion, Pharaoh readjusted his grip on the rifle, ready to fire in the prone position. He squinted hard through the falling snow.

And what he saw left his mouth hanging open.

Khodai had bailed out of the Pathfinder and gone running up the hill, directly between the two machine gun positions. He waved emphatically.

"Khodai! No! Get back here right now! Don't do it! Don't do it!" Pharaoh had instinctively shouted in English, though Khodai understood enough.

Then, without warning, the hills began to quake, the strange rumble working up into Pharaoh's elbows and stomach.

"You hear that?" shouted Rock.

"Up there!" Zulu cried.

A wave of sheep began to pour over the crest, dozens at first, then dozens more, their hooves churning up rubble, their dark heads and pale white coats forming a great breaker rushing down the hillside.

There had to be hundreds of them, a huge flock fleeing madly from the gunfire.

Khodai was nearly trampled by a few strays that crossed his path, but he dodged them, wound up rolling to the ground and coming back up, steering himself farther from their path.

As the grunts and clattering hooves of the flock grew even louder, it dawned on Pharaoh that the machine gun fire had ceased.

Zulu shouted through his laughter, "We're being attacked by sheep! Mutton for everyone!"

Pharaoh crawled from beneath the Pathfinder as ahead, at the top of the hill, Khodai was met by a small group of five men. His body language was very animated, arms flailing, and he pointed repeatedly back down to the two trucks.

"Khodai?" Pharaoh yelled.

But the Tajik wasn't listening.

Ondejko came jogging up, just moments before the road was swarming with ewes. He cleared his throat. "Sir, should we engage the sheep, sir?"

"Good question," Pharaoh said, allowing himself a smile. "Negative, do not engage the sheep. Zu? Let's go on up!"

Zulu wove his way forward, the stench of urine and feces and wet wool growing strong as some sheep turned their heads skyward, into the falling snow.

"It's okay, guys, I'll secure this area," said Rock.

"Thank God for the Agency!" Zulu shot back.

They hiked their way up the hill, noticing that the two men who had manned the machine guns were back at their posts, muzzles following Pharaoh and Zulu.

"Captain, let go of your rifle and slowly raise your hands," said Zulu.

Pharaoh was already thinking that. "*Doost! Doost!*" he hollered to the gunmen. "Friend!"

"Khodai, what's going on here?" Zulu asked in Dari.

The Tajik's tone grew urgent. "These men are shepherds from a village about a kilometer west of here. They say that al-Qaeda fighters have been coming up through Pakistan, sneaking into Tajikistan, and crossing the border here."

"How long has this been going on?" Pharaoh asked the oldest shepherd, who wore a heavy black turban and whose beard was jet-black to match his bushy eyebrows.

"At least one month. They send spies or small groups first. Then they come in larger numbers. They gave out pamphlets in the village. Told us to join them. They do not take no for an answer."

Pharaoh slowly nodded. "I understand."

"They threatened the village elders. Several bodies with no heads were left in the street last week."

"I'm sorry."

"They say that before they kill you, they spend a long time sharpening the knife. A very long time. It is the knife we fear the most. The knife . . ."

"He also told me they've been stealing their sheep," said Khodai. "But now they're ready for them."

"Where did you get these guns?" asked Pharaoh.

The shepherd thought a moment, either not understanding Pharaoh's Dari or contemplating his answer. "We bought them ourselves in Tajikistan." There was no mistaking the challenge in his voice.

"Okay," answered Pharaoh, then, in English, he said to Zulu, "We don't have any more time to waste here. Let's go." He turned to leave.

"Wait," said the shepherd. "Are you here to fight al-Qaeda?"

"Yes."

"Then we will join you. Are you headed to our village? We will have tea and something to eat."

"No, we're headed much farther north. And we have to be going now. I'm sorry."

"Okay," the shepherd said.

"Khodai?"

The Tajik eyed the shepherds, his expression growing more somber. "Even with these guns, if al-Qaeda comes here, these men will die."

"We can't do anything to help them right now," said Zulu, starting down the hill. "But I'll mark this area and their little village on the GPS and see what we can do later on."

Pharaoh dropped in beside Khodai, who lingered behind them a moment. "Khodai, let's go!"

But the Tajik had jogged back to the oldest shepherd. He exchanged a few words, then raced back to catch up with Pharaoh and Zulu.

"What did you tell him?" asked Pharaoh.

"I told him about our militia, about how you trained us. I told him when the time is right, we must join forces."

"Very good, Khodai. That's very, very good," said Zulu. "I told you all that talk about recruitment wasn't a waste of time. See?"

"I also told him you are not to be trusted."

"Oh, come on, we back to that? You can't expect us to

leave you sitting on a weapons cache. And hey, if al-Qaeda comes up here and kills these guys, who gets the guns?"

"If you would keep your word, my men would die for you."

"Khodai, we answer to other men," said Pharaoh.

"Less informed men," said Zulu. "Men who might not understand the whole situation, but we answer to them no matter what. You know we can't change that. We're Special Forces, but we're not in the business of cutting special deals."

They began to push their way through the sheep, shooing them aside. "Back in the trucks! Let's move out!" Pharaoh ordered the entire group.

By the time he resumed his seat inside the Pathfinder, Pharaoh's shoulders and *pakol* were covered in a half inch of snow. He brushed it away, flicked on the heater, then glanced back at Rock and Khodai, who were both red-nosed and exhausted.

"And we're off like a herd of turtles," said Zulu.

The quip was met with silence.

Zulu slowly pushed forward until they cleared the last pair of sheep. He gunned the engine, and they leapt across the barren moonscape and returned to a pockmarked trail winding its way toward another series of slowly rolling hills walled in on both sides by distant mountains.

Rock was back to typing on his laptop. "Well, I wonder what the hell we'll run into next," he said. "UFOs? Pro-life activists?"

"Why don't you tell us?" asked Zulu. "You've been holding out. What are we walking into?"

"We don't need him for that. We still got forty guys," said Pharaoh, bringing up another message from their FOB.

"Forty? I was hoping for fifty. More targets, more fun," said Zulu.

"You might get your wish and then some. We now have a second group."

Zulu frowned. "From Eshkashem?"

"No."

"Yeah, I just heard about those other guys, too," said Rock, rapping a knuckle on his laptop's screen.

Pharaoh continued: "They're heading south from Arakhi in what looks like six pickup trucks. The image here is crap. You can see the trucks right there, but you can't tell how many guys are in back. Maybe twenty in all?"

"So we'll have sixty?" asked Zulu, sounding less cocky and much more concerned now.

"Well, we're not even sure they're invited to the party, but they do have higher's attention . . . and now ours."

"We got anything about the president's itinerary last night?" asked Zulu.

"Not in this dump," said Pharaoh.

"How 'bout you, Rocky Balboa, what do you got?"

The CIA agent made a face. "So far none of my contacts have any idea what the hell Abdali was doing up here."

"Why don't you see if he had any business in Arakhi," said Zulu.

"What makes you say that?"

"Just seems odd for those pickup trucks to be coming from all the way up there, unless they knew something early on."

"We got nothing to lose," said Rock. "I'll put in the query."

"Titan 06, this is Talk Radio, over," Weathers called from the rear truck.

"Go ahead."

"I have Bull on the Shadowfire."

"Put him through."

"Titan 06, this is Tempest. Got my SITREP. We're en route toward the pass, over."

"Roger that. You have an ETA yet?"

"Can't say. All depends, but high winds are slowing us down big-time, over."

"Roger. We just got delayed by a couple of machine guns, but we're back on the road, over."

"Machine guns? Sounds interesting. Everyone all right, over?"

"We're good. They were friendlies, over."

"Roger that. We'll talk later. Next SITREP in thirty. Titan 06. See you up there. This is Tempest, out."

"I got a feeling we'll be late," said Zulu. "Both of us. Very, very late."

"I'm going to request more intel on the crash site," said Pharaoh. "If that bird landed in a real shitty spot, that could work for us by delaying the militia's contact with the president."

"It'll delay ours, too," said Zulu. "And worse, it'll delay us getting our package out, especially if he's immobile."

"If Bull can get the helo in there, he'll scoop him up and bug out for home."

"Don't count on the helo, Captain."

The ground suddenly vanished, the Pathfinder airborne for all of six seconds before dropping a meter to the icy ground with a terrible thud, sending tremors through the entire truck.

"Oh, you little bitch!" cried Zulu.

He lost control, the SUV fishtailing wildly.

Suddenly, he rolled the wheel and straightened them out, the truck bouncing hard once more as he slowed.

"What happened?" asked Khodai in Dari.

"We just hit a little soft spot, and that entire part of the trail gave way. Must be a streambed," Zulu said, then he translated into Dari.

"Who gives a shit, Mr. Geologist?" said Rock. "Just watch the road!"

"You want to drive?"

"Gentlemen," Pharaoh interrupted as his satellite phone began to ring. "Please." He thumbed on the phone, didn't recognize the number. "Hello."

"Hello, Captain Pharaoh?" The man spoke clearly, his English accented but easily understood.

"Yes."

"This is President Abdul Abdali. The men back in Kabul gave me your number and the number of your second in command. I tried to call him first, this Warrant Officer Dennis Bull, but he did not answer. I am told he is the one coming for me."

Pharaoh began to tremble. "Hold on, sir." He covered the receiver. "I have President Abdali on the line, right here, right now."

"I thought his number was to follow," said Rock. "How come they didn't get it first?"

"Because that would make too much sense," said Zulu. "But he's on the line now, and that's outstanding." Zulu's expression grew emphatic. "Captain, pick his brain for intel on the crash site. Bird's-eye view. Everything."

"And ask him what he was doing last night," said Rock.

"And ask him about his injuries," reminded Zulu. "And don't forget to ask him about entry into the chopper. How accessible is it?"

"Are you done?" asked Pharaoh, annoyed. "Shit . . ." He uncovered the receiver and could barely speak. *I'm talking to the president of this entire country.* "Uh, sir, we need as much information as possible."

"I understand. How soon do you think you will be here?"

"I'm not sure yet. The weather's giving my recovery team some difficulty."

"Yes, it is snowing quite heavily up here."

"Sir, first of all, how are you?" Pharaoh caught himself. "I mean, are you injured?"

As the president explained, Pharaoh thought how this would be a moment he would never forget. And, for a few seconds, he found himself considering that instead of paying attention to the very man whose life he was supposed to save.

"Are you still there, Captain Pharaoh? Are you there?"

Pharaoh shuddered. "Yes, sir. I am. Now, I have many more questions."

"Well, Captain. It seems I have time to answer."

20. PLAN A

The UH-60A was the Army's frontline utility helicopter for air assault, air cav, and medevac, and Bull had spent quite a few hours crammed onboard these birds. He didn't mind flying. None of the other operators did.

But it was so damned cold, the ride was so damned rough, and they were flying so damned high, that anyone who wasn't miserable wasn't alive.

He sat facing Hojo, who kept his gaze on the floor. Their knees were only inches apart, and the little jump seat was about as comfortable as sitting on concrete.

Gator, Sullivan, Borokovsky, and McDaniel were locked onto their thrones of punishment, their heads occasionally snapping back as the chopper bit into the wind and their shoulder and lap harnesses grew taut.

Bull was wearing the intercom headset so he could speak directly with the pilots and crew chief, but, for the moment, the intercom was silent. He checked his satellite phone, noted he had missed a call from an unfamiliar number and had a voice mail pending. Though it was hard to hear inside the cabin, and his ears were beginning to pop, he called up the message. A faint voice came through the tiny speaker: "This is President Abdul Abdali. Sorry I missed you. I will try to call your commander. Thank you."

Oh, shit. He'd never live this one down. He would have to call Pharaoh and see if the captain had had a chance to speak with Abdali.

"You all right?" asked Hojo, leaning forward and lifting his voice above the low-pitched cyclical growl of the tail and main rotors.

"Yeah, just missed a call."

"From the captain?"

Bull shook his head. Ah, what the hell. "It was from President Abdali."

"Holy shit!"

"Yeah, I just didn't hear it ring. Now I have to call Pharaoh."

"Hey, Bull?" came the crew chief's voice over the intercom. "Got some new intel coming in from your FOB. Says your interdiction team has made contact with the president. Got some more intel on the recovery area."

Bull unbuckled and shifted between the men, moving up to the narrow space behind the cockpit. The BFT computer sat atop a long metal stowage compartment, its flat LCD display glowing with a map and text messages, its keyboard mounted with big bolts to the metal.

The crew chief tipped his head toward the screen, and Bull crouched down, barely able to fit between the seats so he could operate the computer. In theory, a BFT aboard a chopper like this one was supposed to enhance situational understanding, facilitate command and control, and assist with airspace deconfliction. Bull couldn't speak authoritatively about that, but he could tell you that trying to operate the damned thing in the cramped confines of a Black Hawk was not fun.

Pharaoh indicated in his text message that the chopper was lying on its side; that there were two narrow mountain trails for rapid egress, one east, one west; and that the approach to that area was still unknown. The president and his aide, the only remaining survivors, could be extracted via the copilot's window, so they could leave behind their entry tools. Still, they would need to evacuate the crash site and descend to a pickup zone, since most of the surrounding terrain was hardly helicopter-friendly.

A minutes-old satellite photo displayed the crash site, and Bull zoomed in until the image was blurred with a long gray blob—the chopper—along with the debris trail behind it. He studied the approach, then pulled up a relief map of the area and compared the two.

But it was all academic. They wouldn't know anything until they got there and put human eyes on the site.

As Bull returned to his seat, the chopper began to shudder. He plopped back down and shoved his lap belt and shoulder harnesses into the single, circular lock.

He glanced out the side door window—

And wished he hadn't.

The cold gray blanket enveloping the mountains sent a chill up his spine, and the view ahead turned his mouth to cotton.

Within those great spines of rock and snow lay the Anjuman Pass, the only route into the Panjshir Valley, where more than 300,000 ethnic Tajiks lived in relative isolation.

The good old pilot swore he'd have enough air to get them over the pass, but the chopper shook once more, and Bull's nerves found his mouth. "How we doing up there?"

Simple question.

"Bull, if I can't get you up there, then Jesus Christ himself can't, either," said the pilot.

"So what're you saying?"

"I'm saying don't bother praying. This bird has got just enough ass, and I'll prove that to you."

"It's not the chopper's ass I'm concerned about. Can you get us there or not? This bitch sounds like she's going to fall apart . . ."

"I don't build 'em, son. I just fly 'em. But if she falls apart, you can be sure I'll write a letter to my congressman."

The pilot and copilot chuckled.

Bull glanced over at Sullivan, lost in the world of pencils and puzzles. That was what he needed: some kind of distraction to take his mind off it all.

But he couldn't get the mission out of his thoughts. How could he? They needed a backup plan in case the old fart at the stick couldn't get them over the pass. Christ, they had a hell of a lot of gear. Humping it all the way through a meter-thick layer of snow would kill them.

A sudden updraft sent everyone jerking toward the overhead, their curses drowned out by the engines and their own foam earplugs. Bull had replaced his with the intercom, so he had the pleasure of listening to the pilot and copilot:

"That was a nice one."

"Breath of the gods."

"What?"

"She pulled pretty hard."

"Yes, she did, but that's good."

These freaks were actually admiring the power of the updraft. That they seemed only mildly concerned annoyed the hell out of Bull. Then again, if you were hiring a brain surgeon, you were better off picking the cocky, arrogant guy who believed so thoroughly in his skills that he pictured himself a god among men, rather than going with the tentative guy who spent more time preparing you for the worst than touting his ability to yank out your cerebellum before he played nine holes of golf. Bull would take the arrogant bastard any day.

But cocky sometimes translated into foolish. Bull had seen that, too, among his own operators over the years, especially the younger ones.

Cocky or not, good men would always die, even those who respected the bullet, the knife, the cliff—

And those forced to ride in rickety old helicopters.

21. SPOOKY

Rock sat in the backseat of the Pathfinder, banging on his laptop, but every other word contained a typo. Too many damned bumps in the road. It was like trying to type while having sex, not that his attention had ever been that divided, but he had been with a few women over the years whose enthusiasm had turned his thoughts to work.

The data he was gathering on the militiamen from Eshkashem was not something he would share with Pharaoh or Zulu; that is, not until the time was right—when their services would be needed to help him carry out his orders.

One piece of data he would never share with them was his real name, William Shackelford, or anything more about his background, other than he had been a Force Recon Marine before retiring to join the Agency and train at The Farm at Camp Peary to become a field operative. And the only reason he had shared that was because he didn't want to hear their bullshit about him not understanding their operations or their sensibilities or just what the hell it was like to be them. Well, sir, yes he did.

Furthermore, he would not yet reveal why he had chosen to ride with their group instead of arguing to fly up to the crash site with Bull's team to ensure they did, indeed, rescue the president. Certainly, the Agency would want to take some if not all credit for such an operation. Pharaoh and Zulu obviously assumed that he had chosen to remain with them because of the weight issue. Carrying all those men and all that gear over the pass was a major challenge. But no, that wasn't it at all.

The militiamen in Eshkashem might prove to be much more interesting than these spec ops guys ever knew— perhaps more important to the Agency than garnering some credit for rescuing the puppet president of a country in chaos.

And if Rock was able to exploit the interdiction team to take care of the issue for Langley, hell, everyone would be happy—and Triple Nickel would be none the wiser until the very last minute.

Rock knew he could smooth things over with Pharaoh and Zulu, once the time came to reveal his plans. They would see the light, hallelujah. But at the organizational level, there would be some serious head-banging. Rock's people would protect their sources and agents, and information would be carefully guarded.

The standing joke in Afghanistan was that the CIA could be operating out of a garage fifty meters away from a task force TOC (tactical operations center), and never once would parties from either group actually walk over to share information. Consequently, Rock knew he could do a much better job in the field if he and the ODA teams he worked with shared raw intel, which of course he had done with ODA-555.

One more message to send off and he could take a break. But he needed to rub his eyes, and a glance up was unfortunate. How Zulu could see anything in what now seemed a full-on blizzard was beyond him.

Khodai leaned forward, studying the snow-swept trail through a long cut meandering along the mountain's base. He pointed occasionally for Zulu to make his turns. The Tajik had said they would be nearing their detour soon, but he wasn't sure he would recognize the spot, now that the landscape had become a sea of billowing white.

Why Abdali couldn't have put off his travel plans till late spring was beyond Rock. Now they had to brave this storm, one of many during the winter months. Hell, even the bad guys took winters off. Still, Rock had been in worse weather. And complaining about anything was ridiculous.

You already had to be nuts volunteering to spend years of your life eating shitty food, having no access to hookers, and living in assorted mud-brick dumps in the mountains of Afghanistan.

You had to be out of your goddamned mind to be forging relationships with men who would smile and save your life on Monday, then cut your throat on Tuesday because the situation had suddenly changed and if they didn't kill you, then the "foreigners" would kill their families.

And for God's sake, most CIA case officers lived in the suburbs of Virginia. They watched guys like Rock in the movies. Operations that included diarrhea were too difficult for them.

Which was the very reason why Rock had spent the last half dozen years of his life in a country that no one wanted to visit, a country the ignorant had written off as a drug-producing terrorist camp that should've been nuked a half dozen years ago. They'd never spent any time in Afghanistan; never drank from the cold, clean waters of a mountain stream; never seen the multicolored kites flying over Kabul.

But like Zulu, Rock was an optimist. He realized he wasn't going to change the length and breadth of this country, this culture, this war. Yet he did know that for a short time, he could make life a little better in the villages where he operated, and he could stop, perhaps, a few incidents of terrorism, could make a very small difference that meant something to him . . . and them.

And he liked these people. Liked them a lot. Admired their devotion and determination in the face of utter squalor. They had nothing and smiled. Maybe they had everything: hearts more pure than anyone he'd ever met back home. Survival seemed their only bias. They were human beings who communicated with the earth. They were not cloistered in boxes and trapped behind computer screens. They lived the way nature intended human beings to live.

"Right there!" cried Khodai, jarring Rock from his introspection. "You must turn now!"

"Turn where?" Zulu asked. "I can't see anything!"

"The boulders in the road right there!"

"Zu, turn!" urged Pharaoh.

The team sergeant cut the wheel hard, taking them up higher onto the hillside, but the wheels began to spin, and the SUV lost its footing and slid sideways.

"Shit, I'm losing it!" announced Zulu.

Rock stole a look back. Ondejko's truck was coming up hard behind them, wipers sweeping at full speed, engine roaring loud enough from them to hear with the windows closed. Rock shouted for Zulu to floor it.

But it didn't matter. The Pathfinder slid down several more meters before Zulu regained control, and Ondejko came jostling up alongside them.

Zulu hit the brakes, threw it in park, and lowered the passenger's side window. Ondejko lowered his and said, "This is shit!"

"Get out," ordered Zulu. "Let's see what we got."

Rock set aside his laptop and decided to join them, tugging up the collar on his coat before setting his boot down into calf-deep snow.

"See, there's the main trail out there," said Pharaoh, pointing and staring through his binoculars at a winding path in the valley between two steep, rocky hills.

Covering his eyes from the snow and slight glare, Rock saw the trail. "Looks pretty level down below that ridge. We can try skirting around this shit up there."

"He's right," said Zulu.

"Of course I am. I'm the C-I-Fucking-A."

Zulu snorted. "Let's go."

"This place is . . ." Ondejko trailed off.

"What?" asked Rock.

"I don't know." He grinned. "Spooky."

Rock shrugged and carefully chose his steps back to the Pathfinder, hoisted himself inside, then brushed the snow from his boots. One minute outside, and his nose was already beginning to run. In fact, it felt colder than it had in a very long time. Deathly cold.

Damned Ondejko. Now Rock was getting paranoid.

The engine roared, then Zulu dropped into a low gear and took them forward, up across a rocky hump.

To their left lay the remnants of a massive landslide that had completely obstructed the trail, crumbling boulders a meter or two high amid long shards of gray-and-brown rock encrusted with ice and resembling the shattered ribs of some massive creature.

The engine rumbled once more, and as they worked themselves up onto the more level ground parallel to the boulders, Rock's stomach dropped. And not because he was getting carsick.

But because the shale beneath the truck had suddenly given way. The Pathfinder skidded to the left, turned, then began to plunge nose-first back down the hillside, heading directly for the boulders.

22. PLAN B

Trying to ignore the Black Hawk's rumbling fuselage—a sound that quickened his pulse and made him curse the inventors of rotary wing aircraft—Bull stared hard at the Black Hawk manual balanced on his lap and at the figures he had jotted down in the margin, while Hojo leaned over, watching him intently.

The UH-60A Black Hawk had a cruising speed of about 150 knots and a range of 306 nautical miles. The rotor tips had a tubelike addition with holes that diffused the undesirable blade-tip vortices and increased overall efficiency. The chopper could *normally* (the operative word here) carry an internal load of 2,640 pounds or eleven combat-equipped troops under normal conditions. She *normally* had a crew of four, two pilots and two crew chiefs, but the second crew chief had not been sent along to allow for an extra Ranger on board, a minor blessing.

The distance from Shah-e Pari to the Anjuman Pass was approximately forty-eight nautical miles. They were making about 120 knots bucking a gusting headwind. That translated into six nautical miles every three minutes:

$$48 \div 6 = 8 \times 3 = 24 \text{ minutes to get to the base of the pass.}$$

As the chopper had gained altitude, some icing had added weight to the bird, and now the pilot was busting ass to coax the bird even higher—

But as they reached the base of the pass, and the engine wailed, they couldn't gain any more lift.

The updrafts and swirling winds sent them pitching and yawing, and as Bull slapped shut the manual a sudden scraping noise echoed outside the chopper, like nails on chalkboard, followed by violent shudders that ripped through the overhead and the side doors, moving down into their seats.

Hojo exclaimed, "What the hell was that?" but his voice was consumed by the droning engines and tremendous rattling that threatened to jar Bull's fillings loose.

"Goddamn it," cried the pilot over the intercom. "Rotors brushed that wall! Shit! Tips might be damaged!"

Bull stared wide-eyed through the window.

Oh, Christ.

Beyond the veils of swirling snow lay the rocky mountainside—practically within arm's reach.

Another kind of vibration clutched the bird, and Bull could tell this was not the wind taking its toll—the rotors were damaged big-time, and the chopper's counterbalance had been affected. The shuddering was steady at first, then grew even more violent.

"Bull, this is the end of the line," said the pilot. "I have to put us down."

"Wait! Hear me out!"

Bull checked his figures once more. One hundred and seventy-five pounds average per man times six men equals

1,050 pounds, plus sixty pounds each for gear equals 360 pounds, plus 200 pounds of mountain and other assorted gear.

Their total weight with gear was 1,610 pounds.

The gear weighed only 560.

Most of the weight belonged to the operators themselves.

Time for Plan B.

He got on the intercom. "Drop us off right here. Then get up to the top of this goddamned pass and drop off our gear with a personal locator beacon attached, so we don't have to hump it all the way up."

"Roger that," said the pilot. "I like your thinking, Bull."

"I don't! Gear or not, I still have to haul my sorry ass up to the top! You told me this piece of shit could make it."

"So I lied. Cut me some slack. I'm flying in a blizzard with a bunch of fat-ass hippies."

"Yeah, we love you, too. Just drop us off and get that gear up top!"

"All right, this whole place looks like shit, but I'll see if I can get a wheel on the deck."

Bull shared his plan with Hojo, who passed the word down the line, each operator shouting into the ear of the other. It was time to go—and not soon enough.

From his own pack Bull withdrew a McMurdo 406 MHz personal locator beacon, which was about the size of a cell phone, pulled the red emergency handle, then attached it via the lanyard to the inside of their largest Blackhawk load-out bag, a rectangular-shaped beast that housed their mountain climbing gear. He extended the beacon's antenna through the zipper, then shut tight the bag, pointing at it for the crew chief to take notice of the antenna. He nodded, raised a thumb.

"Hey, Bull, we'll be lucky to get the tail wheel down.

Too damned rocky, and those updrafts are a bitch! You boys will have a little jump."

"Gotcha."

Bull ordered Hojo to pass the word: three guys on each side of the chopper.

After donning their tactical goggles with tear-off lenses, they slid open the aft side doors and extended heavy nylon safety belts across both openings at knee level. Then slowly, one by one, they took seats along the edge, with their boots dangling over the side, the belts pressing against their chests as they swept about twenty meters off the mountainside.

Bull sat between Hojo and Borokovsky. McDaniel, Sullivan, and Gator were shitting icicles on the opposite side. McDaniel glanced back, widened his eyes on Bull, who nodded. Gator repeatedly shook his head: I don't like this. Sullivan shoved up his goggles and rubbed his eyes with gloved hands—too much staring at his puzzle book.

McDaniel was the only guy Bull was a little uncertain about. He was the youngest guy on the team, least experienced, but to have come this far said a lot, so Bull shouldn't concern himself. Hell, old man Bull might break an ankle on the way down, probably the same one he had sprained last week.

Because they couldn't hear shit and could see less, the crew chief would tap them on the shoulders when it was time to bail out of a *not* perfectly good helicopter.

They descended even more sharply, the chopper's nose pitching farther up as they swooped over the uneven terrain, outcroppings like ice-slick fangs wiping by—

Until their wise and wizened pilot saw what he was looking for, not that Bull noted anything even remotely flat or worthy of a single wheel down.

But drop they did—like a rock now—all of the operators

grunting, the snow rushing in at them; for a second, the deck vanished.

They all clutched the safety strap and *bang*, their cold asses returned to the deck with a vengeance.

Someone swore.

The chopper rolled slightly, fighting against another updraft, and now Bull was tugged back toward the others.

Then they leveled out.

Thud. Was the rear wheel down? The noise, the sensation were barely perceptible. There was only the wind and the whomping.

And that hard slap on his shoulder.

Suddenly, the safety strap fell away, and Bull looked down at the slope about two meters below.

A nothing fall.

Unless you hit ice.

He was airborne-qualified. How many damned PLFs (parachute landing falls) had he made?

Two meters.

Borokovsky was first out. He dropped away, hit, fell really hard onto his side, but the snow looked thick.

Even as Bull shoved off, Hojo was a nanosecond behind him, plunging off to his right.

Bull's boots connected with the snow, the hard rock below, and with a breath-stealing thump he was on his side.

Damn, serious pain.

In his mouth. He spit out blood.

And then he realized he'd just bit his tongue. What a nerd.

As the Black Hawk's engine revved higher, the other operators appeared through the waves of blowing snow, their scarves whipping like pennons. Everyone was down. Bull flashed a thumb's-up to the pilot, who climbed away, heading up the pass to drop off their gear.

"Everyone okay?" he shouted.

Sullivan was rubbing his leg, and Bull shifted unsteadily over to the engineer. "What happened?"

"I'm good, Bull. Not broken. Just twisted it a little."

"Let me take a look," said Borokovsky, who'd had no choice but to hump his medical pack up the pass. They wouldn't hike without it. He slid off the shoulder straps and dropped to his knees, while Sullivan released the lace lock of his Warrior Wear light assault boot, slid out the laces from their tongue pocket, and begin to remove the boot.

"All right. Everyone else?"

Hojo and Gator huddled up around him, while McDaniel was on the radio with their pilot. Snow was already collecting on all of their beards, and visibility was shrinking fast. A sheet of gray sky stretched out into nothingness, and for a moment, Bull could only glance around and think, *We're in the middle of nowhere . . .*

"You guys keep an eye on Sullivan for me, all right?"

"You got it, Bull," said Hojo.

"Gator, you carry his rifle."

"No problem. We'll keep him light and mobile."

Borokovsky elbowed his way into the huddle. "His ankle's swelling. I don't think he broke anything. We'll wrap it and keep his boot cinched tight."

"Good."

McDaniel was still on the horn with their pilot, and Bull stepped away from the others, approaching the commo guy just as he finished.

"Gear's down," McDaniel reported. "Got a good beacon."

And now a new huddle formed around them, while Hojo consulted his portable GPS. "Okay, gents, so the news ain't all bad. Right now we're at seven thousand feet."

"My ears confirm that," said Sullivan.

"The old man got the gear up to ten-five, which isn't all the way up."

"You kidding me?" asked Gator.

"Nope. We have about three thousand five hundred feet to reach the gear, load up, and hump another thousand feet with gear to the top."

Gator swore and said, "He couldn't get it up another thousand feet?"

"He probably bailed early because he was low on fuel," said Bull. "He'll be lucky to make it back."

Borokovsky glanced down at Sullivan's foot, then asked, "How far are we from the crash site?"

"About eight klicks," said Hojo, reading the unit's screen. "Or five miles, which sounds better to me." He winked. "Five is less than eight."

"Your math sucks," said Gator. "But let's do this."

Bull nodded. "Time to move out. I want to be up there with the gear before this weather gets any worse."

They all barked a hearty, "Hooah!"

And, with a growing sense of dread filling his heart, Bull joined them as they began their ascent, keeping an excruciatingly slow but steady pace, the snow reaching their shins in a few spots.

All Bull could concentrate on was keeping sight of the man in front of him—Sullivan—since Bull was pulling up the rear. The engineer was trying to hide his limp and doing a poor job. It was hard for any of them to keep their balance in the inescapable icy gale, let alone a man with a sprained ankle.

They had all donned their silkweight underwear to help keep them warm, and the temperature was now hovering around twenty degrees Fahrenheit, yet Bull was beginning to sweat.

Only five minutes into the trek, Hojo, who was walking point, got on the MBITR and called for a break.

The thin air and heavy strain were incredible, and for a moment, Bull felt a wave of dizziness pass through him. He gasped and thought someone had set his legs on fire.

It took at least a minute for him to catch his breath, and within two minutes he was no longer sweating but shivering uncontrollably. He moved up to Sullivan. "Okay?"

The guy's jaw was shaking. "Yeah."

"Liar."

"Really. So cold I can't feel my foot."

"I hear that."

Bull keyed his mike. "This is Tempest, let's go again."

"Roger that," said Hojo.

Ahead lay nothing more than fluctuating walls of wind-whipped snow. They pressed on, one boot after the other, and Bull thought only of the next chance to rest.

23. JOY RIDE

Pharaoh was torn between bailing out of the Pathfinder or just ducking and hoping for the best.

Jumping out could result in him tumbling down the hillside and, perhaps, getting run over by Ondekjo, who was somewhere behind them.

Remaining seated could result in him flying through the windshield and getting ejected as they crashed head-on into the boulders, since he'd failed to put on his seat belt.

Admittedly, the moment of indecision only lasted the span of three seconds—

Before he reached for the seat belt, hung on, and Zulu spun the wheel, hitting the boulders at a forty-five-degree angle, the rocks smashing the front left corner, folding up the hood, shaving off the side mirror.

The SUV kept on moving, carried by ice and inertia and some al-Qaeda or Taliban curse to sideswipe the rest of the rocks, the driver's side window busting out and showering Zulu with glass.

Strangely enough, Khodai and Rock didn't say a word. Zulu was screaming a string of epithets for all of them.

Another loud concussion ripped through the undercarriage, and the Pathfinder fishtailed again, went up on two wheels.

Pharaoh realized what was happening—and he shuddered with helplessness as the Pathfinder tipped a little more and Zulu shouted for them to hang on, which was pointless since they all knew how this ride would end.

With a somewhat muffled thud, the SUV crashed onto the driver's side, the remaining back window shattering, snow and rock blasting inside.

Rock and Khodai, who'd been strapped in, hung from their seat belts, while Pharaoh had been forced to shove one boot behind the steering wheel, the other on the side of Zulu's seat, while Zulu leaned away from his broken window, trying to keep his arm free of the twisted metal below.

Panting loudly, the team sergeant reached below Pharaoh's boot and shut off the engine.

The SUV creaked, more safety glass tumbled from the rims of the windows, and the smell of gasoline and antifreeze grew suddenly thick in the air.

"Khodai, Rock, you guys okay?" cried Pharaoh.

The Tajik, who'd been seated on the driver's side, nodded, but it looked as though he was being choked to death by his seat belt.

Rock, who was already wrestling out of his belt, said, "Nice fucking driving, Zu! Jesus fucking Christ!" He shoved his boot into the side of the seat and began to pry open the passenger's side door, swinging it up into the air.

"Hey, we're coming for you!" shouted Ondekjo from outside. "Hang in there, guys!"

"Hang in there? He's not kidding," grunted Zulu.

"We got to get out of here," said Rock. "You smell that gas? Shit, man . . ."

"Can you get that door open?" Zulu asked Pharaoh.

He reached over and pulled the lever. The door was heavy, real heavy, as he forced it open with one arm, his breath coming hard through gritted teeth. "It won't stay open!"

"Unlock the tailgate!" cried Weathers. "Come on, Zu."

Zulu pushed the button, and the back window popped. Weathers opened the tailgate door. "I'll get the load-out bags! Come on out the back!"

"Go!" ordered Pharaoh.

Rock waited until Khodai had pried himself out of his seat, crawled around, and got on his feet, walking on the cracked side windows to the rear hatch, then slipped in behind him. Pharaoh followed, metal, plastic, and glass crunching under his boots. Ondekjo was there, proffering a hand to help him onto the snow.

Zulu was last out, his eyes telling the story. "Not sure what happened."

The driver's side front wheel was twisted at an improbable angle, the shattered radiator was steaming, and fluids streamed below the wreck.

"Totaled, man," added Zulu, then he swore a few times under his breath.

"Let's transfer all the gear to the other Pathfinder. I don't care if it's hanging off the sides," said Pharaoh, not missing a beat. "Move!" He grabbed the first load-out bag and started for the other Pathfinder along the ridge behind them.

Figueroa and Grimm marched past Pharaoh and went for the rest of the gear.

Rock stepped away from the group and lit up a cigar, much to Pharaoh's chagrin. "A little help, Rock?"

The spook just looked at him, then flashed those crooked

and stained teeth, the cigar jutting from the corner of his mouth.

"You waiting for the magic word?" Pharaoh asked darkly. And suddenly he wasn't quite as cold—because his gut was burning.

Rock chuckled under his breath. "I'll help." He started away toward the shattered Pathfinder, accepted another pack from Grimm, then trudged on toward the second vehicle.

They removed everything they could, especially the BFT computer, but Rock decided to leave behind a little note for anyone who might find the truck. In Dari and in Arabic he wrote: *Special price on this vehicle today! Bad credit no problem! Financing available!*

And he left a bogus phone number. Unfortunately, he was the only one who found the note funny. Pharaoh and his men had too many other things on their minds.

With some carabiners and extra nylon rope they were able to tie down most of the load-out bags to the roof, careful not to damage the Shadowfire's dish antenna mounted there. The SUV looked as overloaded as an Afghan jingle truck, the tires actually sagging a little under the burden of bagged-up rockets, machine guns, and practically a thousand other pieces of gear.

And worse, they had to cram three people up front: Ondekjo at the wheel, Grimm, and Khodai, who sat partially on Grimm's lap. In the backseat sat Rock, Pharaoh, and Zulu. Figueroa and Weathers were jammed in the rear with some of the gear.

It was an ODA field trip from hell, chaperoned by the devil himself.

An inch of snow had already collected on the other Pathfinder, and within a few hours Pharaoh predicted it would be mostly buried, perhaps unseen until late spring.

He stared at the truck as they pulled away, musing that

even the landscape itself did not take kindly to foreigners. They were not welcome here, might never be welcome, and that feeling began to weigh heavily on him. It was a strange thought, not one easily entertained. His whole career was built upon order and training, designed to take him into harsh environments and succeed under the most dire of circumstances. He would do so by critically analyzing every situation and devising creative ways to meet the challenges.

But there was no "creative" escape from the idea that this was not your home, these were not your people, and that aching feeling deep inside was your conscience reminding you that those things would never change.

"Well, we're off again like a herd of turtles," said Zulu.

Pharaoh gave him a look, and the team sergeant shrugged.

24. THE ABOMINABLE SNOWMEN

"We're not crazy. We have to do this. We're the only media up here. If we leave, what'll happen? The truth will become the first casualty, as it always does."

NPR correspondent Sandra Hildebrand was buckled tightly inside the helicopter as it approached the Anjuman Pass, barely visible in the storm. She realized she was panting through the intercom and tried to calm down.

Tracy shook her head. "Listen to the pilot. We need to go back. Your job is not to get killed."

"Just a little longer. Just to be sure. We got such a late start. He said we can push it. You heard him. And we should. This isn't just a rumor anymore."

Tracy clutched her arm. "So now it's Pulitzer or perish? I don't think so."

"It's not just a story."

Rich Oswaller gave Hildebrand a mild grin. "This pilot is good. But your sister's right. We need to get out of here. It's not worth it."

"No, we have to take a chance," said Bill Neggy. "Glick-son has never let us down."

Engineer Neggy was referring to their best military contact back in Kabul, who had provided them with the original lead and who had called only minutes ago via satellite phone to say that he believed that the president of Afghanistan himself was somehow involved and that intel indicated that his chopper may have been shot down; a rescue mission was under way.

So this wasn't just a story. Maybe it *was* a Pulitzer in the making. And braving a snowstorm in the mountains was par for the course. At least that's the way Hildebrand justified it. She and Neggy were on the same page, and she'd thought Rich, as a professional, would be as well, but he, like Tracy, had a deep-seeded fear of flying that had, at this point, turned his ambition and enthusiasm into tremors that occasionally reached his face. Hildebrand had tried to ignore them, but the poor guy looked green. In calm weather he wasn't too bad, but this was, in a word, radical.

"All right, ladies and gentlemen," began the pilot, a merc who went by the name Walsh. "You can stop the debate. I don't believe what I'm seeing, but there they are. Check the port side window as I come around."

The chopper banked and descended, slicing through the winds, gravity tugging on Hildebrand's shoulders in a seemingly unnatural way. Then they began to level off, flying over the pass at just 500 feet or so.

Oswaller found his barf bag; the noises coming from his mouth sounded inhuman.

Poor Tracy also had her barf bag to her lips, and Hildebrand turned away from the window as her sister coughed and groaned.

"Holy shit," cried Neggy.

"What? What?" asked Hildebrand. She peered out the window. Nothing.

"Hold up. He's going to turn."

"Tell me what you saw!" she cried.

"Snowmen."

"What?"

Walsh chipped in: "There they are. Port side."

Hildebrand pressed her face against the glass.

Walsh continued, "Looks like a small party. Lots of gear. Can't tell who they are, but most locals wouldn't be out in this."

"Most radio people wouldn't, either," Tracy managed, sounding even more ill.

"I think they've spotted us," said Walsh.

Hildebrand's pulse mounted. "Can you put us down somewhere near them?"

"Thought you'd never ask. But once we're down, we may be staying a while."

"I don't think that's a good idea," said Oswaller, coming up from his bag. "We don't know who the hell they are."

"Put us down!" Hildebrand insisted.

"It's my bird," began Walsh, his tone growing sharp. "And we're putting down."

It had taken Bull and his men nearly three hours to reach their gear, and he figured at least another hour to get to the top of the pass. Given the altitude and temperature, they were making acceptable time.

And now, as they heard the familiar whomping of a chopper, they wondered why the hell their pilot had come back. There were no FOBs or FARPs (forward ammunition and resupply points) nearby. Bull hoped the guy wasn't in trouble.

"Everybody, hold up," he called over the radio. "Rudy, see what the hell's going on with our chopper." He felt certain that calling the kid by his first name would be appreciated.

"Roger that, Bull." The commo guy broke away from their line, bit off one of his gloves, and began working his radio.

Meanwhile, Bull wiped off his goggles and stared up into the gloom, in the direction of the whomping.

Just a few heartbeats later the chopper burst through the clouds like a dark-skinned demon about to strafe them—

"That's not him! Everybody down!"

A terrific roar and rush of air passed over them; Bull craned his head to watch the bird gain altitude and bank to the right, coming around for another pass.

"That's a civilian bird," said Hojo over the radio. "Looks like an MD600 NOTAR."

The chopper's sleek fuselage and lack of a tail rotor gave it considerable maneuverability in the storm, but even so, Bull could tell the pilot was struggling. He also noted the lack of rockets mounted on its skids, so Hojo was probably right. Damn, the chopper's appearance was a real head-scratcher.

"Everybody hold fire!" he ordered, since every one of them now had his rifle pointed at the sky.

"Uh, Bull?" asked Hojo. "Any idea who the hell they are?"

"No clue. But they're obviously as insane as we are, so I'd like to meet 'em."

Hildebrand waited with bated breath as Walsh set them down on a little ridge with only three or four meters of clearance from a slope that fell away a few hundred meters or more. Walsh made sure to warn them of that, and so, with the rotor blades still spinning above them, they exited the chopper and dropped heavily into the snow.

"Oh my God, where the hell are we?" asked Tracy, tugging on her woolen cap.

"Come on, they're just up there," said Hildebrand, leading the group.

"Sandy, wait," said Rich. "We still don't know—"

"I saw their guns. They didn't fire," she argued.

Then her foot hit a patch of ice and she tumbled hard into the snow. She yanked herself right back up before the others could reach her and returned to her climb, hiking boots plunging into a foot or more of snow.

As her cheeks began stinging from the wind, she spotted the first man about a hundred yards ahead, his silhouette occasionally blotted by gusts of snow. She waved to him.

He didn't wave back. In fact, he had a rifle with a short barrel, a serious-looking one, aimed at her. What was she thinking? Any weapon pointed in her direction was serious.

"I'm an American! NPR! We're media!" She repeated the call in Dari, then in Pashto.

God, should she try Arabic?

"Sandy! Please wait!" hollered her sister, an admonishment repeated by Oswaller.

As she drew closer, she saw that the rifleman wore a thick scarf, *pakol*, and heavy coat. He took one hand off his rifle and removed his goggles, then tugged down the scarf. He was heavily bearded, and when he opened his mouth, she thought he had to be an American Special Forces operator.

"Ma'am? Can I ask you a question? Just what in the hell are you doing up here?"

"Slow down. I'm the reporter. I ask the questions."

"No, ma'am."

Just then the rest of the soldiers, all dressed similarly from the waist up in local Afghan garb and from the waist down in military-issue trousers and sleek, aftermarket boots, gathered around the first man, eyes widening behind goggles. They looked surreal and alien, their huge packs adding considerable girth. For a moment, Hildebrand lost her breath.

From the back came the tallest, who, when he tugged down his scarf, revealed he was probably the oldest, too, with graying beard and deep crow's-feet. He lowered his rifle, approached, and extended a gloved hand. "They call me Bull."

"Sandra Hildebrand. You the detachment commander?"

"Commander? No. But it sounds like you've done your homework."

"Who are you?"

"They call me Bull. And I know you. You're that reporter for NPR. You been on CNN, too. What's your name again?"

"Sandra Hildebrand. This is my sister, Tracy, and that's my producer, Rich Oswaller, and my engineer, Bill Neggy."

Bull's tone turned a little incredulous. "Nice to meet you folks."

Hildebrand smiled. "So, Bull . . . What's up?"

"Not a hell of a lot. We come up here for a little hike. Terrible weather."

"Wait. Isn't this the part where you're pissed off at us for interfering with a military mission?"

"No, this is the part where you're pissed."

"Why do you say that? Because you won't talk to me?"

"No, because this is the part where we take your helicopter."

Hildebrand drew her head back in disbelief.

"Oh, you gotta be kidding me," groaned Oswaller. "You can't do that!"

Bull's eyes grew wide. "Sir, look at us. We can do anything we want."

25. CHOKEPOINT

Zulu, who lay prone in the snow atop the small hill, shoved forward his binoculars and glanced sidelong at Pharaoh, who was still analyzing the cliffs, crags, and ditches of the mountain face about a quarter kilometer ahead.

The windswept snow and his own shivering had wreaked havoc with the images, and Zulu had sworn as he zoomed in, focused and refocused, and occasionally wiped off the lenses.

What he'd seen had looked good.

And bad.

While he waited impatiently for the captain to finish his inspection, he removed his glove and slipped free his Jani-Song from his hip pocket. He deployed the inner handle and blade, feeling the tension rise from his gut and escape out through his hand. *Click, click, click*, and the blade flashed out. Another three clicks, and it vanished back into the handles as quickly as it had come. Over and over. He closed his eyes. His hand grew warm. Muscles took control.

No thought. All muscle memory. And no stress. He practiced several different opening techniques, the inner handle and blade tugging at his hand.

In the hours that had passed, they had cleared the boulders and made their detour, at the cost of one government-purchased Nissan Pathfinder. After that fiasco, they followed an ancient goat path running northwest toward the president's crash site, which lay obscured behind a pair of mountains rearing up from the pale white blanket of foothills.

During all that time in the SUV, Pharaoh had not said more than ten words to him, and that was all right. Zulu had been in no mood to talk.

He'd spent most of his time thumbing through Paladin Press's latest catalog, searching for titles that sparked his interest. Paladin had once been known as "the most dangerous press in America," and over the years Zulu had bought dozens of books and videos on combat shooting, self-defense/combatives, personal freedom, and especially those knife-fighting materials produced by his friend and teacher Michael Janich.

But all the while, as he tried to lose himself in the catalog, making notes in the margin as to which books and DVDs he would next order, he couldn't escape the fact that he, the teacher, had made a mistake. He'd been too cocky, too sure of the hillside.

He was Zulu. Team sergeant. He didn't do things like that. He didn't allow his men to see him vulnerable. Moreover, he'd never made a serious error in front of any of their past captains.

All the cursing in the world wouldn't change what had happened.

Okay, so he'd blow it off as rough terrain, something no one would've been able to anticipate. That was partly true. Technically, you couldn't blame him.

But he was better than that.

Too late now to bitch more about it. He'd just move on. Like he always did. Period. Focus on the mission. The men. And getting back home.

He returned the Jani-Song to his pocket, glanced even farther back, over his shoulder, where their tire tracks were quickly being erased by the storm.

Getting up to this location had been a bitch. They had ventured through yet a second cut running northeast toward a defile between too extremely rocky hills. The militiamen from Eshkashem would, in all likelihood, follow this course.

Khodai, who had taken a similar route to Eshkashem once before, had said the trail through the ice-covered cliffs grew as narrow as three or four meters in some areas and would force that group of forty or so to move single file, which, at first glance, made this piece of terrain a perfect ambush site.

Problem was, the team might not have the time to assume positions along the cliffs because their latest intel dump indicated the enemy force would arrive within three hours—

Which had left all of them breathless. Talk about calling it close. Unsurprisingly, their earlier estimates about the force's speed and location had been off by at least two hours. They were coming faster and sooner. Great.

The team's lack of prep time really pissed off Zulu because they might've been able to establish a superior ambush. Shit. He estimated it would take at least an hour by car to reach the northeastern foothills, then another three hours of hard climbing to put a sniper and a machine gunner on either side of the defile's main egress atop a slope that cut down sharply to the west.

That was an hour they didn't have.

"See what I mean?" he finally said to Pharaoh, trying to break the tension between them.

The captain's voice came evenly. "Yeah, if the intel's good, we can't get up there in time. Still looks like a point ambush, textbook all the way."

"Not exactly. Because we can't take the high ground, we can only hit 'em in the face as they come through, which will drive the rest them back through the defile; and yeah, if we had a force on the other side, we'd trap 'em in the kill zone. It'd be snowing steel until they drop. As is, they can fall back and maybe come around the west side."

"I know, but I have a couple of ideas." The captain gestured toward the truck.

They hustled down the slope, where Ondejko, Figueroa, Weathers, and Grimm were standing watch outside the SUV. Zulu gathered them around and communicated the challenges of the defile to them.

When he was finished, Pharaoh cleared his throat and unfolded a plan that left Zulu nodding—

And wondering how the hell the young captain had matured so quickly. Was it Zulu's mistake that had caused him to rise to the occasion? Maybe revealing that he was human had allowed Pharaoh to draw upon his training and not be so intimidated by the big mouth with the big knife?

Whatever the case, the plan sounded good, so long as the weather and the enemy cooperated.

"Khodai?" Zulu called to the G-chief, who was back inside the SUV with Rock. "I need you."

Rock had volunteered to head forward with Khodai to see if they could observe the militiamen, not because he supported the ODA team's mission, although it'd be nice if they succeeded, sure. No, he wanted to get eyes on those men to confirm some of his own agency's intelligence.

Of course, Zulu and Pharaoh had looked at him a bit

strangely. Even as a split team, they only operated with buddies, and he and Khodai were the odd men out, so to speak, so they might as well form their own little alliance.

"What do you want?" Zulu had asked him.

"Nothing. I dragged my ass up here, might as well make myself useful. Besides, reconnoitering is my middle name."

And so he and the Tajik had been dropped off about two hundred meters below the defile, which was as far up as they could take the SUV.

It was good to have some private time with the G-chief. After all, neither of them fully trusted those operators, so they did have one thing in common. And he and Khodai had a history that spanned some eighteen months now.

As they hiked up the hillside, SCAR-L rifles in hand, faces masked against the cold by scarves, Khodai glanced back, saw Rock was falling behind, and waited up for him.

"You want to die here?" the Tajik asked in Dari, which forced Rock to answer in the same.

"Sure, why not?"

"This is not the place to die."

"I'm not as young as you."

The Tajik tapped his head. "Up here, you are younger."

"That's probably right."

"Tell me, Rock, now that we are away from them, what do you think will happen with my village's weapons?"

Rock raised his head toward the hill. "Let's go."

Khodai lowered his rifle and slapped a hand on Rock's shoulder. "You know what this means."

"I'm sorry, Khodai. Without me there, we can't cut a deal. And I need to be here."

"But you will help us get more, like you did the first time, right?"

"Absolutely. Our mission here is slightly different than

the Army's. You know that. We're still all on the same team, sure, but we do things differently."

"And that's why you didn't tell them that you helped us get the weapons in the first place? And you asked us not to say anything? Told us to lie and act upset?"

"Exactly."

"But then I heard you told Pharaoh and Zulu we had the weapons."

"Yes, I did."

"I'm confused."

"Don't be, Khodai. It's a game we play. I help you acquire weapons, then you help me make the Agency look good by turning them back over to coalition forces. This is what we call politics in America."

"It is a strange game."

"The strangest. But rest assured, once they haul out all that stuff, I'll have your cave restocked within a month—with even better weapons."

"You haven't lied to me so far." Khodai swung around, put his gloved hand on Rock's chest, inches away from his neck. "I hope this is the truth."

Rock shoved down his scarf, withdrew a cigar, shoved it in his mouth. "The truth has nothing to do with it, my friend."

26. A BLEEDING HEART THAT WON'T KILL YOU

"You can do anything you want?" Tracy hollered, glaring at Bull. "Even break the law?" She faced Hildebrand. "Sandy? Come on back to the helicopter. We're leaving."

"No, ma'am," said Hojo. "You're doing whatever we tell you to do."

Tracy frowned, her wind-burned cheeks emphasizing her disbelief. "Do you know who I am?"

Hildebrand shot a look at her sister: don't do it.

But Tracy marched right up to the rifle-toting mammoth. "I said, do you know who I am?"

Hojo snorted. "I wasn't paying attention during the introductions."

"Well, I'm Tracy O'Donnell. I've made a career out of exposing egotistical meatheads like you who, as you've demonstrated, think they operate above the law. Maybe you've heard of us: War Crimes in Afghanistan."

"Oh my God, you run that? What do you people do to keep warm? Burn American flags?"

"Hojo . . ." warned Bull.

But Hojo's words had already caught the attention of every man on the hill, and as the commotion grew louder, Hildebrand stepped forward, getting into Bull's face. "I'll make a call right now to Kabul, telling my contacts what you're about to do. My people have CENTCOM's ear. You leave us to die, and you'll be spending the rest of your lives in—"

"Ma'am," Bull interrupted, raising his hand. "We just want your helicopter to ferry us across to that other mountain. It's not too far. After that, you can fly off on your merry way. I was just being a little facetious when I said we were *taking* your chopper. Jesus . . ."

"No, you weren't. You're just changing your story because now you know how well connected we are. Who are you?"

"We're the bogeymen," growled Hojo, wriggling his brows.

"All right, listen up!" shouted Bull. "Everyone down to the chopper. Let's see what kind of fuel he's got and get ready to move out!"

"Bull, wind's picking up," Hojo pointed out. "I'm not sure about this."

"Yeah, I know."

As the group dispersed, Oswaller rushed up behind Hildebrand and breathed in her ear: "It's a good thing we landed, otherwise the truth would've been the first casualty of war."

"Don't mind him, Sandy," Neggy interjected, hiking up beside her. "This is the biggest news event we've ever covered. We just have to get these guys talking. And we have leverage: the chopper."

Hildebrand turned to the engineer; his nose was cherry red, his breath steaming. "Thanks."

They trudged back to the chopper, each footfall a heavy strain on their muscles.

Tracy made it there first and stood before the cabin doors, shivering. "That's as far as you go," she said to the soldiers.

The group of six did not have their rifles raised, but they shifted into position around the helicopter, as though securing the area. Hildebrand noted that one of them was limping.

Bull walked up to Tracy and sighed loudly. "I want to talk to your pilot."

"Sure you do."

"Let's make a deal," said Hildebrand. "We'll offer no resistance. You tell us why you're up here, what's going on. That's it. Pretty simple."

"We're not bargaining with these guys," said Tracy.

Hildebrand wanted to slap her sister, and if they were teenagers again, she would have. "Shut up!" She regarded Bull. "Why are you out here?"

"Just passing through." He took a step toward Tracy. "Ma'am, please move aside."

Hildebrand grabbed Bull's shoulder. "Come on. We can make this easy for you."

"We don't do easy. So that doesn't matter."

"You're after the president, aren't you? You guys are part of a Special Forces ODA team going after the president of Afghanistan, whose chopper crashed somewhere up here."

"You guys see that movie?" Bull asked his men with a laugh. "That's pretty good. I'd go see it. But what's an ODA team?"

"Don't lie to me, Bull. I'm here to cover this story. And no one can stop me."

"Won't be people doing that, ma'am. You know what Hindu Kush means?"

A smile nicked the corners of her mouth; this guy was a bit of an academic. "Yes, I do. It means Hindu killer."

"Then you know this mountain will kill you way before anyone else does."

"Which is why you can't steal our chopper and leave us here!" shouted Tracy.

"We're just borrowing it, for Christ's sake! Let me talk to your pilot, check his fuel, see if we can't work this out."

"Tracy, let him. It's too damned cold to play games." Hildebrand shifted up to her sister. "No more." She pulled her away from the door.

Bull wrenched open the door and ducked into the chopper, while Hildebrand and Tracy climbed into two of the six back seats.

"How we doing, buddy?" Bull asked Walsh.

"Better now," said the pilot. "Name's Walsh. Nice to hear English instead of Dari or Arabic."

"It is. What's your range?"

"'Bout seven hundred klicks."

"How're your tanks?"

"Little over half full, but that's just enough to get back to Feyzabad."

"I hear you. But I need you to take us and our gear for a little ride about eight klicks northwest. I've got the GPS coordinates. After that, your best bet will be to put down in Eshkashem and see if you can refuel there."

"Well, I should tell you that I'm an independent contractor, and I am armed."

"Good. Hang on to your piece." Bull looked at all of them, his expression softening a little. "All right. I'll tell you this much—we need to get down to those coordinates. Yeah, it's a matter of life and death. You can help make that happen much more quickly for us. I've got a guy with a bad sprain. You guys are a godsend, okay?"

"Well, what happened to Mr. Arrogant?" asked Tracy.

"Look, you want a story? You can write about this,

whatever. I just need to get my men over there. It's a short hop. That's all it is."

"Are you trying to rescue the president?" Hildebrand asked.

"Ma'am, I'm not authorized to talk to the media."

Hildebrand tipped her head toward Walsh. "What, you think he won't talk? He'll have a bird's-eye view of it all."

Just then a tiny beeping noise came from Bull's pocket. He withdrew a satellite phone. "Excuse me."

The voice on the other end escaped from the phone's tiny speaker, and as Hildebrand leaned forward and pricked up her ears, she thought she did, in fact, hear President Abdali's voice. She had spent time with the man, had interviewed him, had eaten with him, and had even politely turned down his offer to move beyond friendship—

But Bull was outside before she could listen further, the wind howling until the door thumped shut.

"I don't care what these guys think. I'm not flying in this shit," said Walsh. "They can shoot me. We'll die anyway. Worst of the front should pass in a couple of hours. We'll have to wait."

When Bull reentered the chopper, Walsh said as much, and Bull, surprisingly, nodded. "This is our best shot, and we do have a little time. So you're right. We'll stand by until the wind cooperates."

"You just spoke to Abdali, didn't you?" said Hildebrand.

"No, that was the guy from DIRECTV. They're trying to sell me more channels."

Hildebrand widened her eyes. "Is the president all right? We're friends, you know that."

"I don't know anything, ma'am, except that I need to get my men and my equipment down to those coordinates."

"And what will you find there?"

Bull just looked at her, then suddenly opened the door and went back outside.

His muffled voice resounded as he barked orders to set up a shelter beneath the chopper. He added that they would rotate spending time inside the cabin.

Abruptly, the door opened, and a younger man with a scrubby beard said, "Ladies, I need you to step outside for a little while. We're setting up a shelter below."

"I'll go, too," said the pilot.

"No, sir. You stay. We need your hands warm for flying."

Walsh shrugged.

"I'm not going out in the cold," said Tracy. "We're civilians."

"Tracy, don't argue. Those guys are freezing. Give them a chance to warm up."

Hildebrand climbed out, dropped to the snow, then took in a deep breath as Tracy reluctantly followed. Four of the soldiers poured into the chopper and quickly shut the doors.

She and Tracy got down on their hands and knees and crawled beneath the helicopter, where Bull and Hojo were finishing tying off some lightweight sleeping bags between the landing skids. The bags flapped violently in the wind.

They had piled all of their backpacks in front and behind the chopper, creating a nice—though drafty—nest below with room for about six people, jammed side by side.

Hildebrand and Tracy took up positions on their sides, facing the two men. Oswaller, Neggy, and a few of the other soldiers opted to hunker down behind the chopper but would rotate inside the cabin and below. Bull said he'd call out the names for rotation, and had jotted them down on a little notepad he had tucked into his hip pocket.

"Thank you for ruining my week," said Tracy. "Do you know how far I'm falling behind now?"

Hildebrand nodded weakly. "It's good to think like that."

"Like what?"

"Like we'll actually live."

"Now *you're* the defeatist?"

"It feels like it's getting colder, and my ears haven't stopped popping. I'm getting scared now."

"That's great. You drag me up here, now you've finally changed your mind. Shit."

"Here," said Bull, offering Hildebrand a stick of gum.

"Thanks."

The big man groaned as she shifted around, sat up, hit his head on the chopper, then cursed.

"Not having a good day, are you," asked Tracy.

Bull smirked. "You mind if I ask you something, Ms. O'Donnell?"

"Go ahead. I'm sure this'll be good."

"Oh, simple question. What's your problem?"

"Excuse me?"

"I said, what's your problem?"

"She's always been this way," said Hildebrand. "It's not a problem. It's a way of life."

"Shut up, Sandy."

"No, I mean, what's your problem with the military? You can't really believe our troops are criminals, can you?"

"*Our troops?* It's your gun club, too."

"We're not talking about me. We're talking about you."

"Do you want me to cite individual incidents, the anecdotal evidence, or would you like me to present to you all of the empirical data that we've collected: reconstruction missions that turned into shoot-outs, bombing missions on civilian weddings and funerals, raids on farmers instead of al-Qaeda leaders, the hundreds of photos we have of the carnage caused by American and coalition forces . . . the list goes on and on."

"So what you're really saying is that you have no idea

what it's like for the average soldier doing a twelve-month—ahem, excuse me, I mean an eighteen- or twenty-four-month tour in A'stan, living in an FOB that isn't much nicer than a cave. That's what you're saying. You sit behind a desk all day, crunching numbers and looking at photos."

"Really? I don't get my hands dirty? Look where I am!"

"I'm just saying that maybe you need to spend a little more time talking to the average troops. I don't think you understand the complexity of what's happening in this country."

Tracy rolled her eyes. "I've dedicated my life to understanding—because these poor people deserve better than what they're getting."

"Has it occurred to you that the military is only as good as the tools it's given? Has it occurred to you that the military here is understaffed and underequipped?"

"And that absolves it from blame? Oh, we bombed that village, we're sorry. We just didn't have enough guys or big enough binoculars to tell us those were civilians." Tracy snorted in disgust.

"What I'm saying, ma'am, is that they need more time. I'm not justifying the mistakes they've made. But it's organizations like yours that will sway the politicians, and our people will pull out before the job is finished—because you focus on only the mistakes, not the successes. The word *crime* is in the title of your organization. That says it all . . ."

Tracy made a face. "You just think we're a bunch of bleeding heart liberals, don't you?"

"At least you have the luxury of a bleeding heart that won't kill you. The men here don't."

Hildebrand looked at Tracy, who averted her gaze but maintained her deep, unflinching frown.

27. VISIONS OF THE SHEIKH

General Malim Kahn's small convoy of six trucks had averaged about thirty kilometers per hour over the rubble- and snow-laden terrain.

A landslide that had probably occurred during the big quake had forced them to make an unexpected turn through a broad valley about a kilometer west of the border with Tajikistan, so now they would be unable to link up directly with the men from Eshkashem and would approach the supposed crash zone from the northwest, while that other group came in from the northeast.

The men in Kahn's lead truck had a portable GPS device, which helped keep them on course through the blinding snowstorm. What Kahn had not counted on was a rebellion from the two men in their flatbed, who had repeatedly rapped on the rear window and asked that they be allowed to rotate inside the cabin. They were covered in snow, blue-lipped, and trembling. Three other men had huddled in one corner of the lead truck, they, too, looking about to freeze to death.

But Kahn would never give up his warm seat inside the cabin, nor should any of the three news crew from as-Sahab, who needed to be in the best physical condition to take video of Kahn's victory. While Kahn's truck was a crew cab, the rest were extended cabs that barely allowed one man and his gear to squeeze sideways behind the front seats. Fifteen men were already crammed into those trucks, so the other five would need to fend for themselves for a little longer.

But Fahim, who repeatedly checked his rearview mirror, had already urged Kahn to reconsider. Now, as he opened his mouth and the rapping on the window started up once more, Kahn knew that he had no choice but to call for a halt.

"All right, all right," he cried, then got on his radio, yelling for all of the trucks to stop.

Fahim was wise to pull over to the right of the trail, anticipating that the truck behind him might not brake in time. In fact, it didn't, the driver rushing forward past them, craning his head, and then seeing he had to stop. The fool.

That incensed Kahn so much that he burst from the truck, stomped over to the other truck in the heavy snow, pulled out his pistol, and began waving it at the driver. "Get out!"

The driver, a kid no more than nineteen or twenty, widened his eyes, opened the door, and raised his palms.

"Pay attention!" Kahn screamed as he put his gun to the man's temple. "Bang!"

The kid flinched as Kahn yanked his gun away, leaving the frightened boy behind. He cried out to the freezing men in the flatbeds to exchange places with those inside the lead and third trucks. The men inside the trucks grunted their protests, but Kahn screamed again, and not a man spoke up to challenge him.

As they made the excruciatingly slow exchange, Kahn stood a moment, grimacing over the tightness in his chest. Was he having a heart attack or was it just anxiety? He felt light-headed, a little dizzy, could no longer sense his legs.

Had he fallen? He couldn't see.

The darkness lifted into a gray veil that seemed to swim over him, then a familiar voice called his name, and his eyes opened further.

He was lying on his back, staring up into the falling snow for a few seconds until a face came into view:

Sheikh Abu Hassan's eyes grew wider to reveal flames in the irises. His mouth opened, revealing gold fangs, and his green, forked tongue lashed out at Kahn and sliced open his cheek. Blood rushed over his chin.

"Brother!"

Suddenly, Kahn's eyes snapped open. Yes, he was still lying in the snow, staring at the sky, but it was Fahim hovering over him.

"Why am I here?" he asked.

"You fell. Come on." Fahim seized Kahn's hand and helped him to sit up.

Several of the men who had been squeezing out of the trucks to give up their seats rushed over, and two dragged him up to his feet. Kahn knew they could not bear the sight of their commander looking so feeble and helpless, and for a moment, he felt embarrassed and ashamed for what had happened.

But then he realized that his heartbeat felt strong and steady. "I am all right," he said loudly, forcibly. "But I will kill the man who sewed these boots!"

The men chuckled heartily, and Kahn waved them off back to the flatbeds as Fahim brushed snow from his eyes and said, "Brother, I think you passed out."

"I slipped. I'm not a young man anymore."

"You called me Hassan. You thought I was the sheikh."

"No."

Fahim stroked his beard. "Yes."

Kahn turned away from his brother, started toward the truck, but his knees felt weak once more, and abruptly Fahim was there to brace him.

"What is it, brother?"

He paused. "I don't know, Fahim. Something inside me is turning like a knife. If we fail, the sheikh will come for us." Kahn began to lose his breath.

"We won't fail. Abdali's helicopter went down. We know this. We will get there before anyone. Believe that."

Kahn took a deep breath through his nose, then nodded. He stiffened and turned back for the truck—

When one of the men in the lead Tundra shouted excitedly for him to come over. "I see something!"

Reflexively, Kahn broke into a jog toward the truck, his body succumbing to his will. And suddenly, he felt very much alive. Two of the men hoisted him up, onto the flatbed, where he was handed a pair of binoculars, and the young man who had shouted for him pointed at the mountainside to their north and said, "There. About halfway up. Zoom in."

With jittery hands Kahn raised the binoculars and, through the blustering wind, managed to focus on a dark blob until the image resolved into—

A fuselage. A helicopter.

Abdali was there, right there.

28. ALL ALONG THE WATCHTOWER

The narrowest part of the defile took Rock and Khodai through a tunnel-like passage, with large outcroppings whose sides were encrusted with ice and whose bottoms bore icicles like teeth threatening to come down on them from several meters overhead. Snow blasted between the long rafters of rock, and it took another twenty minutes of laborious hiking to emerge onto the back side of the mountain, where they both crouched down and rushed along the ridge toward a shallow ravine formed by a now-frozen creek. There, Khodai dropped onto his gut, and Rock slid in beside him.

Before Rock could pull out his binoculars, Khodai was surveying the valley with his. "They're here," said the Tajik.

"You see them?"

"I see their trail. Mule dung. It stands out in the snow."

"I don't see anything."

Khodai pointed off to their right.

"Okay, over there." Rock panned toward the east side of the valley, where scattered, leafless trees rose like bony hands, then he swept up along the hillside toward a thicker cluster of trees behind which stood a collection of dark splotches, four or five in all—

And there . . . he spotted several mules tied to one of the trees. He zoomed in on the splotches, which resolved into jagged cracks in the mountainside: cave entrances, at least four spread several meters apart in a rising and falling pattern like the levels on a stereo equalizer. And there was the fifth, farther west of the first group, a much wider indentation with a snowdrift obscuring one side.

A chill broke across Rock's shoulders as a man emerged from one cave, a typical wiry fighter wearing a *pakol* and clutching an AK-47, his *shemagh* shielding his nose and mouth.

"You see him?" asked Khodai.

"Yeah, I got him."

"They're waiting out the storm. They don't have cold weather clothing like we do. They're all wearing sandals."

Rock swore under his breath. He couldn't get a good look at any of them now. He'd have to wait.

"We should call the captain," said Khodai.

Rock switched on his radio.

Pharaoh couldn't believe what he was hearing from Rock, and for a moment, he couldn't help but look at Zulu and smile. He told Rock to hold on, then said, "You got time to set up your perfect ambush, Zu. You and Ondekjo get up top. I'll get Figueroa to set up his charges."

"What happened? Does he got eyes on them?"

"Yeah, they're holding up along the cliffs in some caves,

probably waiting on this front to pass. He doesn't know how many, but they're about a quarter klick from here."

"Outstanding! Let's go!" Zulu turned away from the sheer wall of rock at the mouth of the defile, then stopped and whirled back. "Wait a minute."

"What?"

"Let's hit 'em now."

"You want to attack? Six of us, Rock, and Khodai, against them? Could be forty down there."

"I know. Doesn't that make it interesting?"

"Sergeant, our job is to interdict them for as long as possible. We have—"

"Sir, I have Bull on the Shadow Fire," said Weathers, rushing up to hand Pharaoh the headset.

"Hold that thought," Pharaoh told Zulu. "Tempest, this is Titan 06, go ahead."

"Roger, Titan 06. We are approximately eight klicks northwest of target site. No visual yet. We have commandeered a civilian helicopter and plan to use it to reach target, over."

Pharaoh frowned. A civilian helicopter? Where the hell had that come from? "Roger that, Tempest. What's your ETA to site, over?"

"Not sure yet. Still waiting on the storm, but I just got a call from the target site. Apparently, they've spotted six trucks moving in from the northwest, over."

"Shit, shit, shit . . ." Pharaoh muttered away from the headset. "Any estimate on their ETA?"

"Not sure, maybe an hour or two. Depends on terrain, how far forward they can get those trucks, over."

"Roger that. You need to get in the air."

"I know. We can get near the site in maybe ten minutes, but the wind is bad, and finding an LZ should be fun."

"All right. We'll see what we can do from our end. Give me a shout once you're in the air, Titan 06, out."

Pharaoh reached into his hip pocket and pulled out his map of the crash site area as Zulu shook his head.

"Well, we got confirmation that those guys from Araki are involved," said Pharaoh.

"I heard. So they're coming in here," Zulu began, tracing his finger over the map. "And we're over here set to interdict these other bastards."

"We'd have to make a half circle around this valley to reach those guys in the trucks," said Pharaoh, drawing the line with his finger around the mountains.

"That'd take all day. The guys in the trucks will get there first, but there's no guarantee we can suppress them before these other forty bastards reach the site."

Pharaoh ground his teeth in frustration, then got on the radio back to Weathers, who was still down with the SUV. "See if you can get an update on close air support. We have a second enemy force advancing from the northwest of the crash site. Here's the grid . . ." Pharaoh went on to feed him the numbers, and Weathers broke off to make the call.

"That's wishful thinking," said Zulu. "I think it's up to Bull to get his ass in and out of there before those guys get close enough. Meanwhile, all we can do is keep these assholes busy." He sniffled, his nose turning even more red. "All right?"

"Yeah, I just don't like Bull going in there with no blocking element."

Zulu shrugged. "If it's any consolation, Bull's the best man on the planet for that job."

Ten minutes later, Pharaoh and Zulu had moved forward through the defile to link up with Khodai and Rock, who were still observing the area while Ondekjo, Grimm, Figueroa, and Weathers got into position. The temperature seemed to have dropped a few degrees, and despite all his cold weather gear, Pharaoh shivered against a chill that had secured a permanent home in his bones.

"We've seen a few guys coming outside to smoke," said Rock, not looking up from his binoculars. "Otherwise, nothing. Khodai says the caves were man-made, a rest area along the route. They knew all about them."

"Guess they're not so highly motivated," said Zulu.

"I think the weather's got more to do with their stop than motivation," Rock countered. "And, hold on, there he is."

Pharaoh squinted through his own binoculars at a tall man who had just come out of the nearest cave. His dark blue scarf had been tugged down around his neck, and his long beard was reddish-blond, not the much more common coal black. Though Pharaoh couldn't make out much more, he certainly seemed far more Caucasian than his counterparts.

And even more remarkably, he shoved a cigar into his mouth and lit it. The tip flared as he puffed away, appearing very much like their own friendly neighborhood spook.

"You know that guy?" asked Pharaoh. "Is he an American?"

"He sure looks like one," said Zulu.

"He is *not* Tajik," Khodai pointed out.

Rock sighed deeply, then rolled away from the ditch and sat up. "Gentlemen, huddle up."

"Aw, shit, Rock, don't even say it," said Zulu.

"The guy down there? We just call him Scorpion. He's the field agent I replaced more than eight years ago. And the latest intel put him in Eshkashem. He went rogue, turned into a merc, and now he's pretty much doing the same thing you guys do, only he gets paid a hell of a lot better and doesn't give a shit about who wins and who loses. He's probably trained and is leading those boys down there."

"And you knew all along?" asked Pharaoh, stiffening in anger.

"I knew there was a chance he could be with these guys. My intel was incomplete. They sent another guy out after him. He's still MIA, presumed dead."

"So who is this guy?" asked Zulu. "What do you got on him?"

"He was a SEAL and developed a rep as one of the most lethal field agents we had. Right after 9/11, he was first in. Two years later, he vanished," explained Rock.

"What kind of bullshit story is that?" asked Zulu.

"I don't care if you guys believe it or not. I'm just saying I could use your help."

Zulu frowned. "With what? Killing him? No problem."

"Langley wants him alive. He's a valuable asset."

"Well, hopefully our claymores, rockets, and machine-gun fire will miss him," said Pharaoh with a lopsided grin. "Then you can move in for the capture."

"I'm serious, Captain. We need to take that man alive. He's got intel on everybody moving in and out of the province. We take him out of the game, and we may be putting a nice dent in drug smuggling."

"Really?" asked Pharaoh with a snort.

"The militiamen he trains are used to guarding drug shipments, securing passes, and even smuggling the drugs themselves. He's become a key player in this region."

"Oh, this just keeps getting better," said Zulu.

"All I'm saying is, let's see what we can do about taking him alive."

"Forget it. We're not holding back fire," said Pharaoh. "You want him so badly? Go down there and get him."

Rock smiled, and sighed once more through his teeth.

"Captain, Captain, Captain. Call your FOB. Ask your CO about Scorpion, and he'll tell you that he's received orders that you are to do everything within your power to bring back this man alive. I didn't want to go there, but there it is. So keeping him alive is part of your mission."

"I plan to confirm that," Pharaoh said, a challenge in his tone.

Rock shrugged. "Go ahead."

"So we're saving Private Ryan," said Zulu in disgust. "Only Ryan is a scumbag who doesn't deserve saving."

29. BY THE HORNS

Bull wrenched open the cabin door, startling the pilot, who'd been dozing off. "Warm her up!"

The guy shook his head as the helicopter shuddered a moment against a strong gust. "Wind's still too strong. Updrafts could slam us into the mountainside. Not good."

"We're out of time, sorry."

"You really want to die."

The pilot wasn't asking.

Bull held up a glove-covered thumb and cracked a broad, fake smile. "I have complete faith in you, Walsh."

"Then you're an idiot."

"Been called a lot worse." Bull grabbed Walsh's shoulder and lowered his voice. "Just get this bitch warm."

"Jesus Christ, you're serious."

"As a heart attack."

Walsh's eyes burned. "Okay."

Bull slammed shut the door, then cried out to the team:

"Police up the gear, detach the sleeping bags, and begin loading everything into the chopper."

"How you want to play this?" Hojo asked.

Bull explained that he and Hojo would take the gear over first, survey the site; then everyone else would be picked up on the second run. The third run would be for the news crew. That was the plan, and he didn't care how much the two sisters bitched and moaned.

"Roger that," said Hojo. "All right, people, let's move!"

Bull ordered the news folks away from the bird as the rotor wash swept across the area, and as expected the women were yapping at him—but it all went in one ear and out the other.

As a terrible husband, he had perfected the ability to ignore women, which, of course, was one of the many traits that had earned him that title.

Bull made sure that McDaniel and his radio gear remained behind (so he could call in the event the chopper went down during the first run). He also made sure that their medical kit and basic food and water remained behind, so, again, in the event of a crash, the folks back on the mountain would have enough supplies until help arrived.

Wouldn't that suck to crash-land in a chopper while trying to rescue the president of Afghanistan who had crash-landed in his chopper?

It did say something about the safety of rotary wing aircraft flown in Afghanistan.

And something about the cruelty and irony of fate.

And something about Bull's misplaced trust in the pilot's skills . . .

To say Bull wasn't nervous would be a lie. But experience and a bit of bravado tempered his fear. A shot of Jack would've really done the trick.

Within minutes the gear was loaded, and just as he turned to join Hojo in the chopper, Sandra Hildebrand rushed up into the rotor wash and shouted, "Don't let us down! Good luck!"

Her well wishes were surprising and a little suspect. He gave her a nod, then leaned forward and jogged to the chopper to climb in. They were already leaving the snow as he donned his headset.

The little group seemed insignificant, pathetic even against a massive humpback of rock and ice. The farther they pulled away, the more Bull appreciated that this god-forsaken mountain range would, without any doubt, kill them if they remained too long.

"All right, it's your call," said Walsh as he banked hard, heading northwest toward the pair of white peaks partially obscured in the blowing snow. A sudden gust sent the man wrestling with the stick, but he course-corrected before Bull had a full-on heart attack.

Hojo gasped. "This is insane."

"Just a little," quipped Bull.

"You want to maintain this course?" asked Walsh.

Bull consulted the portable GPS in his hand. "Yeah, you're good."

"If you got a particular landmark in mind, it'd be nice to share it. Pilots like landmarks."

With a snicker but a keen appreciation for the man's sarcasm, Bull decided it was time for full disclosure. "We're looking for an old Soviet MI-8."

"I flew one of those once."

"She's lying on her side, pieces of her scattered across the hill. Should be one of the rotor blades sticking out, too. Can't miss her, so says the president."

"So holy shit, you *are* trying to rescue the president."

"Not trying. Doing. Take us over that next peak. We're almost there."

"Short hop it is."

"Hey, Bull, look at that," called Hojo, pointing out the portside window.

Below them, just on the other side of the peak, lay a dark gray hump with snowdrifts stretching across its sides.

But it wasn't the main fuselage, just part of the tail assembly, as best Bull could tell. "We're close."

Another wind blast sent the chopper yawing hard, then suddenly they pitched forward, seemingly headed for a nosedive into the mountain.

Bull clung to his seat as the mountainside panned across the windshield and scrolled across the side windows. His shoulders burned against the straps; if they gave way, he'd catapult into the controls.

And then, just as abruptly, the nose pitched up, and they began to level off once more, as though they'd found a large and invisible pocket of calm within the hellish wind.

Walsh hooted and cursed the mountain, telling it how he'd beat its ass.

"We're not on the ground yet," warned Hojo.

"I don't care," said Walsh. "That was the best goddamned recovery of my career!"

"There they are," said Bull, blinking, still recovering himself from the roller-coaster ride but able to see the fuselage now, lying on its side, almost fully buried in the snow. Were it not for that rotor jutting out nearby, they might have missed the downed bird.

She lay at the bottom of a reasonably flat but very narrow ridge, and between all the rocks and debris, Bull doubted the pilot could land there.

"I can't land there."

"You read my mind," said Bull.

"We could get blown off the edge, or our wash could affect the fuselage, maybe send it rolling off, too."

"Shit, what now?" asked Hojo.

Bull told Walsh to make another pass overhead, while he made a call back to McDaniel, told the commo guy that they had found the president's chopper at the exact grid and that he should relay that information back to the captain and to higher at FOB Asadabad. The rookie was on it.

"Look at that shit," said Hojo.

About a quarter klick below the chopper on an adjoining slope stood a two-story mud-brick house with a flat roof wide enough to accommodate the helicopter's skids.

The entire structure was buried in at least a foot of snow, thus it was unclear whether or not that roof would support the weight of a helicopter.

However, that rooftop was the closest thing they had to a helipad. The slopes and ridges nearby looked too steep or uneven, and they might be forced to put down much farther back and have yet another long hike to the site.

"What do you think that's doing up here in the middle of nowhere?"

"Could've been an old lookout post from the Soviet war," said Walsh.

"Maybe so," said Bull.

"All right, you sons of bitches, here goes nothing."

"Actually, here goes something: a perfect landing," Bull corrected.

The pilot chuckled. "Like I said, you're an idiot."

They came around the hut, snow blasting off the lower roof, then, as they hovered, the entire place was caught in the snowstorm created by the wash.

As large pieces of snow peeled away from the roof like broken tiles and tumbled down into the ravine, Bull reported to Walsh that the structure still looked pretty stable but that he should be able to lift off if it begin to collapse.

"Don't worry about that."

With excruciating care, Walsh descended, meter by meter, the rotors whomping, until . . . *thump, thump* . . . they were down.

"Hold up," said Bull, as he peered intently through the window, wondering if the roof was about to cave in.

But nothing. She seemed to hold up well.

"If anyone's home, they should be coming out about now," said Hojo.

"Or they're scared shitless and huddling inside," Bull replied. "We'll see." He waited another minute, then suddenly barked, "All right, Hojo! Let's go!"

They popped open the doors and began carefully and systematically unloading packs down to the lower roofline in front of the chopper. A rickety wooden ladder led below. Bull's best friend, Mr. H&K USP CTV1, was ready to be drawn quickly from his SERPA hip holster, should a not-so-welcome wagon arrive.

Once the gear was out, Bull slammed shut the cabin door and signaled for Walsh to take off.

The guy raised his thumb, nodded; the engine roared while Bull and Hojo quickly descended the ladder, nearly blown off by all the wash.

A door behind the ladder swung half open in the wind. He and Hojo got set with their .45s and Gladius lights, then pushed into the house, sweeping through the shadows to clear the first room.

Some old wooden bowls, empty magazines, shell casings, and empty ammunition crates lay strewn in one corner. They shifted forward, Hojo leading the way, toward a square opening in the floor supporting yet another wooden ladder that would take them below.

Bull shone his Gladius into the gap, while Hojo got on his hands and knees and then peeked down. "Elvis? Is that you?"

"Quit fucking around," snapped Bull.

Hojo glanced up at him with a wounded look, then rose. "Looks empty. I'm going down." He mounted the ladder, descended halfway, then hopped to the wooden floor, timbers creaking.

Bull followed, and below they found more of the same: tattered blankets, discarded ammo, a few broken AK-47s, and a more interesting sight—

A body. Or more accurately, a skeleton lying on its back, still dressed in a Russian military uniform, a pistol clutched in its grip.

"Guess his ride never came," said Hojo.

"This is weird," said Bull. Then he pulled out his radio and called McDaniel. The commo guy said the helicopter was approaching and about to land. Good.

They searched the rest of the house, found nothing, then went back out to survey the mountainside leading up to the president's chopper. They crouched down near the roof's edge and brought up their binoculars.

A quarter klick all uphill. Grade wasn't too bad, though, about thirty degrees, maybe, but a slip could send you into a roll from which there'd be little chance of recovery— until you ran out of momentum or hit a large rock.

Once they reached the top of the slope, they'd need to navigate back down the ridge, across the debris field to reach the fuselage.

"It's going to take us another half hour to forty minutes to reach them," said Hojo.

"That's what I figured. Not good. I need to call Abdali and get a SITREP on those guys in the trucks."

"We might have to extract the president from the bird

while taking fire," said Hojo. "Not sure I want that kind of responsibility."

"And you know, I was disappointed that we wouldn't see much action. Shit." He removed his satellite phone, thumbed the number, waited.

Finally, that familiar accent: "Hello?"

"Mr. President, this is Dennis Bull again. We're just a quarter klick below you and coming up."

"That's excellent news."

"Are you still observing the trucks like I said?"

"Yes. Hold one moment while I check with Rafiullah."

"Hey, Bull, what if we get them moving now?" asked Hojo. "You said he can walk. Maybe a few broken ribs and a broken arm, but he's mobile."

"You kidding me? I don't want him leaving that chopper until Borokovsky checks him out. Just remember: every move we make here will be scrutinized over and over later on. Every goddamned move."

Hojo's frustration came in a deep sigh. "Makes me afraid to breathe. But all right. Rest of the guys should be in the air by now anyway. Borokovsky will be here in five minutes."

"Hello, Bull?" called Abdali.

"Yes, sir, I'm here."

"The trucks have stopped in the foothills; they can't climb any higher. But Rafiullah says there are about twenty men coming up on foot. He says some of them are armed with rocket-propelled grenades. All have rifles. He says they're still pretty far away, but they're coming fast."

Bull wished he were dealing with military men who would've given him a more accurate estimation of the enemy force's ETA, but "far away" and "pretty fast" were what he had to work with, so he'd best get the team's asses moving pretty fast as well.

"Thank you, Mr. President. Just stand by. We should be up there within the hour."

"We'll be waiting for you. Good-bye."

The whomping of a helicopter in the distance caught Bull's attention. "Typhoon, this is Tempest, over."

"Tempest, this is Typhoon, go ahead, over."

"Are you guys inbound, over?"

"Roger that, but we did have a little problem. Ms. O'Donnell got into the helicopter and wouldn't get out, over."

"Oh, shit," Bull muttered under his breath. "We'll talk when you get here. Any word yet on CAS and that Chinook to exfiltrate us?"

"Nothing. Not even sure our extraction bird is off the ground yet. Weather looks like it'll get better for us and worse for them. Front's moving to the south."

"Roger that. Typhoon, out."

"O'Donnell. What an idiot. But at least she didn't throw herself across the skids," said Hojo.

"Ah, they're just worried about getting stuck up there, but now we'll need their bird for Abdali and his aide."

"I figured."

"So what do we do? Hold the pilot here at gunpoint? That'll go over real well. I guess maybe they were right. We are going to leave them up there."

Bull frowned. He wasn't sure they could do that, either. There was no guarantee that he could get a chopper up to them before they succumbed to the elements. Hell, their own extraction bird's ETA was unknown, given the weather.

He took a deep breath, closed his eyes, and made a decision.

30. MORE AUDACITY

Conventional wisdom about planning for any attack was that your plan would not survive the first enemy contact.

If you asked most Special Forces operators, they'd tell you how true that was and cite multiple examples from history and from their own exploits. Sometimes an attack wouldn't even survive the damned planning phase because elements like supplies or transport or close air support were unavailable—which got men so frustrated that they'd just as soon go into the field and improvise. Hell, they might have a better chance than relying upon "planned" assets that never arrived.

Well, be careful what you wish for, Pharaoh thought. Because they were in no-man's-land with no backup, about to initiate an attack they had just devised, one in which they were supposed to keep "Scorpion" alive, the rogue CIA operative turned merc/militia leader.

Let the games begin.

"T-Rex, this is Titan 06," Pharaoh called to Ondejko, who was up in the cliffs with his sniper rifle. "Set, over?"

"Titan 06, this is T-Rex. I'm good to go, over."

"Tarzan, this is Titan 06," Pharaoh called to engineer Figueroa. "All set, over?"

"Titan, this is Tarzan, I am ready to bring down the house, over."

"Roger that. Talk Radio and Trauma, all set, over?"

The commo guy and medic, who were manning the machine guns, also checked in, followed by Rock and Khodai, who were both armed with SCAR-L rifles and had positioned themselves along the backside slopes of the defile.

Pharaoh and Zulu and climbed back up the hillside to observe the caves from a much higher vantage point. A half dozen men had come out of the caves and were climbing into the saddles of their mules. Ten or so more followed, and within a minute, the entire force had gathered outside.

"I count forty-three," Pharaoh said to Zulu, whose attention was riveted on his binoculars.

"I have a confession to make," Zulu said.

"Do I look like a priest?"

Zulu snorted. "Rock and I have known each other for a while. But I don't trust him. He'll take out Figueroa if he thinks we'll kill Scorpion, you know that."

"I've already planned for that."

"What?" The team sergeant set down his binoculars and edged closer on his elbows.

"Ondejko's keeping an eye," Pharaoh explained. "If Rock plays any games, he's gone."

"No shit." Zulu seemed adequately impressed. "Because I tried to work out a little deal with Khodai if the same thing happens."

"You think you can trust him?"

"Not really. He didn't go for the deal. He's playing on Rock's team, not ours. So if we accidentally kill Scorpion, we need to keep an eye on both of them."

Pharaoh nodded.

"So you're okay with all this? I mean, you verified the orders. Rock wasn't lying. We've been ordered to keep Scorpion alive."

After a long sigh, Pharaoh answered: "I'm okay with it."

Zulu nearly laughed. "Maybe you don't want to go on to lead battalions. Maybe you need to stay out here with us."

"Because my pool is as dirty as yours?"

"No, because I finally met an officer who gets it."

"Gets what?"

"It. The mysterious *it* of this."

"Okay, I don't know what you're talking about, but they're starting to move." Pharaoh resumed his gaze through the binoculars.

Zulu got on the MBITR. "All right, everybody. Listen up. They're moving. Tarzan is the cue, then Talk Radio, then everybody else. Stand by . . ."

Pharaoh and Zulu had agreed on the way they would guide the attack. Zulu would fight the men; Pharaoh initially would not engage in order to provide intel to the team sergeant. It was too hard to analyze the overall situation when you were trying to shoot militiamen down in the valley.

And then when all hell broke loose, they'd both engage and call it as it unfolded.

Hopefully, all hell would come after more than half of the militiamen were reduced to pink viscera splattered across the snow. Pharaoh's pulse thundered in his ears.

Ten men on foot spearheaded the group, keeping about a dozen meters ahead, and Pharaoh didn't like that. They needed to get as many of them into the narrowest part of the defile as possible. Shit. In fact, the entire force was broken into four smaller squads of eight to ten men, with the mule guys bringing up the rear, hauling the heavy ammo and supply packs.

Interestingly enough, Scorpion, who of course had his own mule, kept with that last group of eight, his rifle slung over his shoulder, his attention split between the men around him and his own small pair of binoculars.

Pharaoh tensed even more, imagining that the former SEAL would spot them, call for a halt, and suddenly the slopes around the defile would be raked by withering gunfire. He blinked hard, as Zulu got back on radio:

"Wait for 'em, Tarzan. Let 'em get as close as possible. We should be able to get the first ten and at least half of the second party, if they don't spread out any more."

"Roger that," said Figueroa, a slight tremor in his voice.

The lead men started up a trail that snaked to the west, then switched back toward the rockiest part of the slope; there they would turn along the cliff and enter a zone of sheer rock walls where the trail narrowed to just three meters wide, then two, then one: the zone of certain death.

The snow was beginning to taper, the wind along with it. Pharaoh sniffled and glanced over at Zulu, who was a statue holding his binoculars.

For a man about to raise serious and concentrated hell, the team sergeant appeared incredibly calm, and Pharaoh envied the man for that, among many things. Was it just experience that coursed through his veins, turning tremors into a deep, relaxed state, or was he just an expert at hiding it?

Pharaoh returned to his own observation, remembering what Zulu had told him about audacity. More audacity.

One by one the bad guys humped up the mountainside, following the trail toward the west. The team had carefully brushed away any boot prints they had left in the snow, but there was always a nagging feeling that they had forgotten something that would be spotted by even the most inexperienced of fighters.

Repressing the desire to hold his breath, Pharaoh studied the first group as they switched back and began to enter the defile, passing only fifty meters or so west. The closer they came, the deeper Pharaoh tucked himself in the snow.

"You okay, Captain?" asked Zulu.

"Yeah."

"Then please don't move."

"Sorry."

"I'm shitting a pickle, too. Just keep still."

The first group disappeared entirely into the defile, and the second group followed only thirty seconds later, having caught up to them.

"We can't wait any longer," said Pharaoh.

Suddenly, Figueroa's voice broke over the radio. "I see the first guys! Come on! Give me the order!"

"Hang in there, Tarzan," said Zulu.

"Zu, they are right here!"

"Hang tight . . . just a little longer."

"Zu," Pharaoh began.

A shout from below broke the silence, and abruptly the third group and the mule team came to a dead stop along the trail.

"Aw, shit," grunted Zulu. "Tarzan, go!"

Pharaoh gasped—

As multiple explosions from the claymores they had set shook through the mountains.

At the same time, Weathers and Grimm opened up with the M240Bs targeting the third group, muzzles winking atop a bipod and a tripod set firmly on the rock. Weathers was positioned on the left of the defile, Grimm on the right, and even as the men dropped to the snow, another rumble came from the defile—what sounded like a landslide.

"He's brought down the house!" cried Zulu.

More gunfire cracked from the hills overlooking the enemy, and Pharaoh panned his binoculars to see Khodai and Rock laying down more fire on the third group.

Meanwhile, the mule team—including Scorpion—was retreating toward a slope near the east, not far from the caves.

Ondejko's sniper rifle boomed. One man on the mule team, who had just moved away from his ride, dropped as pieces of his shoulder and arm hurtled through the air.

At that moment, Zulu burst upright, bringing the AT-4 launcher onto his shoulder.

Pharaoh scrambled out of the way to avoid the blast that would pour from the launcher's tail end.

Zulu disengaged the two safeties, cocked the mechanical firing pin, then stared down the plastic sights, taking aim at the mule team as it moved within the antitank weapon's three-hundred-meter range.

"Are you going to kill him?" Pharaoh cried, seeing that Scorpion now led the team.

"Who knows?" Zulu shouted back.

Then he pressed the button.

31. CONVERGENCE

Bull studied the faces of his men as they watched the helicopter take off once more from the roof, heading back to the mountain to pick up the news crew. Sullivan was on board, too, to keep the pilot honest.

No one said it, but they were all thinking it: Bull had just sent off their only means to rescue the president. He had decided to have the chopper pilot go back and return the news crew to the mud-brick house, where at least they'd have some shelter and could utilize the team's supplies. He wanted to give those civilians a fighting chance.

He wished he'd had a few days to think it over, play out all possibilities, but he'd gone with his gut, as agonizing as that had felt.

Perhaps he'd regret the decision. Perhaps he'd be accused of favoring American lives over the life of the Afghan president.

The way he figured it, though, the bird still had enough fuel for another run, and in the grand scheme, he'd rather be accused of trying to save everyone than deciding whose life was more important.

But would fate let him have it both ways?

Aw, hell. He and fate were still not talking, and that other guy Murphy and his law? Bull was on the top of his shit list, too. But that was his style: waving a fist against the odds, even if he still felt uncertain.

He cleared his throat. "All right, Cub Scouts, let's get our fat asses in gear!"

Hojo, Gator, Borokovsky, and McDaniel buckled on their packs. With their rifles at the ready, they started up the mountain, Hojo walking point. Bull pulled up the rear, within arm's reach of McDaniel, who said, "Just got a quick call from the captain. They're engaging that militia right now."

"Which could mean we have even less time." Bull lifted his voice. "Hojo, pick up the pace!"

Hojo glanced back and seemed to climb a bit faster, but it was rough going between the thin air, the cold, and the fresh aches in their muscles.

Off to the left, near the windswept mountain, a slight reflection caught Bull's eye: that'd be the chopper, just disappearing behind the mountain.

I made the right decision.

He tugged off a glove, reached into his pocket, rubbed his father's unit coin for luck, then whispered, "We're good to go. All will be well. We're going to do this."

There was no more energy to talk, and yes, it would be at least forty minutes, maybe an hour before they could reach the president's chopper. Hojo's guesstimate was becoming painfully accurate.

They broke their own trail along the slope, trudging higher along rockier, snow-covered ground that drove Hojo onto the radio. "Ice up here. More loose shale. Watch it. Right under your boots."

Not ten seconds later, Hojo's left foot suddenly gave out, and he slipped onto his rump and began sliding down the hillside.

Bull watched helplessly for a moment, forgetting to breathe, until Hojo dug in his heels and stopped, clouds of snow whipping over him. He descended just fifteen meters or so. Good man.

"Hojo!"

"I'm okay!" he cried, then rolled over, got to his feet. And started his hump back up to the others. "Like I said! It's slippery!" At least only his ego had been bruised.

Bull got on the radio. "Everybody sit down, dig out your crampons, put 'em on!"

His order was met by an unsurprising chorus of groans.

So he and Hojo had been wrong about the trail: they'd figured that even if it were a little icy, they could still make better time without attaching the spikes, which would slow them down considerably by adding a more deliberate footfall to each man's stride. True, snow could ball up between the spikes, creating an even more dangerous scenario than just ascending with assault boots, but that wasn't too common.

Oh, well. They'd saved a few minutes and would now waste ten. Bull sloughed off his pack, fished out the spikes, and attached them to his boots. When he was ready, he stood, seeing that Hojo was getting help from Borokovsky.

Within another two minutes, they were back on the trail; the going was a little slower, but Bull felt more secure with the spikes.

After a dozen steps, he was ready for a break, but Hojo and the others weren't stopping. Bull tugged down his scarf and struggled for breath. Six more steps, and he just stopped. Couldn't take another step.

McDaniel glanced back, then called on the radio for them to halt once more.

"Give the old man a rest," Bull said. Then he reached for his satellite phone and called back to the president. "We're coming up, sir. Almost there."

"Rafiullah says to hurry. They are coming, too."

Bull tensed, spoke through his teeth. "Can you give me an exact distance? I mean, how long do you think until they reach you?"

"Hold please."

If the circumstances were different, Bull's condescending tone would have been considered beyond rude, but he assumed the president understood where he was coming from.

After another moment, the president said, "Maybe one hour. But he's really not sure. They keep stopping and going."

"I understand. We'll be there soon."

Bull called for them to move out again. Another footstep. Another. The pack seemed to grow heavier, and his lips were chapped. He grabbed the drinking tube from his hydro pack, took a long sip, licked his lips.

The gray cloak of sky still hung there, unchanging, and the wind began to cut once more across the mountainside and tug on his shoulders and pack.

I want a divorce.

Your girls will never talk to you again.

Quit the Army. You're a fool.

Bull, I'm bleeding bad. Am I going to die?

He gave his life for his country.

They continued to speak to him from the past, all those people who were part of his soul.

His steps grew more uneven, and for a moment, a wave of dizziness passed through him. He told himself to hang in there, to remember who he was, what he believed in, and how far he had already come.

That damned ankle began to throb, and he wondered if

he should have assigned himself back to the mud-brick house to wait for the chopper. Shit.

"I got something ahead," said Hojo over the radio. "Big piece of debris."

President Abdali had been unable to pull himself up through the window to get outside. Rafiullah had tried to help him, but any pulling movement sent pulses of electric pain through his arm and ribs. They would need someone beneath him to lift, while someone else guided him up and out.

For now, though, he stood atop the copilot's chair, watching Rafiullah, who had dug himself a furrow in the snow and kept low, peering through binoculars at the men working their way up the mountain. Far off lay the trucks, tiny specks like a chain of rocks against the rolling foothills.

It felt as though Abdali had spent half a lifetime inside the helicopter, his gaze falling upon the same dark bulkheads, the same oppressive gloom. His thirst had come on strong in the past half hour, but the water was almost out. They had found no food, save for a half-eaten chocolate bar and some mints in the copilot's pockets.

He shielded his face against the wind and squinted toward the valley. His anticipation grew with every minute, as two parties with the same objective fought to converge on the same spot . . . on him.

And somewhere far off, he thought he heard that helicopter again and craned his neck. Yes, it was there, growing closer now. Closer.

Sandra Hildebrand's opinion of Bull had shifted dramatically after she had watched the chopper land and had learned from Walsh that he was supposed to pick them up and transfer them to a little hut. The soldier called Sullivan echoed those instructions.

Yes, it turned out that Bull was, in fact, confiscating their helicopter—and was, in fact, on a rescue mission to save the president of Afghanistan—but he had still wanted to get them to some relative safety. Even Walsh was convinced of that.

So maybe Bull wasn't such a dark-hearted warrior after all, even if he wouldn't admit to being a Special Forces operator, which was written all over his bearded, wind-weathered face.

Now, as they headed toward the hut, Hildebrand addressed Walsh over the intercom: "Why didn't you just land them right next to the helicopter?"

"The slope is too narrow," he said. "All I could do was hover, but he was worried about the rotor wash affecting the fuselage. Could push it over the side."

"What do you think?"

"I think he's right."

"Get us there, right on top of the chopper."

"Are you nuts?"

"You get us close, hover, we'll jump out."

"Ma'am, you'll need to do as I say now," said Sullivan. "We're going to the hut."

"You have no authority over me. As far as I'm concerned, you're a nobody," said Hildebrand.

"He's a nobody with a rifle balanced between his legs and a pistol in that holster right there," said Oswaller.

"Just take us to the crash site," Hildebrand repeated.

Yes, maybe her ambition had burned away her common sense, but if they could land right there in the middle of the rescue, Neggy could get some digital pictures, and she could interview the president seconds before the team took him away.

"Ma'am, you'll need to be quiet now," said Sullivan. "Please."

Hildebrand grinned sarcastically. "We're going up there, he's going to hover, and we're all getting out. You, too, Sullivan. We didn't come this far to cool our asses in a hut."

"I'll play your game," said Walsh. "But it'll cost double my normal fee—if he doesn't shoot me."

"Sandy, give it up," said Oswaller. "You're interfering with a military operation."

"We're not interfering. We're covering."

"If something happens they could hold us responsible. You're not risking your own career here," said Oswaller. "I've been doing this for twenty years! Twenty goddamned years!"

"But if we get this story," said Neggy. "If we're there as it happens, as they rescue the president, Jesus Christ, this will be the story of our lifetimes. Of our *lifetimes*!"

The drama in Neggy's voice did not go unnoticed by Walsh, who said, "He's right. This is a big story. I say go for it. Just remember, it'll cost you."

"This is nuts. Can you take me to the little hut?" asked Oswaller. "I don't want any part of this. I'm out."

"Shut up, you wimp," said Tracy. "You're in. So am I. We're crazy, but we're going down there to cover this story because this woman sitting next to me—my sister?—I've never trusted anyone in my life more than her. And if these goddamned apes screw it up, then I'll be there to watch it happen and present their crimes."

"All right. I need a decision," said Walsh.

Sullivan, who had been quietly listening to their conversation transpire, suddenly lifted his voice—

He had drawn his pistol. "All right, y'all can shut up now. Walsh, take us to the hut." He aimed the pistol at the pilot's neck.

"Don't listen to him," said Hildebrand. "He won't shoot you. He shoots, we all die. In fact, if you discharge that weapon at all in here, we could all die."

Sullivan swallowed, and he seemed to grow a bit more nervous.

Bull lifted his boot, fully out of breath, slammed it down, then glanced back at the approaching helicopter, her rotors echoing across the mountains.

For a moment, he thought his goggles had blurred the image. It looked as though the bird had banked away from the hut and was about to roar right over them.

Nah, couldn't be. He walked a few more steps, the whomping curiously closer.

He whirled back.

Jesus Christ, the bird *had* turned away. She now flew directly overhead. "What the hell are you doing?" he shouted aloud.

Every member of the team froze in his tracks, glanced up, in shock no doubt, as the chopper arrowed directly for the crash site.

"McDaniel! Get that pilot on the horn!"

"Turn up your earpiece," said McDaniel. "I got Sullivan calling in!"

Bull rolled the dial, and the broken voice on the other end communicated everything he didn't want to hear.

In the valley below the crash site, General Malim Kahn led his militia up the mountain, toward the downed chopper.

They had just spotted the helicopter wheeling around the crash site, searching for a landing zone.

Kahn shouted for his man with the SA-7 to come forward, even as Fahim rushed up to him, breathless.

"Brother, we're running out of time!"

"That's not a military helicopter up there," said Kahn, peering through his binoculars. "Strange."

Fahim had a look for himself. "Civilian. You're right. But it doesn't matter. That's his rescue party. We're going to be too late."

"No, we're not."

"Sir, ready, sir!" cried the militiaman with the surface-to-air missile launcher balanced on his shoulder.

"Are you within range?"

"I think so, sir," said the young man, peering through sights. "It takes about six seconds to activate the homing system. I await your orders."

Kahn drew in a deep breath, even as the chopper began to hover near the ridgeline. "Fire!"

32. STILL MORE AUDACITY

At the precise moment that Zulu had pressed the trigger button on his AT-4, four things happened:

The fin-stabilized projectile with shaped charge warhead leapt from the launcher with a whoosh and thunderclap that would unnerve even the most grizzled warrior.

A massive back-blast and pressure wave lit up the mountainside all around Zulu, his neck and back feeling as though they, too, had burst into flames.

Gunfire ripped across the ground within inches of his boots.

And the launcher jerked to the left, sending the projectile wide of his intended target.

The fifth thing that had happened was a shout.

His own.

"Fuck!"

Now, just minutes later, he and Pharaoh were engaging the remaining guys down in the valley, along with the mule team, who had dismounted, although Zulu had taken out the guy with the AT-4, one stinking guy.

The gunfire that had raked near Zulu's legs at the moment of fire could have come from below to be sure, since he had placed himself out in the open to take the shot—

But it could've also come from above, from Rock's position. Had that bastard fired upon him to protect Scorpion?

He didn't know yet. But he'd sure as shit find out.

The remaining militiamen now lay prone, exploiting the rocks, ditches, and low-lying scrub, their *pakol*-covered heads popping up for a second, then disappearing.

And it seemed that every time Zulu rose from his gut and took aim with his SCAR, some bastard below would steal a shot to drive him back down.

"Well, we got us a standoff," he told Pharaoh.

"Outstanding."

"Yeah, but for how long?"

"Hopefully long enough for Bull to get in and out."

"And what about us? I'm not fond of our escape plan."

"Neither am I." The captain grinned weakly, then reached for his mike. "Tarzan, SITREP?"

Sergeant First Class Jonathan Figueroa—call sign "Tarzan"—could, at the moment, give a flying shit about Zulu's voice crackling in his earpiece.

He was pinned down behind a pair of rocks, trading fire with two guys who had somehow miracled themselves through what Figueroa had assumed was an impenetrable gauntlet of claymores that should have torn them up like beets through a grater.

Maybe these guys were from the second group.

Maybe they had supernatural powers.

Maybe Figueroa was thinking too hard.

All he knew was they were about thirty meters ahead, behind a meter-high rock pile created by the explosions; if the sons of bitches had grenades, then Figueroa would've been dead by now.

Fortunately, the situation was reversed. He was the Green Goblin, the one with a small inventory of exploding pumpkins.

And so, with chills fanning across his shoulders, he let fly the concussion grenade in his fist, hit the deck, and anticipated the detonation with a gasp.

The resulting explosion blew free more rock from the narrow walls. Had one of the men screamed? He wasn't sure.

He fished out the second grenade from his vest.

Zulu was still barking in his earpiece. Time to shut him up. Damned guy was distracting him! "This is Tarzan," he answered. "Hold on, my mom's on the other line."

The sergeant would love that.

Crack! A round ricocheted off the boulder to his left. Bastards. At least one of them, anyway, was still alive.

Grenade number two took flight.

Without even waiting for the explosion, Figueroa got back on the radio. "Zulu, this is Tarzan, still engaging some stragglers down here. Maybe more to come, over."

Zulu replied, but the second grenade's boom overpowered his words.

The M24 SWS was referred to as a weapons system because it also included a detachable telescopic sight and "other accessories," most notably a shooter and spotter, the accessories that did the killing.

Sergeant First Class Jason Ondejko, weapons sergeant and team sniper, had a few things working against him.

He had no spotter, who'd have a more powerful scope than the one on his rifle and could help him identify targets.

Additionally, every time he did fire, he advertised his location: hey, militiamen from the fine town of Eshkashem? American Special Forces operator awaiting your return fire for fun and good times. See me here, this location, right now. Bring beer.

And finally, Captain Pharaoh had tasked him with keeping an eye on Rock, who might play games to keep Scorpion alive. It wasn't easy doing that while trying to get a bead on some real bad guys who needed killing.

So as he settled down once more, took his lovely piece into his arms, and peered through the 10×42 Leupold Ultra M3A telescope sight, he decided that the one thing he had working for him outweighed all the negative.

And that thing was?

Well, forgive the less-than-technical description, but he was the baddest mother on the hillside.

Zulu could sit over there and blow mud at the enemy while he babysat the captain—

But Ondejko would unleash his M118 7.62mm NATO Match Grade ammunition from up to 1,100 meters.

Technically, that was impressive. In layman's terms? Heads wouldn't just fly; they'd go into orbit. Space shuttle astronauts would confirm that.

Oddly enough, fellow operators accused him of having a big ego. He couldn't understand why and would tell them that with a shit-eating grin. They'd resort to making fun of his surname.

Damn it, to come out here and do this didn't just take balls; it took a strange, indescribable feeling that you were operating on a higher plane. Eighteen-year-old Marines knew exactly what he was talking about, even if they did call him an old fart. Hell, he wasn't forty yet!

"All right, Mr. Machine Gunner," he whispered to himself as he took aim at a militiaman spraying the defile from his vantage point near the easternmost cave entrance. "Say cheese."

At the boom of Ondejko's sniper rifle, Rock stopped firing, rolled over, and grabbed Khodai, urging him to do the same. Then he thumbed his mike. "Titan 06, this is Rock, over."

After an uncomfortably long pause, Pharaoh answered, "Go ahead, Rock."

"Our target has fallen back to one of the caves. I suggest we move in to take him, over."

"Negative, Rock. We'll hold them here until I get a report from Tempest that the package is moving, over."

"And after that, we move in, over."

"We'll see, Titan 06, out."

Rock swore under his breath, then shifted over to Khodai, hitting the snow beside the G-chief. "We have a saying," he began in Dari. "One hand washes the other."

"We have a similar saying."

"You're going to help me bring in Scorpion, okay? I don't think these guys will do it. And if it weren't for me, asshole Zulu would've killed him already."

"I understand. But there are still too many of them."

"We can circle around the back of this hill, come at them from the top, drop down, and enter the cave."

"It is still too risky."

"About as risky as me working out a deal to rearm your village, right?"

Khodai pursed his lips, then stroked his beard. "You are not a good man. But I understand what you are doing. We should tell the captain."

Rock slapped his hand on the man's snow-covered shoulder and grinned. "I'll take care of that."

Sergeant First Class Jerry Weathers had a rather simple relationship with his machine gun: he liked firing it and the gun seemed to like him back.

In fact, the gun seemed to like him more than his radios did. The Shadowfire's battery was running low, and he wished he had time to swap it out.

But now he and Grimm were on the move, having suppressed the third group with their first wave of fire but having also given up their positions. Their secondary firing locations were just behind them, about twenty-five yards up the hill, near a lone tree rising on the ridge, one they had nicknamed the Tree of Life. He hoped the gnarled and twisted limbs of the leafless sentinel provided more than a little cover; he hoped the tree held true to its namesake.

He and Grimm arrived behind it, drawing some wild fire from below, shots missing them by a half dozen meters or more until the militiamen below got a better bead—

And then bark started flying.

Pharaoh called: "Two-forty Bravo ammo check, over."

That sounded a little official. All he wanted to know was how much machine gun ammo they had left. Weathers consulted briefly with Grimm. "We have about three hundred rounds left apiece, Titan 06, over."

"Roger that. Hold fire for now. But stay hot. Titan 06, out."

Weathers relayed the order to Grimm, and both of them prepared to reload their weapons by first pulling the charging handle that locked the bolt to the rear. They placed their weapons on safe, then pushed the charging handles forward. The feed trays were then lifted, and they began laying rounds inside the feed trays. Once they finished that, they closed the trays and were ready for one last rock 'n' roll show.

"Titan 06? This is Tarzan. I need Trauma over here right now, over."

That was Figueroa. And he didn't sound good.

Grimm looked over at Weathers, then said, "You'll finish the show."

Weathers nodded.

Then the call came from Pharaoh: Grimm needed to haul ass back into the defile, with Weathers providing covering fire.

"You ready, bro?"

Grimm closed his eyes a moment, either saying a prayer or otherwise mentally preparing himself. "Let's do it."

He took off jogging down the hillside.

Figueroa lay behind the rocks, clutching the gunshot wound in his shoulder. He was one man holding back who knew how many climbing over the rocks.

Was it the cold clouding his vision or just the loss of blood?

A figure came forward, and he cut loose with his rifle.

Something stirred above him, pebbles falling, and he stole a look up the second he ceased fire.

A man was up there, hopefully Grimm. *Please be Grimm.*

Two seconds later automatic fire tore into the boulders all around, shards of rock flying as he shielded his face. He thought he had one more thirty-round mag for his rifle, with maybe ten shots left in the current mag.

He needed to provide cover for Grimm's ascent into the

defile, so he took his hand off his shoulder, dragged himself up to the edge of the rocks, then opened up on the unseen bastards ahead.

"Yo, Grimm! Right here," cried the medic, coming up from behind him.

"Dude, the hell with me right now. Get some fire on those rocks ahead!"

"Figueroa and Grimm need help back there," said Zulu. "I'll send Rock and Khodai. We'll let Weathers cover them."

Pharaoh nodded, then swept his binoculars over to Rock's position.

The CIA agent and G-chief were gone.

"They moved," he told Zulu, then got on his mike. "Rock, this is Titan 06, SITREP, over!"

He waited. His pulse mounted. He called again.

"What now?" Zulu asked.

The entire valley had grown eerily silent.

"Something's wrong," said Pharaoh, grabbing his binoculars.

"And I know exactly what it is," answered Zulu, shifting his head, pointing his binoculars along the ridge to their right. "Rock and Khodai are moving up behind the caves."

"Shit, he's going after Scorpion."

Zulu whipped down his binoculars and shook his head, grinning in disbelief. "The audacity of that, huh?"

"No, he can't!" cried Pharaoh.

And just as the words escaped his mouth, about ten militiamen suddenly appeared from behind their ditches and rushed forward toward the defile.

Weathers couldn't get a good bead on them with a slope partly in his way, and while Ondejko's sniper fire boomed solidly, he only dropped a single man.

Fact: the nine enemy guys would reach the narrow passage, with only the injured Figueroa and Grimm in their way.

Pharaoh needed to act. Right now. He looked toward the caves, then back to the defile.

33. PRECIPICE

Sandra Hildebrand and the others, including the soldier called Sullivan, had bailed out of their chopper and were now racing up the slope toward the wreckage of the president's downed helicopter.

Hildebrand glanced back as Walsh banked hard away from the ridge—

And at that instant, a flash of light streaked across the sky, just to the right of the chopper.

"Get down!" Sullivan screamed.

He knocked her to the snow as a massive explosion boomed behind them, a sound unlike anything Hildebrand had ever experienced, a single loud boom, followed by scores of others amid the screaming of the chopper's engine, the now chaotic thumping of its rotors, and the nails-on-chalkboard scraping of metal on metal.

She rolled over, tried to pull away from the soldier. "Let me up!"

"No!" he hollered.

"Oh my God!"

By the time she could actually rise, a thick cloud of black smoke raced over them, obscuring all view, stealing her breath, burning her eyes.

Where were Tracy, Neggy, and Oswaller? She screamed out to them, then waved at her face and coughed, cold tears stinging her wind-burned cheeks.

From his vantage point, Bull had been unable to see the actual explosion, but he'd heard it, and the smoke began wafting down over the edge of the ridge as he and the others drove their spikes deep into the snow and ice, trying to pick up the pace.

Despite being nearly breathless, he called to Sullivan over the radio, but the engineer did not reply.

"They shot down the chopper," cried Hojo. "I know it!"

Or they'd taken a shot from the valley and blown up the president's chopper, Bull thought.

"Can't get the pilot to respond," added McDaniel.

Bull keyed his mike. "All right, just hike! Hike! Hike! Typhoon, you continue to call that pilot."

"Roger that," said McDaniel.

Bull's gut began to twist.

My God. What have I done?

His wife's voice echoed in his head: *"You always want it both ways, Bull. But you can't. You just can't."*

He tugged out his satellite phone, dialed the president as his breath grew more faint. He was barely able to talk now, his nose frozen. He opened his mouth, stuttered. "M-Mr. President? What's going on up there?"

* * *

President Abdali had heard the chopper's approach, and all the noise and vibration through the fuselage had driven him from the back of the cabin and into the cockpit, where he had climbed up on the copilot's chair so that he could peer out the window.

And then the explosion . . .

The terrible, terrible explosion—their rescue helicopter vanishing in a ball of flames—had sent him tumbling back into the cockpit.

He now lay across the sidewall, which had become the floor, his broken arm twisted across the seat and throbbing, his ribs feeling as though they were caving in even more now. He struggled for breath as he clutched the phone to his ear and tried to speak, but only one word could escape his lips:

"Hurry . . ."

Staff Sergeant Larry Sullivan grabbed the woman by the arm, got her to her feet, and led her back toward the president's downed bird, despite his injured ankle.

But she tugged at his grip. "My sister's back there! My crew!"

He tightened his gloved hand on her wrist. "I'll go back for them!"

As they neared the chopper, a young man with a neatly groomed beard, no doubt the president's aide they had heard about, rushed forward. "I'm Rafiullah! I'll take her!"

Sullivan handed off the correspondent, then started back into the smoke toward Tracy O'Donnell, who was staggering toward him, clutching her hip.

"Are you hurt?" he asked, trying not to cough. "Are you bleeding?"

"I don't know!" she cried. "I fell down! I hurt my hip!"

Sullivan dropped to his knees, checked her leg, now saw blood. He wrapped one of her arms over his neck and helped her back to Rafiullah, who took over.

Then he turned back toward the other two men, both of whom lay in the snow, unmoving.

They had been nearest to the explosion, and several pieces of burning debris still lay close, the rest of the chopper having plummeted into the valley, leaving a chute of black smoke in its wake.

He dreaded checking them, and the screaming behind him didn't help matters. But he had no choice. He dropped before the first, the portly guy, Neggy. A wedge-shaped piece of metal had impaled his chest and jutted out from his heavy coat. He lay on his side, his face already turning blue. Sullivan checked for a carotid pulse, but he didn't expect to find one. No. The man was going cold.

Sullivan rose, shifted farther down the slope to the older one, Oswaller, who'd been even closer to the explosion.

A sickly sweat smell made him wince. He pulled up his scarf, dropped to his knees, then grabbed Oswaller by the shoulder, rolled him over.

Sullivan grimaced.

Half of the man's face had been burned away and impaled by dozens of pieces of shrapnel. One of his arms was blackened and hanging half off, and yet another piece of metal had cut through his hip; that was where he had quickly bled out, the snow beneath him melted into a pool. There wasn't much of his neck left to get a pulse, so Sullivan just stood, turned away.

The mountainside spun around him.

I'm all right.

He stopped, yanked his scarf back down, turned into the wind, and breathed deeply.

All right. The world grew level, still. He grabbed his

binoculars, panned to the valley, ignored the throbbing of his foot.

The men below had paused, and as he scanned them, his lenses fell upon the bastard who had shot down the chopper, even as the guy raised his launcher once more.

Oh, my God.

Sullivan knew an SA-7 when he saw one.

He whirled, started running for the bird, swearing over his foot, running, then limping, then running again. "Get away from the chopper! Fall back to the other side!"

And as he ran, there wasn't time to think about his indecision back inside the NPR crew's chopper, wasn't time to consider that if he had been more forceful, if he had somehow used better negotiation skills and not let those media bastards challenge him, then none of this would have happened.

There was only one thought right now: *run or die!*

General Malim Kahn and his men had shouted and raised their fists in the air at the sight of fiery victory.

He had never seen a flower more beautiful blossoming across the frigid landscape.

And now they all watched as their man was ready to take yet another shot, aimed directly for a small group of men coming up the slope.

But the chances of hitting them, he had explained, were slim because of the lack of a significant heat source.

Waving his hand, Kahn had ordered him to take the shot anyway.

So with the SA-7 balanced on his shoulder, and a new missile loaded, their man glanced back, Kahn gave the order, and he pulled the trigger.

What happened next took the rest of them by complete surprise.

The missile did not streak away from the launcher as it should. There was no beautiful tendril of smoke leading up to the mountain and terminating in a magnificent detonation that would turn President Abdali's rescuers into heaps of blackened bones.

And Kahn, who had ordered the cameraman from as-Sahab to capture the unfolding events, was standing beside the cameraman, waiting for the show to begin.

And it did.

Their soldier with the SA-7 simply exploded in a fireball whose concussion knocked most of the other men standing to the side flat onto their backs.

Kahn, who was even farther back, found himself on his rump, the sky alive with fresh flames, his ears ringing loudly.

The weapon had malfunctioned, and a blackened and still smoldering crater appeared where the man had once stood.

Confused shouting commenced as the cameraman sat up, looked at Khan, and said in a shivery voice, "I will erase this tape."

"Brother, are you all right?" Fahim seized Kahn's hand.

"Yes! Everyone, let's go!" Kahn hollered as he allowed his brother to drag him to his feet. "We will take Abdali alive, and then we will show the world who rules Afghanistan!"

Kahn's bravado seemed to inspire his troops, if only a little. Their cold faces still looked stricken as they picked themselves up from the snow, gazes transfixed on the crater.

Bull was the last one to reach the top, the others already rushing down across the slope, weaving between debris and following the fuselage's broad plow mark toward the chopper itself, where Sullivan, another man, Hildebrand, and O'Donnell were huddled.

He shouted for Hojo and Borokovsky to get into the chopper because he didn't see Abdali outside. He sent Gator and McDaniel off to the east side of the slope to observe the approaching militiamen.

And when he reached the bird himself, he wasn't sure who he wanted to strangle first: the two women or his own engineer. He confronted the latter. "You'd best start talking, Sergeant."

"They called my bluff. I couldn't shoot the pilot. We'd all die. I couldn't discharge my weapon at all." Sullivan bared his teeth and glowered at Hildebrand. "She's a smart bitch. I could've tried, but I figured coming up here wouldn't be as bad as risking the whole chopper. But they had an SA-7, and now the bird's gone, so it wouldn't have mattered. Maybe I should've shot them all." Sullivan choked up, and Bull could almost see his mind racing.

He broke off from the engineer, marched over to Hildebrand, then grabbed her by her coat collar.

"What are you going to do?" she asked, challenging him with her tone, her eyes.

Bull opened his mouth, about to hand her a serious piece of his mind, when he froze.

The enormity of the moment took hold.

He let her go. He had priorities and all of this was bullshit. He pushed past her, nearing the chopper. "Hojo? Talk to me." He pressed his face up to the cockpit canopy, where he saw Abdali lying across the side window.

"He's hurt pretty bad. We're going to try to move him, get him out of here."

Borokovsky was already speaking with Abdali, testing to see if they could move his arm.

"Let me know what you need," Bull added.

"What are we going to do now?" asked Tracy. "We're stuck up here, aren't we? The guys who shot down our chopper are coming. And we're stuck up here. And you got no backup, do you? You got nothing!"

"Shut the hell up!" screamed Sullivan. He shouted again, and Bull warned him to calm down.

Bull stepped away from the others. "Typhoon, this is Tempest, over."

"Tempest, this is Typhoon," replied McDaniel. "Observing enemy force. Looks like about eighteen or so men. Mostly rifles, maybe one RPG, maybe two. Advancing on foot. Angle up the slope is in our favor, so they'll have to get in pretty close for small arms, over."

"Roger. ETA?"

"I'd say about an hour, max."

"Roger that. Keep observing. Any change, alert me. Tempest out."

The president's aide came up to Bull. "I'm hearing from the women that their helicopter was the only one. Is that true?"

"No, we've called for a Chinook."

"Excuse me?"

"A big helicopter," Bull said, extending his arms. "But the weather's slowed them down. Haven't heard yet when they'll get here, but they will."

"Yes, but will they arrive before those men down there?" The guy lifted his chin toward the valley.

"Probably not."

The young man's eyes widened, and he raised his voice. " *This* is your rescue mission?"

"You're lucky anyone made it up here."

"The president of this country—"

Bull forced a calm into his voice as he cut the man off. "I know all about it. Don't worry. We'll get you out of here."

The man began shaking his head and trudged back for the helicopter.

Bull tensed, wanting to throttle the ungrateful bastard. At least his satellite phone began to ring, diverting him away from his anger. It was Pharaoh.

34. GUN AND KNIFE SHOW

Pharaoh and Zulu wove hard and fast along the slopes, heading back toward the defile in an attempt to intercept the nine militiamen closing in on Figueroa and Grimm's position. Figueroa was still down, and Grimm was now treating him.

In his heart of hearts, Pharaoh knew they'd be too late, and Zulu probably knew the same, but they had to try. If those men died, he would sure as hell hold it over Rock's head. Had he maintained his position, that bastard could have at least slowed the enemy advance. Pharaoh wanted the CIA agent's neck in his hands. But that would come later.

Right now Pharaoh was on the satellite phone with Bull, getting a SITREP. In fact, Bull had reached the crash site, but the story he unfolded in just a few sentences left Pharaoh dumbfounded.

"Just get out of there, back to that hut. Do what you can to hold 'em off. I'll have Weathers get something more definitive on that Chinook's ETA."

"McDaniel's tried, too. Thanks."

A minute later, Pharaoh and Zulu reached the slopes above Figueroa and Grimm, just as the enemy militiamen were pushing through the narrowest portion between the rock walls.

Maybe he and Zulu were not too late. They had the terrible terrain standing in the militiamen's way to thank for that.

"Grimm, get him out of there," cried Pharaoh over the radio. "We got you covered!"

The medic had already strapped Figueroa into a Blackhawk portable litter. He grabbed the Fast Attack litter's heavy nylon handles and dragged the man away from their cover, gliding over the ice and snow. He moved far faster than Pharaoh had assumed, and his quick exit back through the defile prompted Zulu to leap down into a ditch, then roll and come up with his rifle. He cut loose several volleys, forcing the militiamen to halt and seek cover behind the rocks while Grimm forged on.

Meanwhile, Pharaoh shifted on past the team sergeant to link up with Grimm, even as Zulu pulled the pin and let fly his first grenade.

The resulting boom quickened Pharaoh's pace.

He finally reached the base of the slope, sidestepping his way down to the bottom, where Grimm had just stopped, panting, his face cherry red.

"He's stable," said the medic, his gaze on Figueroa, who was still wincing in pain. "He took a second round in the calf that he didn't even know about. He's got to stay off that leg."

"Sorry, Captain," said the engineer, squinting through his goggles and still clutching his rifle with one hand.

"Don't be. You kicked ass. That's outstanding."

"Thank you, sir."

"Let's go." Pharaoh gripped one of the litter's straps, and they began dragging Figueroa up the slope.

Zulu had one more AT-4 rocket and launcher (they were prepacked, good for one shot), and Pharaoh knew the team sergeant had every intention of making it count this time.

He shouldered the rocket, took aim into the defile.

"Go!" he shouted to Pharaoh.

Pharaoh and Grimm double-timed up the slope, drawing closer to the enemy soldiers lying in wait below, behind the piles of debris.

A few seconds later, Zulu's AT-4 flashed, and that huge shaft of flame extended from his back, as though he were a rocket himself. The entire defile glowed, then—

"Get down!" Pharaoh told Grimm.

They hit the snow, shielding Figueroa as the blast reverberated across the rock ahead, even sending shock waves through the ground beneath them.

"Holy shit!" Grimm shouted, though his words were barely audible through more echoing booms, screams from bad guys, and what sounded like a massive landslide.

Clouds of dust, smoke, and snow rolled through the defile, obscuring the entire area as Zulu did something that left Pharaoh speechless.

The team sergeant threw down the AT-4 launcher, and, with rifle in hand, he burst from the ditch, ran straight down into the defile, then vanished into the clouds.

"Zulu, this is Titan 06, what are you doing?"

Pharaoh could've bet a month's pay that the team sergeant would not reply. He turned to Grimm, gestured they move on.

With sheer rock walls rising up some sixty or seventy feet on either side of him, Zulu charged forward, his goggles protecting his eyes from all the dust, his scarf pulled up tightly over his nose and mouth.

He smiled inwardly as he imagined the expression on Pharaoh's face. He figured that if he died, he might be called a hero for trying to save the lives of his men against a superior-size force.

And if he lived, he might be called a foolhardy idiot for trying to engage the remaining enemy in such close quarters without backup. You always fought with your buddy.

But there were some interesting unknowns that warranted breaking the rules:

He could have taken out every man in the defile with his AT-4, but only scouting the area would confirm that.

He might have killed only a few, in which case it would be imperative for those others to be taken out of the fight, since nothing stood between them and Bull's rescue operation.

And if those men needed to be taken out, then what better way than to exploit the element of confusion and surprise created by the AT-4?

Zulu hadn't come up with that answer, so he'd reasoned that exploitation was the name of the game.

Damning any trace of fear to hell, and riding that beautiful wave of adrenaline, he pushed on, his blood like electricity coursing through him, every sense reaching out as though he had millions of feelers attached to his skin.

Maybe Pharaoh was calling him, but he'd turned off his radio, didn't want even the faintest noise from his earpiece to give him away.

That, too, would be called foolhardy, egotistical, stupid. Or maybe just insanely courageous. Yeah, he liked that description a lot better.

He threaded his way between some rocks, spotted a leg, still on fire, a torso, another leg. He moved a few steps farther, saw a head lying near the wall—

Then just farther up, four meters . . . movement . . . a silhouette near the ground. He longed to fire, but he held himself. The first volley would give up his position.

He drew closer, and the dust cleared a little to reveal two men on the ground, one clutching his severed leg, the other with a hand on his chest.

They spotted him.

One reached for his rifle in his lap.

Zulu leapt forward, his XSF-1 dagger flashing from its Kydex sheath, now in his fist in a reverse grip. He leaned down, grabbing the first man's head with his left hand and yanking it forward to expose the base of his skull . . .

A quick downward thrust into the brain stem, and the man instantly fell limp.

As Zulu retracted the blade, he was already in motion toward the second guy. Zulu's left hand slapped the militia-man's hands down, then he jerked that hand upward to tilt the bad guy's head back, exposing the area under his chin and another route to the central nervous system for a quick, efficient kill.

He withdrew the blade, looked at both dead men, put a finger to his lips. Shhh.

Wiping off the dagger on the guy's shoulder, he silently returned it to its sheath and moved on.

The dust cloud was beginning to fade, and his pace become more urgent. He darted to the left wall to avoid a tall pile of rocks, expecting to find at least one or two men behind it.

He found three.

Rock and Khodai had stolen their way along the mountains behind the caves where that CIA rogue Scorpion had retreated with a small group of men from the mule team.

Rock was certain that the cave several meters below was the one in which Scorpion now sat, directing the battle.

Rock and his Tajik accomplice kept tight behind a long outcropping, and as Rock further surveyed the scene, he realized it would be difficult to move down to the cave entrance quietly without being seen since two men had moved off to the mules and taken up position near the rocks and trees beside them. They had an unobstructed view of the slopes.

Rock had switched off his radio and figured that Pharaoh would have to forgive him for running a little side op in the name of Langley and God and America. In fact, there wasn't a damned thing Pharaoh could do about it. The captain had orders: interdict enemy force, attempt to bring in Scorpion alive. Scorpion was a high value target whose intel could be invaluable to the Agency's efforts in the country—

Which was why Rock stood to collect a six-figure bonus if he succeeded in bringing him in.

"Maybe they will come out," said Khodai. "That was a big explosion in the mountain."

"No, he's waiting."

"Do you want me to go down there and kill those men?"

"Forget it. We don't know how many more are still in the caves. They'll cut you right down."

"Then, Mr. Rock, I don't understand why we've come here if the job is impossible."

"It's not impossible. It's just . . . our timing isn't quite right. We'll sit here and observe a little longer. If they move, then we'll have our chance."

Ondejko's sniper rifle suddenly broke the silence, and one of the men near the mules dropped.

Weathers followed up with machine-gun fire, taking out the second one, and in that instant, Rock realized the time had come.

But when he pulled down his scarf, shoved his unlit cigar into his mouth, then tapped Khodai on the shoulder, the G-chief was already turning around, toward the sound of footfalls behind them.

And there he was, all six feet, five inches of him, Scorpion himself, flanked by two militiamen, coming down the slope.

"Mr. Rock," gasped Khodai.

"Don't move." Rock's arm dropped down to his radio, which he switched on, and keyed the mike.

Scorpion had become a deranged mountain man with a long, reddish-blond beard, bushy brows, and teeth rotting out of his head. The last time Rock had seen him, at least four years ago, he'd sported a crew cut and an Armani suit. "Rock, you old bastard! I heard you were in town. Long time, no see!"

Rock sighed into a curse.

Khodai lifted his weapon.

"No!" Rock slammed down the rifle.

"Good boy," said Scorpion. "Let's all head back down into my office for a little talk."

"Should I call you Scorpion? Or would you prefer—"

"It's okay, Rock. I know how you feel. I was in your shoes. But not anymore."

Zulu opened fire on the three men, hitting them point-blank in the chest, rounds kicking them back into the wall. But as he had feared, he'd just given up his position—

And a round suddenly ricocheted off the rocks behind him.

He hit the deck, returning fire even as he dropped.

Crawling now, he moved to his left, behind one of the

dead men, whose body shuddered as another salvo ripped through jacket and flesh.

Zulu fished out his last grenade, waited. He needed the guy to take one more shot so he could zero in on his location.

Silence. Shit.

"Hey, asshole!"

Bang! A round struck a meter from his right boot.

And that was all Zulu needed. He pulled the pin, wound up, and pitched the grenade into the air.

He counted to himself.

Then, at the exact moment of the explosion, he rolled onto his feet, rifle blazing as he drove forward, past more rubble, to find the guy clutching the stump of his arm, another guy lying in a pool of blood, his legs shattered.

Zulu withdrew his .45 and shot both men, then he dove to the far wall and dropped back down, onto his gut. Silence.

One, two, three . . . he sprang up again, came forward, and realized now that the rest of the defile was clear.

He'd lost count of the men, but he didn't think he'd taken out all nine. One or two must have fled. He'd catch up with them, all right.

He reached the mouth of the passage, huddled near the wall, switched on his radio. "Titan 06, this is Zulu, over."

"Zulu, this Titan 06, where are you, over?"

The captain was pissed. Zulu grinned. "I'm at the opening. The defile has been cleared. I say again, the defile has been cleared, over."

"Are you kidding me?"

The captain's tone was worth a million bucks. "No, Titan 06. The defile is clear, over."

"Uh, roger that. I sent Trauma back to the truck with Tarzan. Talk Radio and T-Rex are still holding the fort. But we got another problem, over."

"Oh, yeah? What now?"

"I think Rock and Khodai got picked up by Scorpion."

Zulu's mouth fell open. "Say again?"

"Rock keyed his mike. I heard him talking. He's with Scorpion right now, inside one of the caves."

"Roger that. Meet you at our original position, over."

"All right. Titan 06, out."

Zulu snorted. "Rock, you idiot. I used to like you." He started out of the defile, moving stealthily along the wall, following the rocky slope to his right, when gunfire from below sent him diving to the snow. That gunfire had a familiar ring to it, an all-too-familiar ring—

Weathers had a bead on him with the M240, and he wasn't letting up.

"Jesus Christ, Talk Radio!" he screamed into his radio. "Hold your fire!"

35. THE GOOD AND BAD TEACHERS

Haji watched with disgust as the last of the crates full of weapons was loaded aboard the jingle truck. The Army Rangers who had come to Shah-e Pari aboard the helicopter had orders to guard then remove the weapons. Haji had hoped that Khodai and the ODA team would return before the soldiers could take away their stash. At least he and a few others had hidden the opium before the squad had arrived.

"Just remember," the Ranger captain told him slowly, struggling for the words in Dari. "This is for your own good and your own protection."

Haji wished Khodai were there to tell this man the truth about where the weapons had come from in the first place, about who had provided them, about the "business deals" Rock had made with them during the past year.

But perhaps Khodai wouldn't do that. He had made his promise to Rock, gone along with the lies to the ODA team, and that was that.

Now Haji had to face the crowd of men, all looking to him for assurance that they could protect themselves from the foreign invaders with only the weapons provided by Pharaoh and his men.

As the truck with all the crates and the Army Rangers started down the road behind him, he cleared his throat.

Abruptly, the old man Zemeri pushed through the others and lifted his voice: "Our men at the pass have called! The enemy is on the move. A large force of nearly one hundred! They will be here in one day!"

"Why didn't you tell us this sooner!" Haji cried. "We could have told the Americans."

"This is our war. Not theirs."

Haji rushed up to the man, baring his teeth. "You old fool!"

Zemeri did not flinch. "We must prepare to defend ourselves."

Haji looked to the men, already imagining their chests exploding under relentless gunfire.

"We will fight to save our village!" Zemeri added, raising a fist into the air.

The men cheered, as Haji stood there and closed his eyes. He would send his wife and two small daughters south.

It was already too late for him.

Pharaoh added his voice to Zulu's, ordering Weathers to cease fire on Zulu's position. The commo guy/machine gunner immediately complied. He apologized emphatically over the radio, and Pharaoh told him to rally on his position, ordering Ondejko to do likewise.

That Weathers had been too alert, too jumpy was hard to blame, and Zulu could have been more specific about his location. That would've been a great irony, if the team sergeant had, after single-handedly taking out more than half a dozen men, been killed by friendly fire.

Stranger and more bitterly painful things had happened. And thank God they hadn't. Yet.

The rest of the militiamen had fallen back to the caves, and once more the valley had grown very quiet, save for the gusting wind and Pharaoh's damned pulse thumping in his ears.

A gasping Zulu met up with him and said, "That AT-4 did a number on them."

"Sergeant, you're insane."

"I wasn't born this way."

"You should've waited, called me. I could've sent Grimm back with Figueroa. He would've been okay."

"But now we're sure, right?"

Pharaoh frowned. "Am I going to put this in my report?"

"Nah." Zulu winked.

"We'll talk later. When Ondejko and Weathers get here, we'll plan our next move. What do you think?"

"Unless those guys down there move, we can just sit tight. If they make another run at the defile, we'll cut them down."

"You writing off Rock and Khodai?"

"You know I thought about that while I was choking on smoke back there." Zulu snorted. "Yeah. Screw him."

"I guess it'd be career suicide for me to order you on a rescue mission to get him and Khodai, and capture Scorpion."

"I don't know about that."

"Weird. You run off alone on a rampage, but you're unwilling to do this."

"You can order me and the rest of us, like you said."

"Khodai's valuable. It took a long time to win over that guy."

"Yeah, the same guy who put a gun to your head. Same guy who's got a deal with Rock, no doubt."

"We do have orders."

"See, Captain, this is where I draw the line."

"But it's not your line to draw. We can't just leave them there. We don't know this Scorpion guy. He could be torturing them."

"I won't refuse an order. But I can't promise that I will perform to the best of my ability. *Sir.*"

Pharaoh turned, looked the man squarely in the eye, and said, "You got some mouth on you, Sergeant. I've been biting my tongue, trying to learn, letting you play teacher, trying to respect experience. But you won't be fighting this team—ever again—if you don't listen to me."

Zulu grinned, yet a new sheen had come into his gaze. "I've been out here a long time. And I've made a lot of friends in low—and high—places."

"Threats? I'm shocked at what I'm hearing."

"Don't be. You sound like me ten years ago. We ain't going down there, us four knuckleheads. He might have twenty or so guys there, maybe more."

"You don't like a challenge? Weren't you a little outnumbered back there?"

"Captain, you let me fight this team. You do what you do best. And we'll all get along just fine."

"So your plan is to sit on our asses."

"Yup."

Pharaoh was about to retort when Weathers and Ondejko came jogging up and hit the ground; all four men crouched down.

"Sergeant, I—"

Zulu cut off Weathers, who looked tortured by guilt. "Have a better reason to kill me before you open fire again, okay?"

"Okay."

"Jesus Christ, it's cold," said Ondejko, putting his gloved his hands to his face and puffing air.

"I do have some good news," said Weathers. "Finally got word on our Chinook. Front's moved through. ETA approximately fifty-one minutes."

"You forward that to Bull?"

"Yes, sir. More good news. They sent up a one-thirty gunship. He's a little farther out, maybe an hour and a half."

"No shit."

Zulu squinted in thought, then regarded Pharaoh. "Maybe, if we play our cards right, your little rescue plan can work after all."

"Rescue plan?" asked Weathers. "I thought we were the interdiction team."

Ondejko snorted. "Oh, how I hate being a jack-of-all-trades."

"Gentlemen, let's get to work," said Zulu, spreading the snow across the ground between them to begin drawing a map.

Although the tension between them was still obvious, Pharaoh glanced at the team sergeant, who simply nodded and said, "We have those caves over there. And here's the only line they can use to reach the defile. So what I'm thinking is . . ."

Bull was having a slightly better day. News of the incoming Chinook and gunship had sent him bounding back for the helicopter, where Hojo and Borokovsky were strapping President Abdali into the litter.

"We're going to take you down the mountain a little ways," he told Abdali. "There's an old hut. Our helicopter will be here within an hour, and they'll take us out."

"Thank you."

Bull nodded. "Feeling any better now?"

"Yes, the pain medicine is beginning to work."

"Good." Bull crouched down. "Can I ask you a favor?"

Abdali raised his brows. "Anything."

"Next time you go for a joyride, would you give us a call first? I want to make sure I'm on vacation." Bull grinned.

"Don't make me laugh. It hurts."

"All right, sir." Bull glanced up at Hojo and Borokovsky. "Ready to move out?" They nodded.

The president's aide, Rafiullah, came up and shook Bull's hand. "Thank you."

"You're welcome. Just watch yourself going down."

He nodded, then joined Hojo and Borokovsky as they started the trek back to the hut.

Bull crossed over to Tracy O'Donnell and Sandra Hildebrand, still wearing stricken expressions. He couldn't blame them. They had just watched their two friends die. And no doubt Hildebrand was telling herself, "If I hadn't been so aggressive to come up here, they'd still be alive."

At least Bull hoped she was asking herself that. During their first meeting she hadn't seemed like a callous, career-bent bitch, but her actions had said otherwise.

"The ground's not real stable. You stay close to my guys. Keep buckled to them. Understand?"

"Yes," said Hildebrand, her voice thin, cracking.

"How about you?" he asked, facing Tracy O'Donnell. "You all right?"

"Yeah."

He took a step back, threw up his hands. "Well, you got your story."

"Bull, I'm sorry," Hildebrand blurted out. "I'm so sorry."

"Me, too." He turned away, heading back to Sullivan, who was busy with the team's twenty-pound load of C-4.

"Bull, I'm going to need your help. Cold weather's making it hard to spread. And we're running out of time," said the engineer.

"Okay, I'm here. Half-inch thick, like we said, right?"

"Yeah."

McDaniel was seated in the snow nearby, hard at work opening up all of the team's buckshot and removing the pellets. A half dozen bars of soap sat next to him, waiting to be converted into shavings.

"How we doing, Rudy?"

"Excellent."

"Let me tell you something, I'm very proud of the work you've done. Both of you."

"Thanks," said McDaniel. "We've had a good teacher."

"Yes, we have," said Sullivan.

"And teacher says, move your asses!"

Bull glanced at the men and grinned faintly as another report came in from Gator, who was across the ridge, his face attached to a pair of binoculars.

The weps sergeant's tone sounded even more urgent. "Bull, they've sent up two guys with RPGs. I'll need to take them out when they get within range, but once I do, the show's on—and I'm out of here."

"Roger that. Just give me a heads-up when you're ready to take the first shot."

"Roger that, Tombstone, out."

Bull finished smoothing out his chunk of C-4, fighting against the cold. He started on the next one, feeling a tremor work its way into his hands.

36. AFTERNOON TEA

As they hiked down the mountain, toward the blurry dot that was the two-story hut lying far below, Sandra Hildebrand kept close to her sister. They were connected to Rafiullah by what the soldiers called Blackhawk 550 cord. Rafiullah, whom Hildebrand had met a few times before, was helping to carry the president.

When they paused for a moment to catch their breaths, she leaned over to Tracy and said, "All this? And for what?" She eyed Abdali. "He wouldn't tell me anything. Neggy and Oswaller are dead. I'm done. I'm finished."

Tracy, who was still limping a little, rubbed her bloodshot eyes. "Don't talk about it."

"I have to talk about it."

"Shut up. What are you worried about? Bad press? You think this ruined your career?"

"I don't care about that. Those guys died because of me. Don't you understand?"

"You had nothing to do with that."

She turned away, shook her head, glanced up the mountain. No one else was coming. She whirled around. "Hey, Hojo? Why aren't they coming?" She glanced up the slope.

"They'll be coming soon."

"What's Bull planning?"

"He's throwing a little party." Hojo looked over at Borokovsky, whose guilt-laden expression was obvious.

"What's wrong?" asked Tracy.

"Nothing, let's move out," said Hojo.

But at that moment, Abdali reached up and grabbed Hojo's wrist. "Bull's not coming, is he . . ."

"Sure he is. But somebody needs to answer the door when the bell rings."

"I see. And I assume all of you wanted to do that?"

"Yes, sir."

"But Bull would not allow it."

"It's his party, sir. He's got one of our best shooters with him, though."

"I understand." Abdali turned his head toward Tracy and Hildebrand. "Ms. O'Donnell. It is fortunate for you that these 'war criminals' were here."

"I never said they were."

"From what I know of your organization, you say it every day."

Tracy just glowered at him.

"And Ms. Hildebrand, I thought much more highly of you—before this. I'm sorry that your career has taken such a bad turn. I really am."

Hildebrand averted her gaze, while Tracy just sighed loudly in frustration.

They resumed their hike, squinting against the wind. Inside, Hildebrand screamed.

* * *

"First, like all good Afghans, we drink tea," said Scorpion, stepping over to his heavy pack and withdrawing some china teacups, saucers, and a tall thermos—all completely incongruent, given their surroundings. They should be lapping at dirty water from clay bowls, not having a most dignified moment of tea.

The former CIA agent's two bodyguards, hardened kids of no more than twenty, stood on either side of the cave entrance. In the saffron glow of two flashlights, Rock and Khodai accepted their tea and took seats on the dirt floor.

The cave was rectangular, about ten meters deep, two meters high, and three or four meters wide, fairly sizable as holes in the mountainside went, though Rock saw no evidence of connecting tunnels or turns to help shield it from American bombers and their bunker busters. It was simply a resting place for travelers through the region, as they had earlier predicted, and the back end was filled with garbage, from abandoned packs to broken weapons to MRE containers to even a few beer bottles amid piles of shell casings.

"And like all good Afghans," Scorpion added, "we don't discuss real business until afterward."

"That's fine with me." Rock reached into his breast pocket. "Cigar?"

Scorpion's eyes grew wide. "Of course."

He accepted the stogie, then he and Rock lit up via Rock's lucky Zippo, one his father had carried in Vietnam.

"Scorpion, this is Khodai."

While Khodai barely looked up, Scorpion spoke to him in fluent Dari: "I'm glad you're here. Maybe you'd like to join us instead of being a pawn for the American CIA."

"I don't think he's interested," said Rock.

"Then let him say so."

Khodai sipped his tea.

Scorpion nodded, seeing that the G-chief had no intention

of answering. Then he faced Rock with a shit-eating grin. "So, my old friend, what brings you to this part of hell?"

"The tea, of course."

"Of course."

Rock took a sip, then said, "I'm surprised you want to sit here and just talk. Aren't you on a schedule?"

Scorpion shrugged. "You got some Special Forces guys out there, huh?"

"No, just a few local guys from Khodai's village."

"With an M240 and a sniper rifle? Don't insult me, Rock. I could tell you that ODA team's number, for God's sake. It's the famous Triple Nickel."

What got into him he wasn't sure, but Rock was too damned old for bullshit games. He bolted to his feet, smashed his teacup against the wall, and asked, "What do you want?"

Scorpion's men charged back into the cave, leveling their rifles on Rock.

Scorpion raised his palms, ordered his men back, then faced Rock. "Whoa. Sit down. Take it easy. You'll get one of these punks too excited, and they'll take a shot at you."

"Then what?"

"What do I want besides a new teacup? Bigger things than you, obviously. Don't you want to know what happened to me?"

"I can already see."

"Sit down, asshole. I've been here just as long as you. And when you hear what I have to tell you, you're going to forget all about that bounty on my head."

"I doubt it."

"You don't know the story."

"I don't care."

"You should. Because you're how the story ends."

* * *

Bull finished dragging and lining up the last of the bodies. He had propped up each man to resemble a dug-in troop from a distance, so as the militia guys approached, they would—for a short time—believe they were being observed and about to be engaged.

Little did these men know that even in death, they would be incredibly useful and might, in fact, save lives.

"Okay, Bull, we're all set back at the chopper," said Sullivan.

Bull slapped a hand on the engineer's shoulder. "Go limp back to that hut down there. You might even have time to play a few games of Sudoku before we take off."

The engineer smiled. "See you down there."

Bull nodded, keyed his mike. "Talk to me, Gator."

"Two RPG guys should be in range in about ten minutes, so stand by."

"Roger that, standing by." Bull then called McDaniel for an update on the Chinook. The commo guy reported all was well, and the helicopter was actually running a few minutes ahead of its prior ETA.

That was good, because the enemy was, too.

Bull then got on his satellite phone, dialed Pharaoh. "Hey, Captain. Recovery operation under way. Our package is en route to the hut." Bull read off the grid coordinates, then added, "I'm holding back here to delay the enemy force. I'll link up with the team afterward."

"Thanks, Bull. Outstanding work. Let Typhoon know that we want that Chinook pilot to hold off picking us up until after the one-thirty arrives. We'll have Jerry contact him directly when we're ready."

"You calling in an air strike?"

"Bull, you have no idea."

"Well, my advice? Keep your head down and make sure they know where you are at all times."

"I definitely hear that. See you soon."

"Yes, you will."

Bull thumbed off the phone. He was about to pull up his scarf when an odd thought came over him. He dialed his ex-wife's number. Wasn't even sure what time it was there. Maybe eight hours ahead? He didn't care. And she answered.

"It's me."

"You? Where are you?"

"Far away."

"Look, I was just going—"

"Melissa, please. I'm standing here on the top of a mountain in the middle of Afghanistan. I'm freezing my ass off, and there's no toilet for hundreds of miles."

"What do you want me to do about it, Bull? That's the life you chose."

"I know. I just wanted to say I'm sorry for being selfish."

"Oh, my God. You called me from halfway around the world to make yourself feel better?"

"Like I said, it's pretty cold here."

"Bull? What's wrong?"

"I just wanted to hear your voice."

"How come you never made a call like this when we were married?"

"I don't know."

"Are you all right? I mean, really."

Bull glanced toward the ridge, wishing he could see the oncoming enemy force. "Yeah. Just give the girls my love, all right?"

"You still have another eight months till you get back, right?"

"Yeah."

"Well, you should call them more often, and do that yourself."

"Okay, I will. Melissa, I swear."

"You're going to get in trouble for this call. You know that."

"It's all right."

"Well, take care of yourself. Call your daughters."

"I will. 'Bye."

He closed his eyes, took a deep breath.

The radio crackled to life: "Tempest, this is Tombstone. Get ready. I'm lining up for my first shot."

The more the young captain gave him a hard time, the more Zulu respected him.

Captain James Pharaoh, newly minted unconventional warrior, had already learned to walk the tightrope, shifting his weight between rank and experience, between courage and recklessness. Good for him.

Of course, Zulu wouldn't tell him that, lest it all go to his young, impressionable head.

So Zulu would continue with his cocky, know-it-all demeanor, which he enjoyed anyway, even as he listened carefully and observed the captain. And admittedly, he was always testing the waters, seeing just how far he could push, both for his sake and Pharaoh's.

He and the captain were now shifting along the west side of the mountain, having left Ondejko and Weathers on the east side. They needed to verify that Rock was, in fact, inside one of the caves, and they needed to know which one so the hell that was about to pour down from the skies avoided that particular little nest.

And therein lay the challenge—getting in close enough to positively ID Rock without being spotted.

The snowstorm that would have helped conceal them

was long gone now, and they knew that the second they were spotted and the shots echoed, it was all over.

They kept low in a dried-up creek channel that ran parallel to the slope. And while the storm was gone, the meter-high snowdrifts that occasionally rose along the channel helped.

After about five minutes of hard double-timing movement, Zulu reached a small mound, dropped to his gut, and crawled up to the edge. Pharaoh picked a spot a few feet away and did likewise. The probing began.

"Well, they can't make it any easier than that," said Zulu, with a chuckle.

"What're you talking about?"

"See the cave entrance with the two guys outside?"

"As a matter of fact I do."

"They got our boys inside."

"I see shadows in there, but I can't pick out any faces."

"Don't have to. That's where they are."

"What if you're wrong? What if they've set up that cave as a decoy, figuring we'll try to come in and rescue our guys?"

Zulu made a face. "I think you're giving them a little too much credit."

"I don't think so. We need to be sure. We can follow this channel down to the trees, where there's another drift. I think we can get a better look inside from there."

"Yeah, but when we get down there, we'll have those other two caves behind us, and we don't know if they're occupied or not."

The captain took a long, hard breath.

"Wait a minute. I have another idea." Zulu got on his radio. "T-Rex, this is Zulu, over."

"Go ahead, Zu," said Ondejko.

"Got two guys posted outside one of the caves, over."

"Already got them."

"Take one of them out, then rally on the west side of the defile. Weathers, you do the same, over."

Both men acknowledged, then Ondejko said, "I have a good shot, Zu. Just tell me when."

Zulu balanced himself on his elbows, glanced over at Pharaoh. "This might flush 'em at least to the edge."

"Yeah, but they're going to open up on our guys. Won't be long till they realize there's only two."

"Well, as they say, you take the good with the bad. You ready?"

Pharaoh nodded.

"T-Rex, this is Zulu, over."

"Go ahead."

"All right, big boy, rub that bald noggin of yours and take your shot."

"Roger that. Stand by for big boom."

37. ZERO HOUR

Staff Sergeant Gregory "Gator" Gatterson was often teased for his southern heritage and for his reputation as the second best shot on the team.

He liked to say there was nothing he could do about being a Georgia boy, but there was a whole lot he would do to dethrone King Ondejko.

Gator's moment had come.

He would live up to his call sign and his nickname. Before those two guys toting RPGs knew it, they'd be dead, and Gator would be on the radio: *"Tempest, this is Tombstone. Two down! On my way!"*

It all played through his head until he could literally taste the moment, like a sweet piece of beef in his mouth.

Breathe. Just breathe.

He lay prone, his SCAR-H at the ready, full magazine, 7.62mm rounds waiting to explode out of his 500mm-long barrel.

Wait till they're in range . . . adjust for the wind, for the bullet drop . . . for your nerves . . .

Gator wanted them to come just a little closer so he could take them both out in a single volley.

But they were beginning to spread apart. If the gap got any wider, the guy in the back could hit the snow while his buddy bought it.

"Bull, this is it," he said over the radio.

"Do it."

And with that Gator opened up, rounds leaping in front of him, racing toward the first guy, who, just as he looked up at the noise, took two rounds in the chest that punched him so hard to the snow that even Gator couldn't believe it.

He panned slightly left, breathing steadily, feeling the weapon grow even warmer, as the next volley streaked past the first guy and punched down the second.

That's it.

He rose, pulled the pin on his first grenade, let it fly—

Then he pulled the pin on his second, chucked it near the first, close to the RPGs, hoping to damage them. He spun around, took off running.

"And that's the way we roll around here!" he cried, as incoming gunfire punched holes in the snow behind him.

Scorpion had just finished telling Rock a story that had left his mouth hanging open.

A story of betrayal.

A story in which both Rock and Scorpion were being set up as the fall guys for the Agency.

And Scorpion had the kind of details, the kind of insider knowledge supported by documents on his satellite-linked laptop that couldn't be faked. He'd gone rogue because he knew the storm was coming.

He'd even tried to warn Rock, but his warnings had been cut off at the knees by those administrators whose jobs were on the line.

It seemed that Operation "Good Press," which involved field agents supplying illegal weapons to militias, only to confiscate them later in order to "claim another victory for coalition forces," had been leaked to the wrong people.

And the usual fall guys were needed. Of course, agents in the field could easily be blamed.

So Scorpion had simply walked away, joined up with a local G-chief in Eshkashem, and been paid to help train his men. Scorpion was fattening his Swiss bank account so he could retire in anonymity within the next two years.

Rock, on the other hand, wouldn't be as fortunate. He would be taking the fall, big-time.

Before Rock could respond to any of this, a round echoed from somewhere outside, and one of Scorpion's men suddenly dropped to the snow, with only half of his head intact.

The other guy freaked out and charged into the cave, screaming and yelling about them being under attack. And at that moment, Rock's satellite phone, which was now sitting inside Scorpion's pocket, began to ring again.

"Why don't you let me answer that, and I can call off that shooter."

Scorpion fished out the phone, tossed it to Rock. It was Pharaoh. "Captain, hold your fire."

"Are you in that cave?"

"Yeah. Tell your boy that was one hell of a shot."

"Can you talk?"

"What do you think, son?"

"Then just listen to me. Stay in there. CAS is on the way. ETA about fifteen minutes. I need you to stay."

"I don't think we're going anywhere."

"Let me talk to your boy," said Scorpion.

Rock frowned, handed him the phone.

"This is Scorpion. Who am I talking to?"

"This is Titan 06," said Pharaoh, loud enough for Rock to overhear.

"All right, Captain, you listen to me. Pull back your men through the trail. Get the fuck out of here. You're outgunned and outnumbered."

"You send out my two guys, and we'll fall back. But you're not coming through that defile, understood?"

"I don't think you understand me, Captain. If you don't fall back within one minute, I'm going to throw every man I have at you, and we'll finish this right now."

As Scorpion spoke, a fact crystallized in Rock's thoughts: The man had to die.

He wasn't Rock's ally. And Rock refused to be the end of this story. Scorpion would be the one and only fall guy, and Rock would make sure that he would be made responsible for all of the illegal weapons transfers to these remote villages and bogus seizures, including Eshkashem and Share Pari. Rock would make sure that his own hands were wiped clean.

Yet Scorpion's man had them covered, his rifle held steadily on Rock, his eyes burning with the desire to blow them away after watching his buddy's head explode. His coat was splattered with blood.

"Scorpion, send out the guys—or send out your men. But trust me. Either way, I'm going to win."

Scorpion covered the phone, regarded Rock with a deep frown. "Who the hell is this guy?"

"He's all right, but the team sergeant has his ear. And you know who that is? Old Zulu. Remember him?"

"Aw, I heard about him," said Scorpion. "Guess I'll have to call that asshole's bluff. He raised the phone. "Captain . . . have a nice day."

With that, Scorpion tossed the phone back to Rock and went over to a radio pack, where he spoke rapidly in Dari, addressing various men with a single word—

"Attack!"

As Gator ran past him, Bull, who had set himself up in a little ditch behind the downed chopper and at the maximum length of his detonation cord—300 feet—was holding his breath until he cried, "Go, Gator, go!"

Bull had already inserted the Ensign Bickford time fuse (named for the British Navy ensign who had invented it) into the fuse lighter, a half-inch-diameter cylinder about five inches long with a pull ring at one end. The time fuse wrapper indicated twenty seconds, which meant a five-foot test segment had been burned and averaged out to twenty seconds per foot. The team only had twenty-four inches of time fuse, so he had forty seconds of fuse to burn until boom time.

Between the time fuse and the detonation cord Bull had placed a #8 engineer cap, which gave him an additional ⅛ second delay and actually ignited the 300-foot detonation cord.

The cord itself was attached to the daisy-chained pieces of C-4 embedded with buckshot pellets. Those four big pieces of C-4 had been attached via duct tape to the side of the chopper, just above the four windows and the fuel bladder.

And that bladder had been sliced open, the soap shavings poured into the JP5 fuel to make good old-fashioned "foo gas," which when ignited and came into contact with human flesh would stick like fiery glue.

Bull had taken some hydraulic fluid from the bird and created a trigger line about sixty feet down the slope from the chopper. He needed a visual cue to be sure as many of those militiamen as possible were within the kill zone.

And therein lay the challenge.

If they didn't see someone up there, didn't feel as though they were under attack during their entire advance, they'd quickly smell a trap.

Which was why he needed to stay there until the very last second.

He ran from his ditch, tossed a grenade, then ran back, firing wildly along the way, into the dust clouds created by Gator's grenades.

With a heavy thud onto his hands and knees, he returned to the ditch, keyed his mike. "Typhoon, this is Tempest. The bird here yet?"

"Not yet."

"ETA?"

"Looks like another ten minutes now. I think we can hear him, though, over."

"Roger that. Look for Gator. He's coming down, out."

Bull pulled the pin on one more grenade, hurling it as far as he could back down the slope.

Boom! Yelling and screaming.

Closer now. They were coming. He dug deeper into the snow, covered his cap and shoulders in the white stuff, then pulled off his right glove, gripped his lighter, and wiped off his goggles—

Just as the first man came over the rise, followed by a half dozen more. They started toward Bull's trigger line, maybe only five meters from it now, not thinking twice about some fuel spill at a crash site. But God, if just one of them came around to the side of the chopper and spotted the C-4 . . .

He could barely control his breathing, the scarf growing hot over his mouth. His eyes were at ground level, watching them come, in twos and threes now, slightly crouched, rifles forward, pushing hard through the snow, fanning out to the left and right, into the trigger zone.

Eight men now. Nine. Ten.

Keep coming, you bastards.

The detonation cord had been carefully buried. There was nothing to betray Bull's location, save for his own movement and perhaps a slight and uncontrollable sheen from his goggles.

Fifteen guys now.

His mouth had gone completely dry. He could barely feel his lips.

Another group. There. And at the back, a fat one, heavily bearded, a warlord no doubt, with three guys close to him.

Bull could already see it happening: the fuse igniting, and, forty seconds later, the C-4 exploding with a massive swell, gases expanding initially at 26,400 feet per second. At that expansion rate, it would be impossible for the enemy to outrun the explosion.

To the observer, the explosion would be instantaneous—one second everything was normal, the next total destruction.

And the militiamen caught even at the far end of the trigger zone would be disoriented in a cloud of thick, black smoke, shredded by pieces of a "shaped" wall of buckshot, then set on fire by foo gas that stuck all over their bodies and burned them to the bone. Those closer to the explosion would have a far more merciful death.

Bull checked his hand; it was trembling violently. He took a deep breath, cleared his thoughts.

And then, taking in another, much longer breath, a peace finally came over him, and his hand grew steady.

More of them came, the whole party, nineteen or twenty, advancing from the far end of the slope.

As the last man crossed the trigger line, Bull grasped the fuse lighter in his left hand and pulled the ring with his right.

He held his breath as he felt the telltale snap inside the cylinder and saw the trace of white smoke confirming he'd lit the fuse.

Good-bye, you bastards.

He let fifteen seconds burn on the fuse.

Then he exploded from his hiding place like some icy Neanderthal frozen for centuries and come back to life.

CW3 Dennis Bull raised his rifle.

The enemy spotted him immediately, and Bull gritted his teeth and opened fire, raking their lines, dropping all of them to their guts.

He didn't care if he'd hit them or not, so long as they had taken cover and would remain right where they were.

Nineteen, eighteen, seventeen, sixteen . . .

The militiamen shouted, and the AK-47 fire began popping and echoing, driving him to his own gut.

Ten, nine, eight . . .

Bull didn't feel the impact of the rounds that struck his arm and shoulder. All he knew was that his arm suddenly gave out, and he could no longer pull the trigger.

Five, four, three, two . . .

38. EXQUISITE BRAVERY

As the militiamen scampered out of the caves like rats cloaked in wool, probably twenty or more in all, two words escaped from Ondejko's lips:

"Holy . . . shit!"

Then he got on the radio and called Pharaoh, wondering if the captain saw the same.

But commo guy Weathers had beat Ondejko to the punch, and Pharaoh ordered both of them back into the defile to hold the line, while Weathers resumed contact with and guided in the AC-130 gunship when it arrived.

"What about the cave?" Weathers asked Pharaoh.

"I'll follow up on that."

Damn, they were writing off Rock and Khodai.

Or were they?

While Ondejko exchanged his sniper rifle for his SCAR-H, he saw Pharaoh and Zulu dart off, weaving a serpentine path farther along the channel, moving behind the oncoming militiamen, and heading for the cave . . .

At that moment, Grimm checked in to report that Figueroa was stable. Grimm would now come up to assist Weathers and Ondejko. Outstanding.

And while Ondejko ran, he called back to Weathers: "Talk Radio, this is T-Rex."

"Go ahead, T-Rex."

"I'll be coming in from the east side, near your two o'clock, over."

"Roger that. I'll watch for you."

Just as Ondejko finished, the snow, dirt, and ice around him erupted with so much incoming fire that he dove onto his gut and crawled forward, searching for anything, even the most shallow depression in the mountainside.

He grimaced and grabbed his mike. "This is T-Rex, I'm taking heavy fire!"

"Hang in the there, Rex," called Grimm. "On my way!"

Suddenly, a distant but powerful explosion rumbled from the direction of the president's downed helicopter.

Pharaoh was right behind Zulu when he heard the boom. He stopped and dove for cover, hitting the snow with a wince. He shoved his rifle around on the sling and tugged down his scarf.

"Come on!" Zulu urged him.

"Hold up! That was Bull up there!" He reached for his satellite phone.

"So he blew the chopper like he said. The president's on his way to the hut."

"I want to confirm that."

"Now?"

"Yeah, now!"

* * *

Gator was hauling ass down the slope and toward the hut as the C-4 shook the mountainside.

When he looked back, expecting to see Bull's silhouette painted across the snow, he saw nothing.

A cold wave of panic hit him.

He whirled and started back up the mountain, calling into his mike, "Tempest, this is Tombstone, over? Tempest, this is Tombstone!"

Sandra Hildebrand stood inside the old hut and glanced up as the walls rumbled and the thunder seemed to reach the distant mountains. Dust trickled down from the rafters, and she waved it from her face. Across the room sat Tracy, her knees pulled up to her chest.

"You hear that?"

Tracy nodded.

Hildebrand pursed her lips. "That was him."

General Malim Kahn had spotted only a single man with a rifle firing upon their position.

Just one man!

And that man could have been Abdali himself.

Kahn had ordered his troops forward, screaming at the top of his lungs, along with Fahim.

But then, one of his men had pointed to the side of the chopper, and Kahn had raised his binoculars to see the four large pieces of C-4 attached to the fuselage.

His chest caved in.

"Get out! Get out of there!" he cried.

But it was too late.

The gloomy mountainside was gone, replaced by a brilliant white sun that swallowed the chopper in a massive ball of flames rushing toward him.

And suddenly shrapnel or pellets or something else woke a thousand points of pain in his chest, arms, and legs as they ripped into him.

He shrieked in agony, glanced back, and saw an equally terrible sight in the distance:

The news crew had kept far back, the cameraman now filming the entire scene—filming his ultimate failure.

Kahn turned back, raised his arms, both on fire now, and tried to ball his hands into fists before he collapsed in another wave of flames.

Bull had known all along that getting out alive would be a small miracle, but he had buried that fact deep in his mind, in a place that operators often refused to acknowledge—because when there was a will, there was a way.

Special Forces operators never gave up.

They never admitted defeat.

And they never said die.

They were not kamikazes. They were tacticians and warriors who freed the oppressed.

And part of Bull had still wanted to believe that he could put enough distance between himself and the explosion, enough distance between himself and the stragglers who might've only been wounded, enough distance between himself and death.

He had believed it would all come down to distance.

But he hadn't figured on getting shot before the big bang even went off.

He hadn't planned on losing so much blood that he'd fail to get up.

And he certainly hadn't thought he'd be within 300 feet of the chopper when it exploded.

At least when Gator found him, he still had enough energy to say, "Good work."

"Hang on, Bull. I'm going to get you out of here." Gator keyed his mike, started talking rapidly, the words beginning to mash together into a deep, almost soothing tone.

Bull wanted to raise his hand, tell Gator that it was all right, that he was too tired to be carried. Just leave him here. He'd be all right.

He closed his eyes and thought of Melissa, of his daughters, and reaffirmed that promise to call them.

Gator finished his radio report, then scanned the area. Two or three militiamen on the far end of the slope were stirring.

"Bull, I'll be right back. Hang in."

Gator ran forward through the smoke and terrible stench, weaving through the still burning corpses, to find those soldiers. He drew his pistol and quickly finished each man.

Before he headed back, something caught his eye in the valley below, his hand already going for his binoculars.

Three people were hurrying back toward the trucks. If they were armed, their weapons were concealed. One man had a camera tucked under his arm.

Gator frowned, then glanced toward the scorched graveyard around him.

Bull had taken all of them out, all but those three down there. He must've stayed in place till the last possible second, and that's why'd he'd been shot up. Gator wasn't sure if he could ever be that brave.

After a deep sigh, he jogged back to Bull, but when he got there and put a hand on the man's neck, he knew immediately that his fellow operator and friend was gone.

And he could barely speak through the mike as he called back to Hojo: "Thunder, this is Tombstone, over."

"Tombstone, where the hell are you, over?"

"Up top. Militia force has been taken out. Repeat, all enemy forces are gone, except for three heading back to the trucks. One had a camera. I'm coming down, and I'm bringing Bull with me, but we lost him, over."

"Say again, Tombstone."

Gator choked up. "We lost Bull."

Pharaoh couldn't get through to Bull, and seeing that Ondejko, Weathers, and Grimm were under attack by at least twenty militiamen, there were more urgent matters at hand than an unanswered call.

"We have to stall them till CAS arrives," said Zulu. "Forget the cave for now."

"I agree," said Pharaoh as he clambered up the side of their mound, hit his elbows, and began firing at the backs of the militia guys headed for the defile.

About six or seven of them hit the deck, while the others kept on toward the slope and defile beyond. Smart bastards. They had broken up into two groups, and now the six or seven did a 180 and began to engage Pharaoh and Zulu.

"I'm down to my last mag," said Zulu, slapping it home into his rifle.

"Me, too," said Pharaoh. They each had a couple magazines for their sidearms, and Pharaoh had two grenades, but they had expended everything else. He reached for his mike. "Thunder, this is Titan 06, over."

"Go ahead, Titan 06," replied Hojo.

"You guys rally on the truck and drive away, heading east. Weathers will direct that 130 onto the defile and those troops, over."

"Roger that. You don't want us to hold the line, over?"

"Negative. Change of plan. Just get out of there. We'll link up after CAS arrives."

"Okay. Bugging out."

Zulu cut loose another volley, rolled back into the channel, just as shards of ice and snow sprayed into him. "You still have two grenades, right?"

Pharaoh nodded.

"Let me have one. On my mark, we throw 'em both, then we come up firing, dive down into the next ditch ahead, then split up, you right, me left. They'll be firing forward. While that's happening we flank 'em, move in point-blank, take 'em out, boom."

The team sergeant made it sound like a training course; Pharaoh just sat there a moment, mulling it over.

"Captain—"

"You got it all figured out, huh? I mean, you think it'll go down just like that?"

"Visualize, man. Just visualize." Zulu wriggled his brows, then added, "You're not scared, are you?"

"You're damned right I am."

"Good. Me, too. You ready?"

Pharaoh grimaced. "Aw, shit. Here goes nothing."

"On three," began Zulu. "One, two . . ."

Rock sat on the cold, hard cave floor, Khodai at his side, with Scorpion's man leveling his AK-47 on Rock's head.

Mr. Scorpion himself lay on his belly near the cave entrance, surveying the valley below with his high-power binoculars. "Looks like they've fallen back."

"I wonder why," Rock sang in a knowing tone.

"If we stay here, we will die," said Khodai.

Scorpion glanced back from his binoculars. "What makes you say that?"

"Because the storm has passed."

The man nodded. "And they'll be calling in their close air support. But wait a minute. What's that down there?"

Rock stiffened as twin booms resounded: grenades exploding down in the valley.

Zulu emptied the rest of his magazine, then pulled his sling strap and quickly dumped his rifle.

With a meter-high mound of dirt and ice between him and the enemy soldiers, he crouched down and broke to the left, just as they had planned.

He stole a second's glance right, where Pharaoh was doing the same.

All right, so he'd pulled this plan out of his ass, but sometimes they worked. Sometimes . . .

Meanwhile, as expected, the incoming fire blasted through the clouds of smoke, targeting an area between them. These guys were decent shots but had predictably poor reaction time.

Gasping for air, Zulu ripped down his scarf, drew his pistol from his hip holster, then broke toward the six men, seeing two guys skulking along the rocks to his right, another two in the middle, and two more out near Pharaoh, who were still firing into the smoke.

Zulu would take out the nearest two, praying the captain had his pair. The middle guys were up for grabs.

It was crazy. That was all he could think as he ran right at the two guys, letting out a scream and squeezing off two rounds at the first guy, hitting him, then turning toward the second as that heavily bearded fighter leveled his weapon. They were no more than five meters apart.

Within the next eye blink, gunfire cracked around him as he added the boom of his own pistol to the music, firing and hitting the ground. He came up out of his roll, gaze probing:

He'd taken down the first guy and had wounded the second, who let out a cry and fumbled with his rifle. Zulu fired again, three more rounds, knocking the guy to his back.

Pharaoh had taken down his two with his rifle and was drawing his pistol, just as both guys in the middle broke from their positions and went after him, crawling on their hands and knees behind the rocks.

Aw, shit, Zulu thought. *The captain doesn't see them!*

39. ALMOST HOME

The Chinook's pilot had descended, wheeled around, and, with McDaniel's guidance, carefully set down the heavy-lift chopper's two rear wheels on the hut's roof, while he kept the front wheel hanging in midair. Hojo couldn't hear much above the whomping of tandem rotors and the howling wash.

At the moment, his attention was divided between the helicopter's remarkable partial landing, which was being photographed by Sandra Hildebrand, and the sight of Gator, still far up the mountain, with Bull slung over his shoulders.

While Sullivan and Borokovsky began to load President Abdali, Rafiullah, Hildebrand, and Tracy O'Donnell into the chopper via the wide loading ramp at the rear of the fuselage, Hojo climbed down the ladder and went below, where McDaniel was getting ready to come up and board.

"I need to talk to that pilot," Hojo said.

The commo guy nodded and put him through over the radio.

"I have a man coming down the mountain. Can you wait for him, over?"

"Negative. One updraft, and we're history. Let him get down, and we'll come back once he's down here. But I'm not sure I can get lightning to strike twice!"

"All right. I'm going up to help. You'll need to come back for both of us."

"You don't make it easy, Sergeant."

"No, I don't. Thanks!"

Hojo raised his chin at McDaniel. "Good work, get on that bird. You're out of here."

"All right. Sure you don't want help?"

He widened his eyes. "Go."

McDaniel nodded and ascended the ladder leading up to the rooftop. You couldn't mistake his somber tone. All of them were struck hard by Bull's death, but they were professionals and knew there was a time and a place to grieve.

Once Hojo reached the ground, he dug his boots in deep and headed back for Gator, letting the operator know he was on his way to help.

"Thanks, man," came Gator's breathless reply. "Thanks."

Ondejko, Grimm, and Weathers were on their way back to the truck when the AC-130 checked in with Weathers, who led the others behind some rocks so he could help guide the plane's pilot and gunners.

Ondejko and his fellow operators only needed the gunship to get its 105mm howitzer on the defile. Unless they sought hiding positions, those militiamen wouldn't stand a chance against all of that firepower.

And although big, lumbering gunships weren't best used during daylight hours because of their poor maneuverability, the remoteness of the region and the limited number of combatants worked to the crew's advantage.

Ondejko listened carefully as Weathers put that 130 crew on the target, then the commo guy glanced up at them. "All right. We get out of here now!"

All three charged down the last part of the trail, following their beaten path in the snow.

Below, the SUV sat near the tallest two boulders, Figueroa hanging out the window, bandaged up and looking drugged, his weapon at the ready.

And just as they reached the truck, the mountain behind them rumbled.

The gods were angry. Very angry.

Then several massive explosions resounded, followed by huge clouds of fire, as though the peaks were erupting, debris hurtling through the air.

Ondejko turned back and gaped at the devastation.

Zulu did two things at once: he reached under his heavy coat for his second pistol magazine and shouted to Pharaoh, "Get down!"

But Zulu's second mag wasn't in the pouch buckled at his waist.

Then it dawned on him. Bull had been low one magazine, and Zulu had given his second away.

So he screamed once more at the two guys, took his pistol and literally threw it at the first one, even as he leapt off a snow mound, driving his forearm across the man's weapon just as he fired over Zulu's shoulder.

Pharaoh's pistol boomed, and he had better be putting lead in that second guy—because Zulu sure as hell couldn't see jack as he tumbled across the ground with the guy still in his clutches.

With one hand locked onto the guy's rifle, Zulu used the other to wrench out his XSF-1 dagger. As the guy pushed off of him, trying to get enough distance to tug free his rifle, Zulu drove the dagger into his chin, forcing the chisel-tipped blade all the way up, into the guy's head in an "apple on a stick" maneuver.

In truth, Zulu had only practiced the maneuver on dummy targets of foam rubber and duct tape; a living, breathing man was a very different experience: the noises, the hot breath in his face, the look of utter terror in the guy's eyes . . .

And for the first time in quite a few years, he felt a little light-headed as he drove the blade even deeper, gave it a little wrench, then brought up his knee and pushed the guy away, the dagger ripping out and dripping blood.

Pharaoh, who couldn't have seen what Zulu had just done, emptied his magazine into the guy, even as Zulu shouted, "No! Save your ammo!"

As the captain stopped firing, it was only then that Zulu looked up and saw the explosions rising from the defile, mushroom clouds of orange-blue flames licked by black smoke and unfurling down the slopes.

And up there, far above them, a dark shape cut smoothly across the gray.

"We got 'em all," grunted Pharaoh, as his satellite phone began to ring.

Zulu could barely nod.

Pharaoh took the call from Weathers, and the captain's tone grew soft as they caught their breaths. He hung up and swallowed, then spoke through his teeth, beginning to once again lose his breath: "President's on board the Chinook. But we lost Bull."

"What do you mean, we lost him? No contact?"

"No, he's gone. Gator's carrying him down from the crash site. Hojo's going up to help."

Zulu lay back in the snow, tossing his head, closing his eyes a minute. Old Dennis Bull. God, he'd spent a lot of time with that man.

Suddenly, gunfire raked across the ground less than a meter from Zulu's head.

They both rolled, tucked themselves down, then Pharaoh turned onto his side, and with his binoculars in hand, slowly edged up and stole a quick look. "Shit, there's three, maybe four coming back down the slope!"

"Time to go!"

He and Pharaoh bolted down into a ravine that spanned the length of the valley and would take them back up toward the caves.

Pharaoh was back on the radio with Weathers, trying to get that AC-130 on their position.

Meanwhile, it dawned on Zulu that they hadn't grabbed at least one freaking rifle before bolting off. How could he be that foolish?

Bull would've said, *"Because you always work too fast."*

And he did.

But Zulu wasn't thinking straight. He'd just lost a friend. He swore at himself, swore again, thought of running back. Probably too late already.

Zulu dodged behind some rocks forming a jagged hedge and caught his breath there. Pharaoh joined him.

"All right, Weathers will get that gunship on those guys, but we have to keep moving, back to the cave," said the captain.

"With no ammo," added Zulu.

The captain's eyes bugged out. "I thought you grabbed an AK, some mags?"

"Should've been the first thing we did."

"Jesus Christ!" Pharaoh's gaze swept right and left, as

he groped for an answer. "Well, screw it, we're still going back to the cave."

"With no ammo."

Pharaoh reached over and pulled the dagger from Zulu's sheath. "I'm armed. And you got your switchblade."

"Jani-Song."

"Right." Zulu grabbed Pharaoh's wrist before he could tuck the dagger in his belt. "Captain, you don't bring a knife to a gunfight."

Pharaoh's face had grown ruddier, somehow older. He just looked at Zulu and, in a voice so steady it was unnerving, said, "You scared?"

"You're serious?"

"You didn't answer my question."

Zulu couldn't believe what he was hearing: he'd just met a man as insane as himself, and an officer no less. The kid was supposed to be a scared shitless academic who led men with PowerPoint presentations, not knives.

Zulu shook his head, dumbfounded. "Let's go, you crazy bastard."

Pharaoh nodded. "For Bull."

As they took off, Zulu removed his gloves, pocketed them, then withdrew his Jani-Song, flipped it open.

Then he reached into his hip pocket, where he kept another special blade, a custom balisong designed by renowned knife maker Darrel Ralph, a Venturi IX with a beautiful twist handle design, dagger-style blade, and some custom grooves or "jimping" filed on the "safe handle" so that Zulu could distinguish it by feel from the "bite" handle, which, if he held unknowingly, could result in a bad cut. This knife was his baby, a good-luck charm and a fully functional piece of art.

Yet he'd never thought that one day he'd be snapping

tight both handles, locking the latch with his pinky, and gripping the blade to defend his life.

With knives jutting from his fists, Zulu led them on, breaking across the channel and drawing more gunfire that fell just ahead of them.

* The sound of plane engines from somewhere above boosted his spirits.

The thugs behind them weren't about to attend a bonfire—they would be the bonfire.

Scorpion had ordered Rock and Khodai out of their cave and back toward yet another cave entrance about twenty meters south on the mountainside.

Although Rock had demanded answers about their destination, Scorpion just cursed at him and urged him on with a pistol.

When they got into the second cave, and Rock saw that a deep tunnel went who-knew-how-deep, he raised his palms. "Where does this go?"

"It leads through several more tunnels, out the other side, then on into a second valley we can take back to Eshkashem."

"I'm not going."

"My gun says otherwise."

"Why don't you shoot me?"

"Because I need you. Because you and I are going to blow the lid off this bullshit, and a whole lot of people back in Langley are going to hang for it. But not us. Not fucking us. Understand? I'm here to help you. Now move!"

"I have something you want. That's why you're not killing me. What do you need? My passwords?"

Scorpion turned away.

"That's it, isn't it? You just want my passwords. You're not going to clear me. You're going to clear yourself. And you're going to use me as the fall guy. Call me killed in action—because that's the same thing I'm going to do to you."

"You give me what I want, and maybe we'll pair up. You don't have to die, Rock. You don't."

Rock steeled his voice. "No, but you do."

40. WHERE LOYALTIES LIE

As they approached the cave from the east side, Pharaoh could neither see nor hear if anyone was inside. They crawled forward on their hands and knees as silently as possible, the wind helping a little to dampen their rustling, the rocks shielding them from the men darting from ditch to ditch below—

And then the AC-130 began pounding the hell out of their pursuers with thunderous explosions.

Zulu froze, turned back, and cried, "Put the dagger away! Draw your pistol!"

Pharaoh frowned. "Click, click, no ammo."

"They'll be looking at you, while I go to work. And if I know Rock, he'll help, no matter what kind of asshole we think he is."

"All right. Ready? Go!"

They burst up from the snow and rushed into the cave, Pharaoh yelling, "Hold it right there! Nobody move."

No one did.

Pharaoh swept right and left, thinking of the dagger at his waist, itching to pull it out.

Zulu, who was holding another fancy knife as well as his Jani-Song, lowered both hands.

Only the cave walls confronted them.

"They had to go back," said Pharaoh. "Another cave. Next one up. Come on!"

With the booming still going on, they returned outside, spotting the next cave entrance. They crossed a rocky and ice-laden path there, paused, got set, and burst inside.

Empty.

Zulu cursed.

"Wait." Pharaoh tugged out his Gladius and thumbed it on. A tunnel appeared in the back. "This is it." His light played over the fresh boot prints. "Has to be."

"I'll roll those dice," said Zulu, following Pharaoh to the back.

The musty tunnel was only about five feet high, three feet wide, but it grew more narrow as it turned left into another tunnel. They had to shift sideways, pushing through for several meters until the passage opened up into a much wider section that ran about twenty more meters toward a shaft of dim light in the distance.

"I just had a weird thought," said Pharaoh.

"Oh, yeah?"

"What if Rock and Khodai have joined up with Scorpion? What if Rock's been playing us all along?"

"He uses ODA teams as tools to accomplish his missions. No big surprise there. But I don't know about him joining this guy. I think he wants to make the big capture."

Pharaoh shrugged and kept on.

When they reached the exit, they hunkered down and reconnoitered the mountainside. A fairly steep slope lay to their left, a more gradual one to the right, and Pharaoh directed his binoculars there—

Where he saw Rock, Khodai, and two other men crouched down behind some boulders. The taller man with the blue scarf was, indeed, Scorpion, who spoke on a phone and repeatedly glanced to the AC-130 making a slow turn overhead.

"They're afraid to run," said Pharaoh. "Worried about the gunship taking them out."

"Rock has a blue force transmitter like we do," Zulu said. "Scorpion should know that."

Pharaoh shrugged. "Maybe Rock turned his off or broke it. Or maybe he doesn't trust it."

"Who knows." Zulu traced his finger over the landscape. "Look there. We can get in from behind them. Let's go."

They slipped from the cave, taking the steep slope down, allowing the ridgeline to conceal their advance.

They had about twenty-five meters to cover, and the descent burned in Pharaoh's legs. It was all he could do to keep his balance, sidestepping and carefully choosing his steps, the ice and gravel giving way at the slightest mistake.

As they approached the boulders, they could still see Scorpion on the phone, getting upset.

Then Rock said, "Forget them. We're humping back to Eshkashem. Your people don't give a shit. I told you."

If there was a moment in the past two days when Pharaoh's heart threatened to rip through his ribs, this was it.

He ordered himself to breathe.

Don't embarrass yourself in front of Zulu.

The team sergeant gave him a hand signal: Pharaoh should go to the right and come around, while Zulu would spring on them from the left, near the guy with the rifle pointed at Rock.

Pharaoh nodded, took a deep breath, and suddenly

bolted around the boulders, waving his pistol—the one with the empty magazine.

Hojo and Gator carried Bull the rest of the way down to the hut, and it was hard for Hojo to take his eyes off a man who had once been so full of life.

Gator lifted up his goggles and rubbed the corners of his eyes. "I don't know what to say."

"I do. You did outstanding work up there, man. Outstanding."

Gator nodded as the Chinook came back down, getting ready to try that hair-raising landing yet again.

"If this guy can pull off that stunt twice, then somebody up there likes us."

Hojo grabbed Gator's shoulder. "Somebody does."

And with that they tied a sling under Bull's arms, and together, hoisted him up the ladder and onto the roof. The task left both men completely exhausted.

But their efforts were worth it. The Chinook made an even more graceful landing the second time, two wheels on, one hovering over the abyss, and together, Hojo and Gator carried Bull up the ramp and on board.

Zulu sprang from behind the rock and used a vicious backhand slash of the balisong in his left hand to cut the throat of the guy with the rifle. Sweeping his arm over the top of the weapon to trap it and deflect it downward, Zulu simultaneously drove the Jani-Song in his right hand up through the man's diaphragm, toward his heart.

But even as the militiaman stiffened with the impact of the Jani-Song's thrust, he convulsed, fired a shot, and the captain dropped onto his side.

He got Pharaoh?

Scorpion whirled, turning his pistol on Zulu.

But in that instant, Rock seized Scorpion's wrist, giving Zulu enough time to drop his knives and take up the bleeding militiaman's AK-47. He spun, directing the rifle on Scorpion and shouted, "Neither of you move!"

"Zulu!" cried Pharaoh.

He hadn't seen Khodai, whom he assumed wanted to be rescued, come up from behind him and lock both gloved hands onto the AK. "What're you doing?"

As Zulu began struggling against Khodai's grip, from the corner of his eye he saw Pharaoh, crawling toward Scorpion.

He'd been shot. Pharaoh knew it. That pinch in his left arm, just above the bicep, wasn't a muscle spasm.

But he didn't care. He threw himself forward, wrapped his right arm around Scorpion's legs, and knocked the man off his feet, while Rock still wrestled with him, trying to get his pistol.

Pharaoh released his grip, was about to slide out his arm—

When the pistol cracked loudly in his ear, startling him.

Suddenly, Scorpion fell over Pharaoh, thudding to the snow, gasping, clutching his chest.

Rock, who was now holding the pistol, grimaced, opened his mouth, then pursed his lips and sighed.

"I'll shoot you, Khodai, I swear to God!" Zulu cried. He'd tugged off the G-chief and now had the muzzle of his AK jabbed into the Tajik's chest.

"Zu, back off. He was just protecting me," said Rock.

"That right, Khodai?"

"Yes, you can't shoot Rock. He has done a lot for my village. I would not allow it."

Zulu snickered and lowered his rifle. "Well, Rock, you got your prize."

Rock crouched down beside Scorpion and opened the rogue agent's jacket as the color faded from Scorpion's face. He glanced over at Pharaoh. "He won't make it."

"Well, there goes your intel dump," said Zulu. "You don't look too upset."

"Know what?" Rock began. "I'm not."

Pharaoh sat up, clutching his shoulder, and that was when Zulu remembered. "Captain? You all right?"

"Wasn't sure you cared. I don't know."

Zulu rushed to him, and Pharaoh didn't want to look as the sergeant examined his wound. "Clean entry and exit. If you have to get shot, this is the way to get it."

"I'll remember that, the next time I walk in front of bullets."

"Rock, see if he's got a med kit in his pack," Zulu said to the spook, whose gaze was still locked on the now-unmoving Scorpion.

"What?"

"I need a med kit."

"All right."

"Can you call Weathers?" Pharaoh asked Zulu.

"Roger that. We'll get that Chinook over here. Definitely time to go home."

"Khodai?" Pharaoh called.

The G-chief came over, and Pharaoh extended his hand. The Tajik removed a glove, and Pharaoh took his hand, squeezing it tightly and drawing the man down to him, so he could look him straight in the eye. "He used us. And he's using you. Rock is not your friend."

The Tajik snorted. "Neither are you."

41. AFTER-ACTION REPORT

Back at Forward Operations Base Asadabad, President Abdali was transferred to another helicopter bound for Bagram Airbase. Before the president left, Pharaoh and the rest of the interdiction team, who hadn't spoken to him during the evac, shook his hand and told him they were glad he was all right.

Afterward, outside the tent, Zulu turned to Pharaoh and said, "Good work up there."

Pharaoh snorted. "Really?"

"It's too bad you're a captain. You could've been a pretty good team sergeant."

"Pretty good?"

Zulu stroked his beard. "Let's not get carried away."

Pharaoh nodded and started off, wincing at a needle of pain that worked up into his shoulder. They had patched up his arm, and he'd only need a couple of weeks to recover. Figueroa, too, would be back in action within a few weeks.

The rest of the day was a blur: a long meeting with Major

NurenFeld, an after-action report, a rumor that Rock was being detained and shipped back to Bagram Airbase for questioning, and some news about a large force of al-Qaeda–backed militiamen moving in on the village of Shah-e Pari. Pharaoh was able to press NurenFeld to send help up there, along with another AC-130, and he was able to sit down with Khodai and explain that he was doing his best to help protect the village. Khodai was still not convinced. At sunset, the G-chief left aboard a Blackhawk, along with another ODA team, heading for Shah-e Pari.

Pharaoh watched their chopper turn and disappear, eclipsed by the mountains, and wondered if Khodai—if all Afghans, for that matter—would ever trust them. He shook his head and tried to think of something less depressing.

Zulu drifted off to the edge of the base, far up a slope near a wall of sandbags, where he could watch the sun set over the jagged, snowcapped peaks.

He reached into his pocket and pulled out some battered pictures, thumbed through them, and found one of him and Bull, taken only a few months back, right here in Afghanistan, sitting on the hood of their Pathfinder.

He considered what he would say tomorrow at the service for Bull, and everything seemed cliché: a great warrior, an inspiration to the men he led, and so on.

What he would never talk about to anyone was the bitter secret, the one that tore him up inside.

He closed his eyes and rubbed the burning away, the questions still unanswered.

Sandra Hildebrand and Tracy O'Donnell had been taken back to Camp Civilian at Bagram Airbase, where they had chosen to stay for a day or two, trying to organize a mission to recover the remains of Oswaller and Neggy.

She and her sister were inside one of the "B-huts," which at least had a portable heater and fairly comfortable bunks. At the moment they were sipping on tea and just staring through each other.

"Did they call you back?" Tracy asked out of nowhere, referring to Hildebrand's bosses at NPR headquarters in Washington.

"Not yet."

"Well, at least the military won't leak all the details. It's Abdali you have to watch. He could say we almost botched his rescue."

"I don't think he will. He's disappointed in me, but I think he still respects me enough not to do that."

"Well, that's a little naïve . . . but all right . . ."

Hildebrand closed her eyes. "I can't get him out of my head."

"Who, Abdali?"

"No, Bull."

Tracy snickered. "His ego got the best of him."

"Excuse me?"

"You have to wonder if guys like that throw away their lives because they really want to save us—or because they want to go out in a blaze of glory. Is it self*less*ness or self*ish*ness?"

"I don't believe you."

"Maybe he was a hero, but for every one of them, there are a hundred thugs wearing the uniform."

"You owe him your life. If I were you, I'd put my politics aside, find out who his family is, and write them a letter."

"Is that what you're doing?"

"No."

Tracy frowned—

And Hildebrand added, "I'll be thanking them in person."

From his hospital bed in Kabul, President Abdali spoke to reporters about his ordeal in the mountains. Rafiullah suggested that he say a coalition forces rescue team had saved them, making for good press all around.

Instead, Abdali reported that an *American* Special Forces team had flown him off the mountain, and that a chief warrant officer named Dennis Bull had sacrificed his own life in a moment of exquisite bravery.

Abdali had never met a man more brave.

And with reporters still there, Abdali placed a call to Washington and personally thanked the president of the United States.

Afterward, Abdali learned that Governor Hajji Mohammad Omar had been found beaten and locked inside a small hut near the village of Arakhi.

As Abdali had suspected, Omar had been coerced into the meeting, blackmailed by the warlord Malim Kahn. Consequently, Abdali vowed to call the man within the next day or two because he still fervently believed that there was a path to even the highest mountain.

Department of the Army Form 638 stared back at Pharaoh from the folding table inside his tent.

Six-thirty-eight was the preprinted document on which he would write up an account of Bull's actions, and he had every intention of nominating Bull for the Medal of Honor. He'd already imagined how the citation would read:

The President of the United States in the name of The
Congress takes pride in presenting the MEDAL OF
HONOR posthumously to

CHIEF WARRANT OFFICER
DENNIS R. BULL
UNITED STATES ARMY
for service as set forth in the following
CITATION:

For conspicuous gallantry and intrepidity at the risk
of his life above and beyond the call of duty while serv-
ing as Assistant Detachment Commander, Special Forces
Detachment ALPHA, 5th Special Forces Group (Airborne), 2nd Battalion Company C, Team ODA-555.

On 22 February, Warrant Officer Bull's team was
conducting a strategic rescue mission at a remote helicopter crash site in the Hindu Kush Mountains, thirty-
five miles southwest of Eshkashem, Afghanistan. In
peril of being overrun by a numerically superior force
of seasoned militiamen, Warrant Officer Bull ordered
the construction and placement of improvised explosives in a manner designed to deliver a devastating,
lethal blow to his attackers. With a clear understanding that one individual must remain at the crash site to
initiate the desired outcome and with full knowledge
of the lethality of the resulting explosion, Warrant Officer Bull remained at his post. In an ultimate and self-
less act of bravery in which he was mortally wounded,
he saved the lives of his fellow soldiers and Afghani
citizens.

By his undaunted courage, intrepid fighting spirit,
and unwavering devotion to duty, Warrant Officer Bull
gave his life for his country, thereby reflecting great

credit upon himself and upholding the highest traditions of the United States Army.

Pharaoh was about to get started when Zulu pushed through the tent flaps and said, "Want to take a walk?"

Pharaoh rapped a knuckle on the form. "I'm busy right now. I'm going to recommend Bull for the Medal of Honor."

"Jesus Christ, you serious?"

Pharaoh nodded. "We have plenty of witnesses and first-hand accounts like Gator's. I think we have a chance here. CENTCOM says Abdali called the White House and told the man Bull did everything but walk on water. Back in 'Nam, seventeen Special Forces operators were awarded Medals of Honor. We're long overdue here."

The team sergeant nodded. "Damn right we are. That's incredible." Zulu stood there. He wasn't leaving.

So Pharaoh sighed and rose, grabbed his coat, and stepped outside with him. They started down a long dirt trail between the tents, a magnificent sheet of stars flickering overhead.

"What's on your mind?"

"The service tomorrow. I'm not good with speeches."

"Neither am I."

"You kidding? I thought all you officers loved to hear yourselves talk."

Pharaoh chuckled. "Not all of us."

Zulu shrugged. "I don't know what to say."

"And you're asking me for advice?"

"I guess I'm too embarrassed to ask anyone else. They all know me too well. I know one thing, though. Bull didn't die alone up there. We were all with him. Every guy who ever served with the Fifth."

"That's right. So when you get up there tomorrow, you

remember the same thing, and then the beers are on me, as promised."

Zulu pursed his lips and offered his hand. They shook, then he reached into his pocket and slipped out his Jani-Song. "Here."

"Your knife?"

"It's yours. I'll teach you how to use it."

Pharaoh accepted the blade with reverence, knowing how much it meant to the team sergeant. "I'm honored."

They continued walking down the trail, Zulu explaining how to avoid becoming a blood donor through careful manipulations.

The knife felt awkward in Pharaoh's hand, just as awkward as commanding an ODA team had, but he vowed to learn, to keep on learning, because that was what effective operators did.

And because he'd never felt more proud.

ABOUT THE AUTHOR

Peter Telep is the author of more than thirty novels. With the help of dozens of technical advisors from all branches of the service, he has documented the exploits of Force Recon Marines in Pakistan; U.S. Army tank platoon commanders in Korea; and mercenary fighters in Angola, Uzbekistan, and Vladivostok. Mr. Telep has written under the pen names P. W. Storm, Pete Callahan, and Ben Weaver, and his heavily researched work has been translated into Spanish, German, French, and Japanese. In addition to his writing career, he is also an English instructor at the University of Central Florida, where he teaches creative writing courses. He invites readers to visit his website at web.mac.com/ptelep.